VANILLA
RIDE

VANILLA RIDE

JOE R. LANSDALE

ALFRED A. KNOPF   NEW YORK 2009

THIS IS A BORZOI BOOK
PUBLISHED BY ALFRED A. KNOPF

Copyright © 2009 by Joe R. Lansdale

All rights reserved. Published in the United States by Alfred A.
Knopf, a division of Random House, Inc., New York, and in Canada
by Random House of Canada Limited, Toronto.

www.aaknopf.com

Knopf, Borzoi Books, and colophon are registered trademarks of
Random House, Inc.

Library of Congress Cataloging-in-Publication Data

Lansdale, Joe R., [date]
Vanilla Ride : a Hap and Leonard novel / by Joe R. Lansdale.—1st ed.
p. cm.
"This is a Borzoi book."
ISBN 978-0-307-27097-9
1. Collins, Hap (Fictitious character)—Fiction.   2. Pine, Leonard
(Fictitious character)—Fiction.   3. African American men—Fiction.
4. Drug dealers—Fiction.   5. Mafia—Fiction.   6. Texas—Fiction.
7. Adventure fiction.   I. Title.
PS3562.A557V36 2009
813'.54—dc22   2009008821

Manufactured in the United States of America
Published July 2, 2009
Second Printing, July 2009

For all you Hap and Leonard fans. Bless your little weird hearts.

The pistol is the devil's red right hand.

—Steve Earle

Man turns everything into a weapon. Even his tongue.

—Hap Collins

VANILLA RIDE

1

I hadn't been shot at in a while, and no one had hit me in the head for a whole month or two. It was kind of a record, and I was starting to feel special.

Brett and I were upstairs in our little rented house, lying in bed, breathing hard, having just arrived at the finish line of a slow, sweet race that at times can seem like a competitive sport, but when played right, even when you're the last to arrive, can make you feel like a winner.

In that moment, life was good.

Brett sat up and fluffed her pillow behind her back and pushed her long bloodred hair to the side with one hand, shoved her chest forward in a way that made me feel mighty lucky, said, "I haven't had that much fun since I pistol-whipped a redheaded midget."

"You don't know how romantic that makes me feel," I said. "I think Little Hap just went looking for a place to hide."

"I thought he just came out of hiding," she said, and winked at me.

Thing was, she actually *had* pistol-whipped a midget. I was there. She was trying to find her daughter and save her life, but still, it was ugly, and I was a party to it. I will say this, however, in favor of the midget: he took his beating with stoic pride and refused to take it while wearing his cowboy hat, an expensive Stetson. He wanted it right on the skull and that's where he got it.

"You know, I think they prefer being called *dwarf* instead of *midget*, or *little people*," I said.

"No kidding. I don't know about the rest of them, but the one I worked over, I just call him Pistol-Whipped."

"Do you ever feel bad about it?"

"Nope."

"He died, you know."

"Not from the pistol whipping."

This was also true. He ended up dead another way, but, man, that had been some pistol whipping. She had also set her ex-husband's head on fire and put it out with a shovel, which is a far cry from a water hose. My sweet baby, at times, could make a man nervous.

She said, "Speaking of little guys," and took hold of my crotch.

"Little guys?" I said. "That's supposed to fire me up?"

"No. I'll fire you up."

She chuckled and slid over close and I took her in my arms and we snuggled. Things were looking operational when there was a knock on the door.

Typical.

I looked at the clock on the nightstand. Eleven p.m.

The knock came again, louder.

I got up and pulled on my robe and bunny slippers, and cursed. "Keep that thought. I'm going down to kill a late-night Bible salesman."

"Will you bring me back his head, please?"

"On a platter."

2

Downstairs, I went to the window, eased back the curtain and took a peek. Two big black guys, one supported on a stick, were standing on the steps. My best friend, Leonard Pine, and an ex-cop buddy, Marvin Hanson.

I opened the door.

"Sure isn't good to see you," I said to Leonard.

Leonard pushed on in. He was decked out in cowboy boots, jeans, a faded snap-pocket shirt that was a little stretched across his broad shoulders, and a shit-eating grin. "Now that's no way to be," he said.

"Your timing as usual is impeccable, brother," I said.

"Thank you."

"Leave your horse and hat at the corral?"

"The horse is wearing the hat," Leonard said. "After the fun me and him had, I thought he deserved a little token of my appreciation. You can bet he'll call tomorrow."

"You're funnier earlier in the day," I said.

Marvin came in more slowly, using the cane.

"Like them foot rabbits," he said, nodding at my shoes.

"Yeah, me and them are buds," I said. "You're getting around good."

"You should have seen me before we went dancing. Those hip-hop steps have a way of making you weak."

"We went for tacos," Leonard said. "This guy, you can't get him to do nothing fun. His idea of a good time is chewing gum with a fruity flavor."

"Where's the love of your life?" I asked Leonard.

"John?"

"No. Winston Churchill."

"He's mad at me."

"Imagine that."

"It's nothing much. I think we called each other bitches and then I got mad enough to take a dump in the middle of the bed, and did."

"Overshare," I said.

"We both forget what started it, and we're both holding out for an apology. I will, of course, cave, and then we'll be back to normal. You got anything to eat?"

"I thought you ate tacos?"

"Two, maybe three hours ago."

"I'm not feeling all that friendly right now," I said. "Why would I want to feed you?"

"Interrupt something?" Leonard said, sliding into the kitchen to open the refrigerator.

"Yeah, me and Brett were just setting up the checkerboard. Marvin, why do you hang with this riffraff?"

Marvin found a soft chair and was sitting there, stretching out his leg, rubbing his knee. "I hang with him because I pity him."

"So why let him bother me?"

"Leonard said you love late-night company."

"He's a lying sonofabitch."

"Hey, boys," Brett said.

I turned and saw her coming down the stairs. She had on a white shorty robe and her hair was bed fluffed and her legs were long enough to make a giraffe drown himself. Her eyes were half closed and she was beautiful.

Leonard came back into the living room, empty-handed.

Brett finished off the stairs, said, "Hi, Leonard."

"Hi, Brett. You got anything to eat?"

"John lets you out to play this late?" she said.

"I'll make it up to him tomorrow," Leonard said. "I've got some moves, honey. If you like, I could show Hap some of my tricks, though it would be purely theoretical, of course."

"Your biology sucks," I said. "John. Brett. Different plumbing. Wouldn't work."

"Hi, Marvin," she said.

Marvin smiled, gave her a little wave.

"I'm having milk and cookies," she said. "Anyone else?"

"Me. Me," Leonard said. "Are the cookies by any chance . . . vanilla?"

"They are," Brett said. "Hap keeps them just for you, baby. There's also your favorite. Dr Peppers. These are from the only plant where the original formula is used. We drove over there special to get them."

"We were passing by the plant," I said, "so I thought, why not."

Leonard looked at me and batted his eyes. "You are the sweetest bastard ever squatted to crap over a pair of shoes."

"Cookies aren't just for you," I said. "I like them too. And Dr Pepper."

"He's a liar," Brett said. "He keeps them for you. He drinks that diet crap. Go sit down. Milk or Dr Pepper with your cookies?"

"Need you ask?" Leonard said.

"Marvin?" Brett said. "How about you?"

"Milk and cookies sounds fine."

"Great," she said. "Hap, get your ass in there and get the cookies. Some for me too. Chop-chop."

I started toward the kitchen. As I passed her, she grabbed my arm. "Just kidding," she said. "I'll get them. I was just evaluating your training. You get an A. Later I'll give you a treat, and it won't be a dog biscuit."

She leaned forward and kissed me on the lips.

As I started back into the living room area Leonard said, "Good dog. Next you'll be off the newspapers and using the yard."

"That's my goal."

I sat down on the couch, the far end from Leonard, who had kicked off his shoes and was stretching his legs out.

"I can't see what Brett sees in you, Hap," Leonard said.

"It's the parts you don't see," I said.

"Nor do I want to."

"I'm thinking, maybe," I said, "you didn't really come over here to interrupt my sex life and have milk and cookies."

"I'm having Dr Pepper," Leonard said. "Dr Pepper that you got special just for me."

"Go to hell, Leonard."

"You're right, Hap," Marvin said. "We didn't come over to have milk and cookies. It's a little more complicated than that."

3

We finished up our milk and cookies, Leonard his Dr Pepper and cookies, then Brett went upstairs to bed. The treat she offered me would have to be held in abeyance. I considered the delay Leonard's fault, and gave him a black mark on my mental chalkboard. No star for you, asshole. Next time I'd get RC instead of Dr Pepper, see how that pulled his chain, maybe get some of those nasty coconut cookies he hated. I hated them too, but the punishment was worth consideration.

We went out in the yard to talk so Brett wouldn't be bothered by our big mouths. She had bought some metal lawn chairs and put them out there, and I kept expecting to come out some morning and find they'd been chair-napped, as our part of the neighborhood was getting bad. Used to, you could leave your wallet on the porch swing and no one would bother it. These days, you left a cheese grater out, someone would steal the holes.

It was a nice night and there weren't too many lights on our street, and the sky was clear so you could look up through the limbs of the elm tree at the edge of the yard and see stars. It was too cool for crickets and there wasn't any traffic on the road out front. The air smelled fresh and a little sweet, like a baby's breath, and in that moment I was glad we lived there in that house with that yard and that big elm, in what the old books about the South used to call genteel poverty.

After seating ourselves in the lawn chairs, I crossed my legs and dangled a bunny shoe.

Leonard said, "Man, you could have at least put on pants. That robe is a little too peekaboo."

"My motto," I said, "is if you've got it, flaunt it."

"What you're flauntin' is enough to make a man turn a gun on himself," Leonard said.

Marvin said, "I got a job proposition to discuss."

"You're gonna love this, Hap," Leonard said.

I looked at Marvin. "Am I?"

"I don't think you're going to throw a parade, but here it is," Marvin said. "My daughter's daughter, her boyfriend, he's been beating on her."

This fit in with the theme Brett and I had been discussing. Maybe I should just send her over there with a shovel. If there was a dwarf, I could send her with a pistol.

I said, "Boyfriend? Your granddaughter? What is she, like twelve?"

"Eighteen."

"Get out," I said.

"They grow fast," he said.

"And she's a cutie," Leonard said. "You should see her. A dirty old hetero man like you, you'd love her."

"You've seen her?"

"Photograph," Leonard said.

I turned to Marvin. "So what exactly is the deal?"

"Well, he whipped up on her and I went over and caught him pulling into his place and he got out and I beat him a little bit with my cane. It wore me out and it didn't do my cane any good and I scuffed up a good pair of shoes. I had to get a new cane and have the shoes shined. That ain't a quarter no more. White boys are doing it now, by the way. They like at least five dollars."

"Inflation," Leonard said.

"How old is the boyfriend?" I asked.

"Twenty-five or so," Marvin said. "I don't know exactly. Old enough to be a better person than he is. Old enough for me to kill him and drop his body in a hole somewhere."

"So you beat him with your cane, and now you want . . . what?" I said. "Sounds like to me you took care of the problem, gave him an attitude adjustment. Did you leave the old cane up his ass and you want us to fetch it?"

"Deal is," Marvin said, "he didn't like it much, that beating, and he has friends he can go to. And my leg, it's just getting good, but it's not that good. I can whip one ass easy enough, but multiple asses, not so sure. And I'm only up for one ass at a time, maybe once a week during certain hours after lunch and well before sunset when the stars are aligned just right . . . I was lucky I caught him alone, without his posse."

"Call me foolish," I said, "but since you used to be a cop, did it occur to you that you might want to call the law and maybe have them go over there and do the domestic violence thing?"

"Therein lays the Shakespearean rub," Marvin said.

"That sounds like something I'd like on my middle leg," Leonard said.

"You see, my granddaughter, Julia, we call her Gadget, this guy she's with, he's kind of a drug dealer."

"Kind of?" I asked.

"Okay," Marvin said. "Absolutely he is. And if the law gets involved, well, she could get involved."

"I'm not loving this at all, Leonard."

"I was being facetious."

I turned to Marvin. Fearing I already knew the answer, I asked, "Why would she get involved if the law got involved?"

"Because she is selling grass out of their trailer, and they, as I said, are drug dealers. As for the law, they are in the drug dealer's pocket, in there with the lint and the pocket change. So it could really turn out bad."

"I probably should know this already," I said, "but what about Gadget's father? Maybe he can do something."

Marvin shook his head. "No reason you should know. I don't make a point of talking about him much. He ran off when she was a fetus, and now her mother is at her wits' end."

"So what you need from us is . . . ?" I asked.

"I need someone to do some serious ass whipping, and bring her home. If you can get by without the ass whipping and just bring her home, that'll do. But I'd like to think there will be an ass whipping. Not meaning her ass, of course."

"What if she doesn't want to come home?"

"I think she will. I think she would have the other day, but at the last minute she didn't. I'm not up to snuff. I burned myself out and didn't have any energy left, so I had to let her go. There wasn't anything I could do. I bluffed my way out to the car and got out of there. But you two, you can do it. You can bring her home."

I studied on this a moment, looked at Leonard. He gave me a small nod. I said, "We'll do it, but she doesn't want to come home, I don't know what to tell you. That's the case, we bring her back, she'll just run off again."

"I understand that," Marvin said. "But I saw something in her eyes before she got pulled away. She wanted to come home. I'm not sure she knows it outright, but I could tell."

"I don't trust things you see in people's eyes," I said. "You might be seeing your own reflection."

"Me neither," Leonard said, "but I'd sure like to whip that guy's ass. We could make it a weekly tradition."

"You mentioned that he has a posse," I said.

"He does. My catching him alone . . . I understand that's rare."

"How many?"

"From my sources, I hear four, sometimes less, sometimes more. But generally, four. They stay in a trailer out in the woods. That's where I caught him. I wasn't using my head. Had they been there with him, my picture would probably be on a milk carton, people out beating the bushes, digging up anything looked like a grave. I don't think they're all that rough-and-tumble, but I don't want you to think they can't be dangerous they catch you just right."

"Who are your sources, far as the size of his posse goes?"

"Formerly bad people gone straight. Or so they say. They may still be bad people. But I trust them on their head count."

"Four is a lot," I said.

"Hey," Marvin said, "you two against a trailer full of scum, that's not fair to the scum."

"Don't blow me, Marvin," I said.

"I wouldn't think of it. But you show up in that robe and bunny slippers, you're bound to have them licked. They'll laugh themselves to death."

"You're kind of nasty for a man wanting a favor," I said.

Marvin grinned at me, then his face let loose of the smile and his eyes narrowed. "Look. I need your help. I'm asking . . . Hell, I'm begging a little, just not so that you can tell, all right?"

"This guy, what's his name?"

"Oddly enough, I don't know. I know where he lives. He has one of those sixties-style Afros, maybe not as big as the really big ones, but you know, out there, Jimi Hendrix like. But I can put you right at his trailer."

I looked at Leonard. He gave me a nod.

I said, "We'll scope it out. See what we can do."

4

The place where Gadget was selling grass and her boyfriend was selling meaner drugs when he wasn't using Gadget for a racquetball was not in LaBorde but just outside a nearby town called No Enterprise, where the law was two fat guys in a used cop car with so-so tires. They took the town's cop checks, but they didn't do much for it, except maybe catch a speeder now and then, maybe talk some gal into a blow job to get a pass on a ticket. The real money was in crooked enterprise. Or so Marvin told us. And Marvin isn't often wrong about stuff like that. He was a cop for years. First in Houston, then in LaBorde. He said he knew about those guys and told us about them, and I took his word to be as true as the turning of the earth.

We drove over to No Enterprise in my pickup. The truck is one of those Dodges with a backseat and four doors and a short bed. I had recently traded for it and it ran good.

· It was raining and it was a cool day, especially for early fall. Just the night before we had been sitting in my yard in shirtsleeves, and now it was cool enough to wish for excess hair on your chest. As for women, I don't know exactly what they'd wish for. Probably a nice coat and a pair of shoes. I know Brett liked coats and shoes, especially shoes. She had enough in the closet to shoe a couple of monster-size centipedes, as long as they liked their footwear to come from Payless, Wal-Mart or Target. Equating women with shoes might be an old sexist cliché, but it didn't change the fact Brett had a lot of shoes.

What Leonard and I had were some windbreakers. Mine was blue. Leonard's was beige. We made a point of making sure we weren't wearing the same colors. It's hard to be convincing as tough guys when you're wearing matching outfits.

We had the address from Marvin, and of course the thing to do was not to just drive right up on the place, as that would be foolish and dangerous, but, since the two of us together sometimes can only manage the IQ level of a ground squirrel, that's exactly what we were going to do. We tried to come up with some nifty sophisticated plan on the way over, but we kept getting distracted and singing along with the CD player. We had to listen to Leonard's music. If I didn't want to, he pouted. He can pout big-time. Since we were in my truck and it was my CD player, I should have chosen some of the music. I wanted to play Amy Winehouse. He didn't.

Anyway, we drove over there singing to Kasey Lansdale's *Back of My Smile* CD, some Hank Williams, and a bit of Ernest Tubb. All good stuff. Then we listened to Patsy Cline. Neither of us had the balls to sing along with Patsy. That just isn't done. By the time we were five miles outside of No Enterprise it occurred to us that we had yet to concoct some kind of strategy, so we stopped off in town at Big Burger, a local place that served food and was also a filling station with an open garage. Inside the garage was a lube rack and a lonely-looking guy in blue khakis sitting on an old-fashioned Coke crate turned on edge. He was reading without fear of insult a sex book titled in bold letters *Poontang Palace*. The book was probably older than the reader, and considering the size of the town he probably read more books than he lubed transmissions.

Inside, they took our order and a lanky guy in an apron brought it to the little table where we sat, placed the hamburger plates on the plastic checkered tablecloth, and went away. They made a good hamburger and some French fries that tasted as if they had been put out on the drainboard and pissed on the night before and left to dry. We both bought potato chips as a replacement and pondered how a place could make such good hamburgers and such shitty fries. What kind of cook could fry a burger and couldn't dip some French fries in a deep fryer without screwing them up?

At that moment it seemed like a question equal to "why are we here?" We came closer to solving the French fry enigma than coming up with any kind of plan to deal with our problem concerning Gadget and her keepers.

"We're just going to rough him up, aren't we?" I said.

"He hit Gadget."

"We don't really know Gadget."

"She's Marvin's granddaughter, isn't she?"

"She is."

"All I need to know, Hap, ole buddy."

"So, we punch him in the head a little and we take Gadget with us."

"We can punch him lots of places. He's got friends, we got to punch them too."

"Okay, so we punch him and anyone else gets in our way, and we punch them all kinds of places, and then we take Gadget."

"Always been the plan, far as I'm concerned."

"And if she doesn't want to go?" I asked.

"We could take her."

"That wouldn't be smart, and it wouldn't be any good. You know that. We told Marvin that."

"You told him," Leonard said, sipped his coffee and looked out the window at cars going by on the highway.

"But you know it's true," I said.

"Yeah, I know it. But I don't like bastards like this guy and I don't like what he's done to the granddaughter. . . . Ever notice how many cars are red these days? That used to be bad luck, a red car."

"No. I haven't noticed. We don't know this guy has done anything. She might be making him do it."

"Making him do it? Sayin', 'How's about hittin' me upside the head'? That what she's doin'?"

"I don't mean she deserves it. I mean it may be some kind of sexual ritual. He punches her in the eye, then she sucks his dick. Then she punches him in the eye, and he goes for the taco. Then they start all over again."

"That what you think?"

"No."

"Just like to hear yourself talk, don't you, Hap?"

"Pretty much," I said.

"So we're back to roughing his ass up and seeing she wants to go with us."

"Yeah, that's pretty much it," I said. "That is the plan. I mean, why do something smart and safe and well coordinated, when we can just drive up on them and start throwing knuckles."

"Sometimes it works."

"Sometimes it does. And sometimes we get our asses kicked around."

"I know," Leonard said. "I've seen it happen. But that ain't often, is it?"

"Once is too goddamn often."

"Point taken. Chocolate pie?"

5

We finished off our lunch with chocolate pie and more coffee, considered having another slice and another cup but talked ourselves out of it, reminded by the fact that we had a job to do, a promise to keep, and we didn't want to do it toting too much weight in our bellies.

Outside I took a peek in the garage. The reader was still sitting on the upturned Coke crate, engrossed in his book. I sort of hoped no one would want a tire changed or a manifold replaced. I'd hate to think such intense concentration might be broken. A car backfired out on the highway. The dedicated reader didn't move. He didn't bat an eye. I guess he was at the good part, where someone was about to put the arrow in the target.

Leonard came over and stood by me, said, "Come on, doofus. I been standing out by the truck waiting. Let's roll."

Following Marvin's directions over to the place, we listened to some more music and sang along some more, this time with Willie Nelson. I thought I did a pretty good "Blue Eyes Crying in the Rain." Leonard didn't think so. We sang "In the Jailhouse Now," which I thought might be a form of prophecy, considering what we were about to do.

Where we were going was kind of a peckerwood suburb, which was pretty much a clutch of fall-defoliated trees, some evergreen pines, a listing mobile home, and a dog hunched to drop a load in what passed for a yard. The dog was medium-sized, dirty yellow, and looked like the last meal he'd eaten was what he was dropping. He was working so hard at dropping those turds, his eyes were damn near crossed, had the kind of concentration that made you consider he might be close to figuring out the problems of string theory. He didn't look owned. Had the look of a freelance dog. Maybe there was something to be said for that.

The yard wasn't much. The rain had stopped and windblown leaves had bunched up all over the place. There were some cars parked there, and there were some people standing next to the cars. Eight guys, to be exact. They looked pretty young. There was a fellow standing in the doorway of the trailer in Scooby Doo shorts scratching his nuts like a squirrel sorting acorns. He was young too. I didn't see anyone I thought was Gadget, unless she had been disguised as the stray yellow dog or was in that fellow's shorts hiding next to his nut sack.

We parked and Leonard got my .38 snub-nosed revolver out of the glove box and stuck it in his pants and pulled his shirt and windbreaker over it. I have a gun permit, as does Leonard, but that gun wasn't on it. It wasn't even registered. It was for nefarious deeds.

I said, "Don't use that."

"Hey, better to have and not need than not have and need."

"What about me?"

"You didn't want me to use it, but now you want to carry it? I don't think so."

"It's my gun."

"Tough shit. Use your suave and debonair fucking charm."

We got out and started walking toward the trailer. The people in the yard rapidly divided into two camps: the scared and the nervous. Some of them got in their cars and drove away quickly. They would be the buyers. The rest started inside the trailer. They would be the drug-selling posse. The guy in the shorts let them pass, then took his position again, hand in his drawers. He looked at us like he thought he was tough enough to chew the edge off a Buck knife. I didn't think he looked as tough as he thought. However, sometimes looks can be deceiving.

There was what passed for music coming out of the trailer. Rap, I guess, but it sounded like someone beating an active washing machine with a log chain.

I said to Leonard as we walked up, "Take it easy, play it cool."

"Cool is my middle name," Leonard said.

"No," I said. "No, it isn't."

We were close to the front door when the man holding his balls, a black guy with pale skin and a longish Afro that made him look like a time traveler from the late sixties, early seventies, said, "Man, you two are fuckin' my game. You didn't come here for what we sell, I can tell."

"Ain't this where they're having the revival?" Leonard said. "I been wanting Jesus in my heart, or up my ass or somethin'. Way you're digging, is he in them Scooby shorts with you?"

"You a funny nigger," the black man said. "You don't know shit. Scooby is cool. What the fuck you want?"

The idea that our bad guy guarding the door was worried about our dissing Scooby amused me a bit. We had stopped about four feet from the door. The trailer was up on concrete blocks, so the guy in the doorway was standing above us. He was still playing pocket pool. By this point, my nuts would have been chafed and my hand would have been tired enough I would have had to call in reinforcements. His legs had bruises on them. I figured that would be from Marvin's cane. Behind him, in the slight darkness, I could see movement, and the sound of the music was loud enough and bad enough that the idea of kicking someone's ass was beginning to appeal, if for no other reason than their lack of taste.

"I don't like being called a nigger even when a nigger calls me that," Leonard said.

"That some kind of joke too?"

"You see me laughin'?" Leonard said.

Another man, a lanky but muscled white guy with a close-shaved scalp, appeared at the Afro guy's shoulder, looked out, said, "You want I should take care of them?"

"I ask you shit?" the Afro man said. "You hear me ask some shit from you? Go on in there and sit your white ass down. Pet the fuckin' dog or pat my old lady's ass, but don't be gettin' in my game unless I call on you."

"Have it your fuckin' way," the white guy said, and disappeared back inside the trailer.

"I'm pettin' your gal's ass," the white guy called from somewhere inside.

"That was like just a fuckin' thing to say. Don't you do it, asshole," the Afro guy said, glancing inside the trailer. Then he looked back at us.

I said, "Could you ask him to turn down the music? I think I saw a bird fall out of a tree."

He ignored me. "You cops?"

"We look like cops?" Leonard said.

"He does," he said, pointing a finger at me.

"He's white," Leonard said. "All white guys look like cops."

"I resent that," I said.

"We ain't cops," Leonard said. "Now, get your hand off your bulbs, we maybe can do a little business. But you and me. No matter what the business. We ain't shakin' hands."

The Afro guy didn't pull his hand out of his shorts. His eyes narrowed. "All right, you buyin' somethin' or not?"

Leonard said, "You're right. I fess up. We don't want to buy anything. To be precise, we're here to take somethin'. It's Gadget we want."

"Gadget?"

"Yep," I said.

"You guys are nuts. Ain't nobody around but you two, and there's four of us and a badass dog, and you're tellin' me you're takin' my woman?"

"If you had two dogs," Leonard said, "now that would be different."

"There's a dog?" I said.

The guy in the doorway shifted his nuts to the other side of his shorts and looked exasperated. "Gadget ain't goin' nowhere, man. She's my hole."

"Damn, that's a romantic reference," I said. "You say you got a dog in there?"

"She ain't goin'," the man said.

"Only if she wants to go," I said. "And maybe even if she doesn't want to. We're kind of up in the air on that part . . . What kind of dog is it?"

"Ah," he said, "I get it. You two from that old nigger. Her granddaddy. That fuckin' cripple."

"Whipped your ass with a cane, didn't he?" Leonard said. "That was some lively old cripple, wouldn't you say? Your legs look like a fuckin' zebra with them bruises."

"He caught me off guard."

"He hit you with that stick like he was dustin' a rug, Tanedrue," the white guy said from somewhere inside.

"You shut the fuck up," Tanedrue said.

He turned back to us.

Leonard laughed a little. "Tanedrue? That's your name? Your mama made that name up, didn't she?"

"It's African."

"Naw it ain't," Leonard said. "If that don't scream ignorant backwoods nigger, I don't know what does. That was my name, I'd stick a sharp stick up my ass and impale myself."

"That's it," Tanedrue said, and reached back into the trailer with his right hand. For a slight moment he was distracted, which of course was what we were waiting for.

Leonard moved quickly, caught Tanedrue by the feet, jerked them up and out. Tanedrue's head smacked on the bottom of the trailer doorway and then Leonard dragged him down the metal stairs so that his head bounced on each and every one of them. I saw a bit of blood fly out from Tanedrue's skull, then he went limp and tumbled off the stairs, his hand still in his shorts. No doubt about it, he was one tenacious ball handler.

We kept moving, straight into the trailer.

6

The white guy with the shaved head was the first one at the door. Leonard hit him between the eyes with a swinging elbow so hard I'm sure a distant relative in bad health in the old country crossed his eyes and died. The blow made the goon spin around and away from us. He went down on one knee and held his head, just to make sure it was still attached. While he was on his knees, his legs slightly spread, Leonard kicked him in the balls like he was making a soccer goal.

I was in right behind Leonard. As I entered, the music smacked me like a fist and the stink of the place draped over me like a blanket. Then a dog jumped at me from the shadows. It was a big, dark, growling dog and it was part of the stench. It went for my throat. I moved to the side slightly and caught the dog by the collar with one hand as its teeth snapped in the air, and saliva from the snap popped across my fore-head. With the other hand, I caught its hind leg and picked it up high as I could manage. It was a heavy dog. I saw a window out of the corner of my eye, just over a stained kitchen sink. I tossed the dog at it, hard as I could. The window cracked and the dog went through it in a shower of black and tan fur and a tinkling of glass, its body doing a kind of horseshoe maneuver from the impact. The dog let out a whelp and a yip and then I heard nothing but the sound of its body striking the earth outside. There was blood and fur on the jagged glass. I suspected fleas had pulled parachute cords.

I heard Leonard say, "Come to papa," and when I turned my head, I caught sight of Leonard holding a big bushy-headed white guy by the back of the neck, slamming his head into the wall so hard a mirror fell off and shattered.

As I turned, a thin black guy came down the hall at a rush, clubbed me in the ribs with a right hook that nearly caused me to piss myself. I tried to kick him, but there wasn't any room. In a reflex action he shoved out with both hands, hit me in the chest and knocked me down on top of the guy Leonard had kicked in the balls. The ball-kicked dude was resting politely on the floor whimpering like a little girl who had lost her dolly, hands between his legs.

"You hurt my dog," said the guy who shoved me.

I rolled up and he kicked at me and I scooped my hand under his leg and grabbed his face with my other hand and used my closest leg to sweep his standing leg out from under him. He hit his head on a counter, his teeth snapped together on his tongue, and he went down, blood foaming out of his mouth. I smelled something that made me think he'd bent a biscuit in his skivvies.

I heard a shriek from the back, looked down the hall. A young, long-legged woman was running at me. She was a dark-skinned girl with a lot of processed hair, maybe some extensions, and for all I knew a recent manicure and a toe ring. She jumped on me with her legs spread and straddled me, her ankles locked around my back; she had hold of my hair with one hand and was clawing my face with the other, still shrieking.

I hit her with a right cross between the eyes and she let go, though her legs stayed hooked. She fell back on her head, then her legs came undone and they sort of melted toward the floor with the rest of her.

Leonard was still working on the big hairy guy, had him by the mane and was smashing his head into the wall, cracking the paneling. All I could tell for sure was the guy now had a very flat nose and his lips looked like fat fishing worms that were coming apart. One of his teeth was embedded in the paneling and there was blood on the wall. One more slam and a big crucifix fell and bounced on the couch and then bounced on top of the ball-kicked guy and then onto the floor.

The ball-kicked guy had gotten some juice back. Maybe the crucifix revived him. He tried to get up, made it to his hands and knees. Leonard, without letting go of the guy whose head he was bouncing, kneed the other dude in the face, knocking him back down. He winced, did a kind of push-up, tried to come up. I got him from behind, right in the snickerdoodles again. He farted and went down and didn't get up, either knocked out, dead, or hoping to God we thought he was. Right then he was probably wishing he had been thrown out the window with the dog. I was too. That was quite a fart.

I took a breath and put a hand on my side, then my face. I was bleeding from where the girl had scratched me.

I did a quick reconnoiter. It looked as if the trailer occupants were all pretty much Nap City. Leonard whirled the guy whose nose he had flattened around and hit him with a hard strike to the neck with the side of his hand. The guy went down. Not that he really needed that neck strike. He was going to fall anyway. Leonard kicked him once just to keep himself flexible.

I picked up the CD player on a shelf over the couch and slammed it against the wall. The CD flew out of it and I stepped on it. It felt good to have the air filled with emptiness.

That's when the now awake Tanedrue came wobbling through the door, his hand no longer in his shorts. He reached for what he had been reaching for before, something just inside the door on top of the refrigerator. A little automatic. He got hold of it. As he brought it around, Leonard pulled my .38 and shot Tanedrue in the right thigh, just below the shorts. Tanedrue dropped the automatic, grabbed his leg, let out a yell that made my asshole pinch tight, then went down shrieking, holding his thigh, blood squirting everywhere.

"Goddamn, Leonard!"

Leonard gave me an exasperated look. "I started to let him shoot you, but I thought Brett would be mad."

"Goddamn, Leonard."

The guy who had bitten his tongue was closest at hand, so I grabbed his shirt by the front and pulled hard. It ripped off of his unconscious body, and I stuck it in Tanedrue's wound. Tanedrue cussed me and struck out at me, so I hit him in the head a couple of times. "Lay down, you stupid fuck, before you bleed to death."

"You shot me!" he said.

"Technically, he shot you," I said, jerking my head at Leonard.

Leonard tossed my .38 on the couch, grabbed Tanedrue by the Afro and lifted him off the ground a little, slid behind him, and slipped his forearm around his neck, pushing in tight on the arteries there. He slid his choking hand into the bend of his other elbow and locked the other hand behind Tanedrue's head, compressed while he expanded his chest.

Tanedrue passed out quicker than an asthmatic octogenarian fucking a sheep in a stuffy hayloft.

"Now fix him," Leonard said, letting Tanedrue drop.

"I don't know he can be fixed."

"It ain't through an artery. I'm a better shot than that."

"No, you're not."

"Yeah. Okay, I was lucky."

Leonard was right. Tanedrue was hit through the meaty part of the thigh and he was losing blood from the hole in his leg, but the main artery had been missed. I tore some more of the shirt off the guy on the floor and wrapped Tanedrue's leg as best I could, put my ear to his chest to make sure he was breathing. Leonard had used a blood choke, but sometimes they don't come back.

"I guess that's Gadget passed out over there," I said.

"She wasn't as glad to see us as I had hoped," Leonard said. "I saw you hit her. You hit her hard. If she was wearing a Tampax, I bet you knocked it out of her ass."

"She rearranged my looks a little," I said, touching the scratches on my face.

"You look like an old-fashioned German duelist."

I picked up Tanedrue's automatic and went to the back of the trailer, just in case someone was hiding back there with a shotgun and a machete. There was no one else left. On a chest of drawers in front of a mirror there were some bags of white powder that I didn't mistake for self-rising flour. There were some boxes of baby laxative there too, for cutting the stuff. On the floor were empty cheese cracker boxes, lots of wrappers for sweets and empty soft drink cans and bottles and a near-empty jar of peanut butter with the lid off. There was a box of half-eaten Cracker Jack. That would be the property of the health nut of the bunch. What remained of the peanut butter had turned dark as dried dog shit. And there was plenty of that to go around too. Dog shit in the corner, on the floor by the bed, at the edge of the dresser. There was a footprint in that pile. Not mine. This footprint was bare. There were some other piles that someone had thoughtfully covered with paper towels. Whoever did that was probably considered prissy. A fat roach crawled out of the peanut butter jar and scuttled under the bed.

Taped to the mirror on the dresser were birthday cards, an old Christmas card. They said "To Tanedrue" and were signed "Mom." I felt a little sick looking at those, had to wonder how his mom felt about how her boy had turned out. For that matter, if my mother was alive, how would she have felt about me, hitting people and throwing dogs out windows? It wasn't a line of thought I wanted to linger on.

When I looked up, I noticed the walls of the trailer were moving. I had seen it before in white trash housing and poor black folk shacks. Cockroaches. They were so thick in the walls they made the paneling flex like it was breathing. Yuck.

I went back to where Leonard was slapping Tanedrue briskly on the cheeks to either bring him awake or give his cheeks a touch of color.

"Wake up, nigger," Leonard said.

"They got some real bad stuff back there," I said. "And perhaps, as a nod to political correctness, I should note, for your own good, that you're using the N word."

"I've been busy with words and slapping in here," Leonard said. "I've done run out on the cocksucker word, and I wore out mother-fucker, and sonofabitch seems so lame, so I'm going for the gold . . . Ah, Sleeping Beauty awakes."

7

Tanedrue woke up. We were squatting down beside him. Leonard said, "Every time I think of Gadget's grandpa beating your ass with a cane, I get a kind of warm feeling all over. In fact, my dick gets hard."

Tanedrue said, "I'm bleeding to death."

"You ain't bleeding to death, dumb ass," Leonard said. "Not yet, anyway. It got the fat part of your leg, went all the way through. Bleeding has mostly stopped because Hap, who is like goddamn Florence Nightingale with a pecker, stuck your buddy's shirt in the bullet hole and stopped the bleeding. Course, you might want to worry about blood poisoning from the dye in the shirt, that would be my concern. Oh yeah, and the bullet."

"You could have shot my balls off."

"You'd have to have some first," I said.

Tanedrue was sitting on the floor with his legs stuck out, his back against the refrigerator, looking around. "You fucked everybody up, you done killed them."

"No," Leonard said, "nobody's dead. The fucked-up part is right, probably a concussion here and there, so I'd wake them up pretty quick. Word is on concussions . . . you shouldn't sleep. Do that, sometimes you don't wake up, and what a shame that would be. Think of the loss to art, science, and literature. Oh, and the big guy there, with all the hair. He may not have a real profile anymore, so photo shots of him might be best from the front, him wearing a bag over his head, standing somewhat at a distance."

"They could die," Tanedrue said. "You might have hurt them real bad. And me, I don't feel so good either."

"Boy, that's a shame," Leonard said. "Considering you were going to shoot us, you fuckin' asshole! Pour some monkey blood on it and shut up. Now listen here: Leave Gadget alone. Stay away from her. And if you have a day where you think maybe we've forgotten about you and you decide to bother her again, that's the day we kneecap you, asshole, and then I'm gonna put your ass in an ant bed after I stuff it full of Gummi Bears, and then I'm gonna set your head on fire, and then I'm gonna get mad. Savvy?"

"Gummi Bears?" I said.

Tanedrue was almost crying, but he was still defiant. "You don't know what you're up against, nigger."

About that time the guy whose shirt I had torn off woke and tried to sit up. I said, "Lay back down, ball sweat."

He lay down and closed his eyes and stretched his arms out at his sides with the palms down and was quiet as a dead mouse.

"Now," Leonard said, standing, "we'll be taking Gadget with us, and before I go, I want to leave you with one more piece of wisdom."

Leonard kicked Tanedrue in the head, hard, knocking his noggin back against the refrigerator. Without knowing it was going to come out of my mouth, I said, "Ouch."

"You get my drift, dick cheese?" Leonard said.

Tanedrue nodded, blood dripping from his mouth, his hand held to the side of his head.

"Say it," Leonard said.

"I got you," Tanedrue said.

"That's good. And you know, this place . . . you ought to get some nice curtains, a little better lighting, one of those de-stinkers that plug into the 'lectric socket, a friendlier goddamn dog. This joint is fuckin' depressin'."

"You ought to see the dog shit in the back room," I said. "It's not a pretty sight."

"Clean that up too," Leonard said. "Goddamn dog don't want to see that, wonder he hasn't committed dog-acide. Better yet, set fire to this whole place and start over."

"Your little white powder in the back," I said. "I'm gonna have to get rid of it."

I put Tanedrue's automatic in my waistband without blowing my dick off, went back to the bedroom. I could hear Tanedrue calling out, "Don't do it, man. There's people gonna be mad and they're so bad they make you two look like weenies. I ain't jerkin' you. Come on, man. We can work some kind of deal."

I heard Leonard give Tanedrue a whack and then the guy went silent.

I got the bags one at a time and took them to the bathroom and used my pocketknife to cut them open and flush the contents down the toilet, which was a nasty little number with a dark ring inside the bowl that wasn't some kind of design.

I could hear Tanedrue groan every time he heard the toilet flush. I kept at it until I was finished. I took a leak and washed my hands and came back and stood over him. Leonard was squatting beside him.

I said, "All down the crapper. Thousands of dollars' worth of blow."

"You're gonna wish you hadn't done that," Tanedrue said. "Them guys we work for, they ain't got no sense of humor."

"That may be," Leonard said. "But a fashion tip. Them Scooby shorts, on a grown man, they aren't that cool. Trust me." Leonard sniffed at the air, looked at the guy on the floor without a shirt, wrinkled up his nose. "And maybe you ought to wipe that fucker's ass."

I looked down at Gadget. She was lying on her back, breathing deeply. She was wearing a tank top that barely kept her unfettered breasts in check and a pair of shorts that were cut so high and were so tight, if she yawned the damn things would have sucked up her ass. She was not bad to look at, though her eyes had dark circles like a raccoon's around them. I had only hit her once, so I figured Tanedrue or one of his brethren had done the bulk of the knocking. My shot had given her a knot in the center of her forehead about the size of a turnip, so I too could be proud.

I got the .38, leaned over, and picked her up and threw her over my shoulder. She was very light, maybe a hundred and ten pounds. That's great, Hap, you just punched out a little girl about half your weight.

I carried Gadget out to the truck and we looked around for their dog, just in case he was vengeful. But he was either on the other side of the trailer in a heap or had run off to join the circus. I hoped the latter. I liked dogs. I put Gadget in the backseat and Leonard got in the front and I drove us out of there. As we went, I saw the other dog, the yellow one, sitting beside the road. He turned his head to watch as we drove by.

Leonard turned to me, said, "Now, see. That worked out fine."

"I hate you," I said.

8

Leonard leaned back and looked over the seat at Gadget. He said, "She looks like some kind of angel got caught up in a fan."

"I hit her," I said.

"And boy did she have it coming."

"I feel like a bully."

"You had to do it."

"I still don't like it."

"Had she been wearing a nose ring, would you have felt better?"

"Just a bit," I said. "I really hate those things. Seriously tattooed arms would have helped too."

Leonard grinned and shook his head. "You worry too much about things that are done, my brother. She's taken beatings for no reason and you punched her because you wanted to keep your eyes in your head and get her away from those boneheads. Give yourself some slack."

"Hitting women is not on my list of gentlemanly activities."

"Well, whipping people's asses and throwing their dog out the window might not be on the list either."

"Yeah . . . well . . . At least I didn't shoot anyone."

"That's right, point that out, put it all on me. But unlike you, I don't feel guilty . . . Listen, man. You did what you had to do. And now we got to do something else. The .38 and dickhead's automatic."

We drove down some back trails and stopped by a little run of water that was just off the road and flowed out into the woods. The road was pretty messy and I figured if it rained harder it would be difficult to get down it, and even more difficult to get back out.

Climbing out of the truck, Leonard got some gloves from the toolbox fastened to the bed and wiped the .38 clean and threw it into the woods, into the shallow water there. He took the automatic and did the same.

We got back in the truck and I got back on the main road. "They find that stuff," Leonard said, "it don't mean a thing. We didn't own the automatic. And your .38 was as cold as the cunt between a dead nun's legs . . . Hey, Gadget. She's coming to."

Gadget sat up in the back and I watched her in the rearview mirror. She had a hand to her head. Right where I had hit her. "You hit me," she said.

"Right between the eyes," I said.

"He feels bad about it," Leonard said.

"That don't mean a damn thing to me. My head hurts."

"He did it with love," Leonard said.

"Who the fuck are you?" Then it struck her. "Ah, I know . . . My grandpa's friends. Hank and Larry."

"Hap and Leonard," Leonard said. "I'm Leonard, and he's Hap. You can remember the names because he's a white guy and I'm a black guy."

"I can see that . . . I know who you are."

"Yeah, but can you remember which of us is which," Leonard said. "Black guy, Leonard. White guy, Hap."

"Why did you do it?" she said.

"Your grandpa asked us to," I said. "And he's a friend, and we remember when you were a baby and everyone thought you were going to grow up to be worth something."

"That don't mean nothin'," she said. "I don't even remember you guys."

"In truth, you may not mean all that much to us," Leonard said, "but Marvin, he means a lot. Come on, gal. What the hell you doin'? We know you got raised better than that."

"You don't know nothin'."

"We know that," I said. "We know you weren't raised to bang drug dealers in a trailer with roaches in the walls and dog shit and a near empty jar of cheap peanut butter on the floor."

"Don't forget the cocaine," Leonard said.

"That too," I said.

"And a criminal dog," Leonard said. "That pup y'all got, he has done gone over to the dark side."

Gadget took a deep breath, narrowed her eyes. "I remember Grandpa said you two thought you were funny."

9

As we arrived in No Enterprise it started to rain heavy and the sky took on a hazy green look like nature had vomited into the heavens. The wind hit the truck hard enough to move it. Looking at the town through wet swaths made by the wipers, it was even more depressing, a weak hope thrown together with brick and glass. Someone thought the railroad would come through there many years ago, and it didn't. What was left now was nothing more than a hope and a dream.

The rain was running deep in the streets and in the gutters. My gas gauge pinged. We drove back to the place where we had eaten and parked under the overhang where the fuel pumps were. Leonard got out and began putting gas in the truck. The rain pounded on the overhang. The water splashed all around us. It was pretty dark for the time of day. I glanced at Leonard standing by the pump working the gas nozzle. He gave me a weak salute. I shot him the finger. He shot me the finger back. I never said we were mature.

I looked back at Gadget.

"How'd you get that name, Gadget?" I said. "I used to know, but I forgot."

She was slow with the answer. "I liked fixing things when I was a girl. I had a knack . . . Look, Grandpa shouldn't have asked you to do this. This isn't good for me or anyone. Other day, when he hit Tanedrue with the cane—"

"Hold up," I said. "How many times did he hit him? I just got to know."

"A lot. He did it quick. I thought Tanedrue was going to shoot him. I begged him not to."

"Your boyfriend sounds like aces. Goddamn, I bet you're proud."

"You got to take me back, Leonard—"

"I'm Hap."

"Whatever. Or let me out here, and I can call someone."

"We're someone."

"I mean someone Tanedrue knows. I can't call him. Cell phones don't work out there, and that's all they got. Cell phones. They like it that way. Hell, I don't even have a phone. Just let me have yours, so I can call someone in town they know, and then you can go on. I see them, I can tell them something, whatever you want, make it some kind of misunderstanding, and I can say you apologized—"

"Not likely," I said.

"You don't want to get into this any deeper and drag me down too. You do, and hell will be coming."

"Too late," I said. "Did you really like it out there, Gadget?"

Again, hesitation. "I don't know."

"That means no," I said.

"I loved Tanedrue."

"Loved?"

"Love. I love him."

"You want to go back because you're using. That's it, isn't it?"

"No."

"I think it is."

"I said it isn't."

"It isn't Tanedrue you want, it's the monkey."

"I just like it. I'm not hooked."

"That's what they all say."

She held her stomach.

I said, "You hungry?"

"I don't know."

"Let's start with the idea that you are."

"Sometimes, I try to eat, I throw up."

"That's the drugs, or . . ."

"I'm not pregnant. I been careful about that."

"So, you do have some common sense. Damn, girl. You don't have to do this, live like trash."

"You a social worker?"

"No. Unlike social workers, I really care."

She took a long time to respond again. That was okay. I was getting used to it.

"Tanedrue, he said he was gonna quit dealing, soon as he got us a nest egg."

"A rotten egg."

"He meant it. He loves me."

"You are young, aren't you?"

"You don't know everything."

"I don't know anything. Older I get, less I think I know. But I know this, and I'm going to be crude to make my point. What Tanedrue has is a dumb bitch he can screw and lie to and feed drugs to, and when he's through with you, when you get so fucked up you can't tell the difference between a fat mouse and a full-grown elephant, he'll get rid of you, kid. You won't be fresh meat to him no more. You won't be pretty, and you won't be nothing but a whining whore with a habit. Maybe just some dumb dead bitch in a ditch somewhere."

"I ain't no whore."

"You will be. That's how it'll work. He'll turn you out, baby. So he can make a few more bucks off his horse before it dies. He'll tell you how you're doin' it for the two of you, and it don't mean nothin', not really—"

"Shut up! You don't know everything."

"You said that already, and I even agreed with you."

Leonard opened the door, said, "Give me some gas money."

"You pay."

"I haven't got any money."

I gave him some money, hesitated, said, "Let's get some coffee. Gadget here, she might could eat something."

"I'm not hungry," she said.

"Then watch us drink coffee," I said. "And if you run off, we'll just chase you down. We don't care how it looks or what anyone thinks. We are wild and crazy guys."

"What if Tanedrue and the rest of them come and find you?" she said.

"That would be bad for them," Leonard said. "Didn't you just hear Hap say we were wild and crazy?"

10

I parked us near the garage between some yellow lines and under the overhang. The rain plunked on the aluminum above us like buckshot. The guy who had been reading *Poontang Palace* was still inside the garage, but now he was digging around in a toolbox, probably trying to find a big enough hammer to beat some sort of automotive problem into submission.

Inside the joint we got the same table as before and the guy who waited on us before came over, said, "You must like it here, back in the same day, and now with a friend."

"We don't like the fries, just want to go on record with that," Leonard said. "But the hamburgers do the alligator rock. And she's not a friend."

"What?" the waiter said.

"He likes the hamburgers," I said. "He doesn't like the fries. The girl is not a friend. She's a friend of a friend."

The waiter didn't look at me. He studied Leonard for a moment. Leonard smiled. There was always something about that smile. It was less like a smile and more like a snake trying to grin up a frog right before it struck and ate it.

The waiter looked away from Leonard, looked at me. "What happened to your face?"

I reached up and touched the scratches on my cheeks. "Briars."

"You ought to see his ass," Leonard said. "That's where the real work was done."

"That right?" the waiter said. "Sorry I asked. Here's menus."

When the waiter went away, I said, "What you going to have, Gadget?"

"I'm not hungry."

"That crummy way you feel, that's because you're so hungry your belly thinks your throat's cut. Have some soup. They got soup here. I don't know how it is, but stay away from the French fries. Soup, any kind of soup, if it's fresh, it's pretty hard to mess up."

She didn't order anything, but when the waiter came back I ordered a cup of coffee and a bowl of chicken soup and Leonard ordered another hamburger, minus the fries, potato chips instead.

When the waiter was gone, I looked at Leonard, said, "You just ate couple hours ago. Maybe less. You want another hamburger?"

"Whipping the pure-dee-dog-doodie out of people makes me hungry. Don't it you?"

"A little."

The food came and I drank the coffee and pushed the soup over close to Gadget. I said, "I don't want the soup after all. Why don't you give it a taste? It smells pretty good."

She shook her head. "I know what you're doing."

I nodded. "Suit yourself."

Leonard dug into his hamburger. "Oh, Jesus, this is so good it makes you want to hold down a wild hog and fuck it in the ass."

"That passes for manners at his house," I said to Gadget.

"I've heard worse."

I noticed she had picked up the spoon and was starting to stir the soup. I pushed the crackers over close to her. She opened one of the cracker packages and bit a corner off the cracker. She crumbled the rest in her soup. I turned at an angle so I wasn't watching her. I got up and went over and ordered some pie and a glass of milk. When my pie and milk came, Leonard had to have the same, and now Gadget, finished with her soup, wanted some pie and milk too.

By this time she was starting to look better. I had a feeling it had been a long time since she'd eaten anything besides cheese crackers, potato chips, peanut butter and Cracker Jack. My guess was she was the neatnik who put the paper towels over the dog piles.

I paid the bill because Leonard didn't have any money, or said he didn't, and we drove out of there. The rain had died out and everything, even the crummy little town, looked better than before, spit-cleaned by nature. We hadn't gone a mile before we looked back and saw Gadget had gone to sleep in the backseat, her belly full, and maybe, for a moment, satiated.

Of course, there was that hairy old cocaine monkey, and when she woke up, it was sure to chatter and show its ass.

I tried to tell myself we had done all we could do. What Marvin had asked. But somehow I didn't feel satisfied that we could say "job well done." I kept thinking about what Tanedrue had said, about what Gadget had said. About how we didn't know what we had done and that hell was coming.

11

When we got back to LaBorde, Gadget was still sleeping. We drove through the wet town on out into the country where Marvin Hanson stayed. He lived there with his daughter and his wife. They had once been a very close family, then Marvin's pecker had gotten excited about a young woman; the same young woman I had liked. She was dead now, and Marvin had gone back to his family, and I had gotten over my feelings of wanting to skin him and nail his hide to the side of a barn and throw knives at it. Got over it long ago. Me and him and Leonard had gone through a lot, and we were bonded, as they like to say.

Marvin and his wife, Rachel, had gotten back together, and they were doing all right. But during that time, their daughter, JoAnna, had gone through some stuff, and then she had a daughter of her own, Julie, aka Gadget, by the guy who had run off. I didn't know that until Marvin told me. I knew I had never met him, but then again, much as Leonard and I liked Marvin, his family didn't hang with us, didn't even send us a Christmas card. They could have had three more kids, and close as the three of us were, we might not have known.

Now they all lived in a small two-bedroom house out in the country, trying to pull everything together and live happily ever after.

The house was off a rain-slick red clay road, and we started down it just as Gadget awakened and sat up in the backseat.

"If you hadn't had such a bad day," I said, "I'd have made you wear your seat belt, and I should have anyway."

"You're not my daddy," she said.

"No," Leonard said, "and from what I've heard, your daddy, who-ever he is, isn't claiming you either. You weren't nothin' to him but a hump and a squirt."

Gadget crossed her arms and sat back in her seat and looked mad. I gave Leonard a look that could have paralyzed a chicken at twenty paces. If it bothered him, struck a nerve anywhere inside that hard black hide, I didn't notice it.

We drove up to Marvin's house and I got out and opened the back door of the truck. Gadget got out with her arms still crossed and walked briskly toward the house. I tried very hard not to notice that from the rear in those very short shorts she had what might be a championship butt. If not, it was certainly a top contender.

Marvin came out on the porch with his cane, and Gadget walked by him like he wasn't there, went inside and slammed the door. Marvin looked back at her through the screen. I could see his shoulders slouch. JoAnna, Gadget's mother, came out on the porch. She looked at us and tried to smile, then went back inside. I heard her call out for her daughter.

We hadn't moved away from the truck. We leaned against it and waited. Marvin came out and nodded at me. "Thanks." He looked at Leonard. "Thanks."

"We didn't have anything else to do," Leonard said. "Me and him, we usually save this day for a little Bible study, but all the dirty parts we've read so much they don't do anything for us anymore."

Marvin ignored Leonard, as was often his custom, looked at me, said, "You got her back, but other than that, how did it go?"

"Let me see," I said. "We went to the trailer, and the guy you beat with the cane was playing with his balls, which he kept in a somewhat overly snug pair of Scooby Doo boxer shorts. Leonard jerked him out of the trailer and bounced his head, and then we went inside and some guy got kicked in the balls a few times. A guy got his face flattened on a wall. The guy who was playing with his balls pulled a gun and Leonard shot him and I stuffed the bullet hole with a shirt."

"Bullet hole?" Marvin said.

"Yeah," Leonard said. "I shot the guy you beat with a cane."

"You shot him?"

"In the fat part of the thigh."

"He was shooting to kill," I said. "But he missed and only wounded him."

"He was going to shoot us," Leonard said.

Marvin shook his head. "Damn, I'd have gone myself, guys. You know that, hadn't been for this bum leg."

"You think we don't know that?" Leonard said.

"You could catch some shit for shooting someone, even if it wasn't life-threatening," Marvin said.

"Yeah, maybe," Leonard said. "Hap, he threw a dog out the window."

"It was trying to bite me . . . We got rid of the guns and Leonard lectured them on fixing the place up a bit. Gave out a fashion tip . . . Oh, and there was dog crap all over the place. Oh yeah, I broke their CD player and stomped the shit out of a really bad rap CD."

"That's an oxymoron," Marvin said.

"They had drugs," Leonard said.

"And not just a little," I said. "Not some baggie of grass. Gadget . . . she's got some juice in her moose, man. She's hooked on the snort. She's not just smokin' weed."

"No," Marvin said.

"I'd recommend some kind of clinic, and quick," I said. "You give her any slack, she'll be back out there snorting some of what I flushed down the toilet. She thinks she's in love with numb nuts, Tanedrue, but down deep I think she knows he's what nature wipes its ass on. Just isn't ready to face it. Not yet. Way I figure, Tanedrue has got her hooked on drugs so he can use her until he doesn't want to use her. Hell, man, I don't need to tell you that. You know how it works. Sorry we got to lay it on you like this."

"Yeah," Marvin said.

"It ain't good news," Leonard said, "but it's the news."

"I think we're home free, far as those yo-yos are concerned," I said. "All done."

Marvin thought for a moment, then said, "Cops over there are dirty as a wino's drawers. Drug dealers own them, so don't be so sure they won't try and screw you over, bring in some artillery, a mechanic to go with it, and it'll be my fault. I shouldn't have asked you."

"No one else to ask," Leonard said. "No one else would be so stupid."

"You have a point," Marvin said.

"My take is the dirty cops might not like we fucked with their guys," I said, "but I can't see them doing anything about it. They don't really know who we are. Gadget didn't tell them, 'cause she didn't even get our names right. They know we're connected to you, though. That I'm sure of."

"I sort of let slip how much I enjoyed you beating Tanedrue's ass with the walking stick," Leonard said. "But then again, I wasn't really trying to hide. We didn't do no sneakin'. I did want to mention, however, that Gadget said you said we thought we were funny, as if it weren't confirmed."

Marvin ignored that.

"It was pretty much our usual plan," I said. "We just went in there and beat the hell out of 'em, tossed a dog out a window, shot one of 'em in the leg, and messed up the paneling. It got a little wilder than we thought. I know that's a synopsis of a synopsis I already gave you, but that part about us not being really funny, that really hurt, man, and I didn't want to revisit that territory."

"I see scratches," Marvin said, nodding at my face.

"He tried to fuck a cat," Leonard said, "and the cat didn't like it."

"Those look like some pretty good claws," Marvin said. "Like maybe Gadget did it."

"Now I remember why you were a good policeman," I said. "I had to hit her. I'm not proud of it."

"You did what you had to do, I'm sure," he said.

"We got to go," I said. "Gadget, she's got to have some serious detox, buddy."

"That costs serious money," Marvin said.

"Maybe so," I said, "but unless you're going to lock her in a room and feed her soup through a straw while she's tied down to a bed wearing a straitjacket, you got to find a way, man."

"I know," he said. "And I will. But I am worried about you guys. When I asked for help I was thinking about Gadget, and not much else. I should have known better. I did know better. All I could think about was her, and the only people I knew to ask were you. I knew it could have consequences for you, for all of us. But I had to get her out of there. Listen, I know two, three guys we could get for protection. There's Jim Bob, and maybe that friend of yours, Veil."

"I hope Veil doesn't hear you address us as friends," Leonard said. "He might shoot us all. As for Jim Bob, no need to stir him up."

"And there's another guy that owes me. He could help."

We shook our heads.

"You fellas sure?"

"We been over this," Leonard said. "We don't need anyone, and you don't owe us a thing. Besides, those guys today, they don't want to mess with me and Hap again because we are two badass motherfuckers. Didn't I tell you Hap threw a dog out a window?"

As I drove us away, I said, "Two badass motherfuckers?"

"Sound convincing?"

"It sounds like you have been watching too much *Shaft* or *Superfly*."

"Marvin has enough to worry about. We knew what we were getting into when we took the job."

I nodded. "Absolutely."

We chatted a bit about how we actually thought things would be okay. About how they were small-time goobers and they wouldn't mess with Marvin either, 'cause there was no mileage in that.

By the time we got back to LaBorde, we had almost convinced ourselves that we were in fact badass motherfuckers. Had we felt any tougher, we'd have stopped by the side of the road to shit in plain sight and wipe our asses on dried grass with sticker burs in it.

12

By the next day things seemed to have gone back to normal. You know, the basics: killing another perfectly good day and knowing you weren't going to get it back.

Brett was working at her nurse job, and I at a typically shabby day job at a construction site. Actually, it was a crummy two-day job picking up lumber and nails and all the stuff the major workers dropped. When I was hired, my boss, a black guy, told me, "You're just one of the niggers, or wetbacks. Used to be they did what you're doin'. I did what you're doin'. Now you got to do it. That's the job, take it or leave it. You're late, I hire a beaner at half your price."

I took it. I got paid by the day, and that was good. I still had a little money from another job I'd done that had to do with the sort of stuff Leonard and I excelled at. Intellectual work, like kicking someone's ass up under their ears and convincing ourselves it was for the greater good. It was rough on the knuckles, bad on the shoes, and tough on the conscience, or at least it was on mine.

Anyway, in the money department, Brett and I weren't rich, but we had most everything paid off and weren't hurting. And, as always, another job would pop up. Also, Marvin was starting a private investigations company and Leonard and I had been promised work from him once he got that up and running. I couldn't wait to peep in windows and take pictures of the wrong couples coming out of cheap motels.

I got off work and went home and showered the sweat off and read a little from a book by an author who didn't use quotation marks and was scared to death his work might be entertaining. I gave up on the book and put it in the to-be-swapped pile for the used bookstore, went upstairs, and watched TV.

There was some good History Channel stuff, and some Discovery Channel stuff on, but I watched a show about some dumb blondes who had access to a lot of money and didn't do much of anything all day but plan ways to spend that money. I couldn't take my eyes off the program. I told myself down deep they couldn't be as dumb as they seemed and that there was something spiritual about them. I think their most spiritual aspect was their lack of clothing. Their benefactor was an eighty-year-old gray guy who walked around in a house robe and took Viagra so he could bang all three and sleep in the bed with them all at the same time. He was my hero.

When I heard the front door slam, I switched the channel. Brett was home. I found a history program about Genghis Khan. I had seen the program before and had enjoyed it. Seen it twice even, but by this go-round I knew Genghis was dead and he wasn't coming back.

Brett came upstairs. She looked cute in her nurse's uniform. Her flame-red hair had slipped out from under her cap and was hanging over one eye. She took off the cap and sighed and threw the cap on a chair. She came over and turned her back to me. I sat up on the bed and unzipped her dress. She wiggled out of it.

"I want to order pizza," she said, "and then fuck like a couple of greased weasels."

"My lucky day."

"And don't you forget it."

She sat on the edge of the bed and picked up the phone and called the pizza place. I unsnapped her bra and played with her breasts while she called.

When she hung up, I said, "Bet we could do it before the pizza delivery gets here."

"He's ten minutes away," she said. "What fun is there in that?"

"About ten minutes' worth."

"You are correct, sir," she said. She rolled onto the bed and I took her in my arms and we kissed. "Will you wear the bunny slippers, baby?"

"Oh, hell yes," I said.

But I didn't. The rest of it just happened naturally.

13

We ate the pizza downstairs and Brett read the newspaper and I read part of a Western novel and thought it was pretty good, even if the author did talk about starting his herd with two steers; that didn't exactly endear me to his Western lore or his grasp of basic biology, but the story was all right. Then there was a knock at the door. I went to the curtain and pulled it back and looked out. The glass was fogged over from the cold outside. I had to wipe it a bit, and then I could see Leonard standing by the door, looking toward the curtain. When he saw me he lifted a hand.

I let him in, and felt the air blow past. It had really turned chilly.

"Winter's here," Leonard said. "My nuts have frozen up to the size of raisins."

"Now, don't brag," I said.

Brett got up from her chair and came over and hugged Leonard, said, "We still got some pizza, baby, you want it."

"No thanks," Leonard said. "Well . . . how much pizza?"

"Couple of pieces?" Brett said.

"I can do that. And then I could maybe have some of those cookies Hap got for me and some of the Dr Pepper he got me special too."

"I like that stuff myself," I said.

Leonard winked at me. "You are so cute," he said.

I sat at the kitchen table with Leonard while he ate and Brett went back in the living room to finish reading the paper. When Leonard finished eating the pizza and was ready to start on the cookies, I put a pot of decaf on, said, "Okay, what's going on?"

"What?" Leonard said.

"Why are you here?"

"Because you're my bestest goddamn buddy in the whole damn world. My brother. My doppelganger. My—"

"Yeah, but why are you here?"

"I always come over."

"And you're always welcome. But where's John? Why haven't you mentioned him? You know better than to jack with me, Leonard. I know you better than anyone in the world. Better than you know you."

"Yeah?"

"Yeah."

Leonard pushed a vanilla cookie around on his plate. "John and I aren't doing so good."

"Could it have anything to do with you crappin' in the bed?"

"I was mad."

"You? Oh, say thee not such foul lies about your own sweet self."

"I said some things."

"Another surprise."

"I've sort of been staying somewhere else."

"Where?"

"Motels. I get off the security job, I been picking a different one each night. Quite the thrilling experience. One of them, it has one of those old-time beds where you put a quarter in a machine and the bed vibrates. . . . Course, it doesn't work. But the mechanism is still there, and you can't imagine how the nostalgia comforts me. Hey, and there's this one cheap motel, the sheets, they got shit stains on them. I stayed there twice, two different rooms, shit stains on blue sheets. I guess it saves on laundry soap, leavin' them like that."

I got up and poured us some coffee and got some sweetener and cream. We fixed our coffee. I stirred mine longer than was necessary. I said, "Have you tried to talk to John?"

"I have."

"And what's the sticking point?"

"He doesn't like me."

"Bullshit. What's going on?"

"The queer stuff."

"You're both queer, Leonard."

"Really? Well, that puts some things in perspective."

"So, John feels guilty about being gay?"

"John's brother hates him because he's gay. He tells him he doesn't have to be gay. He's telling him God doesn't want him gay."

"Even if God made him that way?" I said. "Provided there was a God."

"If there was one, and he made someone gay, wouldn't God his own goddamn self be responsible?" Leonard said.

"In my book, yes. But in the Christians' book, that rascal can do no wrong. Someone survives a hurricane, it was God's mercy. Someone drowns, it was God's will. I don't like him. He's a bully."

We touched fists. It's a manly bonding thing.

"Or maybe," Leonard said, "God is gay and it's the rest of you people who are messed up and going to hell. You ever think about that? Maybe there's another Bible out there that tells us to stone you guys and not to lie with women because it's strange. It is, you know."

"Brett and I like it."

Leonard sipped some coffee. "You see, John is starting to feel he's not supposed to be gay, and unlike us, on some level he believes that God stuff. He thinks he's violated God's law, so he's going to church counseling to get straight."

"Oh, for heaven's sake."

"That's what he thinks. For heaven's sake."

"It's a figure of speech."

"I've tried to tell him that even if there is a God, the New Testament is the one to go by, and it's not tough on us queers. It's just the old mean version of God that gives us a hard time. Motherfucker in the Old Testament won't even let us have a pork chop."

"God must have finally got laid between the Old and the New Testament," I said. "'Cause between those two books, he sure mellowed out."

"Who'd he lay, male or female?"

"Either . . . Look, Leonard, I'm sorry about John."

"Not half as sorry as I am. I've called him, I wrote him a letter. I even did an e-mail from one of the hotels on my laptop."

"You got a laptop?"

"John bought it for me. At home I even got a printer and some paper to print out on."

"You are so cosmopolitan."

"Tell me about it. But the thing is, he's going to take these classes so he can tell his brain and his dick that he's been confused and he likes women. I can't think of anything yuckier than learning to like that old pink snapper. . . . No disrespect to you and Brett."

"I get your point. You want me to talk to him?"

"I don't know. I thought about that, thought about asking you. But it won't matter. He thinks he's on the road to hell and wang and butt hole are no longer on the smorgasbord."

"Leonard, thy middle name is romance. You and Tanedrue, you should get together, write a book on courting. Look here, you're not staying in any motel. You'll park your happy ass on the couch tonight."

"Thanks, Hap."

"I'm just afraid you keep trying to hook up those motel Internet connections to your laptop you'll put your eye out. So I want you here, safe and sound."

"Thanks, brother. Can I have the last cookie?"

"No."

We sat there and looked at the cookie. I said, "You haven't given up on John yet, have you?"

"No. But I got a rule. If you're ashamed of being gay, I'm ashamed of you. I say, Queer up. I take into account John's getting some shit and was raised in such a way as to not think he's on the right path, but I was raised that way myself. I got over it by the time there was hair on my balls. Actually, John shaves them for me, but you know what I mean."

"Too much information, partner. Besides, I think a man ought to have hair on his balls."

"Now that John won't be doing that for me anymore, are you interested in doing the shaving?" Leonard said, and smiled.

"I'd just cut them off, problem solved. Actually, several problems solved. Your relationships would be less strenuous and that pesky hair problem would be over with. You could just hang out with Bob and be happy."

Leonard sighed. "And if things aren't bad enough, Bob died."

"Oh, man. Sorry."

Bob was Leonard's pet armadillo. They had been close. Well, Leonard had been close to Bob. It was hard to tell how Bob felt. But he did hang around and would sniff Leonard's hand and eat out of it. He lived in Leonard's closet a lot of the time. Went outside to do his business, like a dog. Had a bowl with his name on it.

"It was like his little clock ran down," Leonard said. "I buried him out back near a little wallow he had made. You know how he liked to dig."

"He was an armadillo, Leonard. It's what they do."

"I know. But he was kind of cool. I liked him. . . . Hell, Hap, I don't know. Short time back, life was good, felt like I was fartin' perfume and crappin' chocolate candy. Now things suck the big ole donkey dick. John, the way he's actin', and now my 'dilla goin' down. It sucks the oxygen right out of you."

I couldn't tell if Leonard was more upset about John or Bob. I studied his face, decided it was a draw.

"Sorry, man," I said. "Really."

"Thanks. It don't help worth a damn, but I'm glad you said it," and his voice wavered a little. "Actually, I'm thinking of trying to write a soap opera, call it *Lives of the Homos*."

"Leonard?"

"Yeah."

"You can have the last cookie."

14

Leonard stayed with us about three days. After work we played chess, talked nasty, read books and discussed them; we talked about which was cooler, Marvel Comics or DC. Leonard thought Marvel. I thought DC. Brett liked Archie Comics. That immediately excluded her from the discussion and a bit of respect was lost. We listened to music. We rented movies and played Monopoly. Brett proved to be adamant about having the silver dog as her token, and she won a lot. I saw her steal some money from my pile once, but let it go. I called her on it when we went to bed and she made it up to me and the authorities were not called, though Archie Comics was not entirely forgiven.

It was fun having Leonard around for a while, and we hated to see him go, but he finally rented a little apartment on the other side of town, said he was calling John daily, that they were talking and he was guardedly optimistic, hoping things would resolve quickly because the hair on his balls had grown back.

I came home from work one day, sweaty and dirty and feeling like something the dogs had dragged under the porch and gnawed on, and there was a police car parked out front of the house at the curb. There was a big black guy with a cop's uniform and a cowboy hat about the size of a life raft sitting in one of my lawn chairs smoking a cigar big as an erect horse dong. When I parked in the driveway and got out, the stench of that damn cigar wafted over to me and damn near curled the hair on my eyebrows.

I went over, said, "Let me guess. No Enterprise Police Department."

"Ah, hell, man, you ain't that smart," he said, turning his head as if he wanted to pin me with just one eye. "You read that off the side of my car."

"You're right." I sat down in a lawn chair and looked at him. I said, "So, you took a wrong turn or what?"

"No. I'm in the right place. They said you were a smart-ass, both of you were, and I figure you're the white guy."

"That's observant."

"Yep. I had a whole month of cop college and I read a book on fingerprinting once. I took a couple of courses in identification too."

"Wow!"

He grinned at me around his cigar. He had strong creases around his mouth when he grinned and his eyes were slightly bloodshot. One ear floated out from the side of his head as if signaling for a turn. He didn't strike me as over fifty. He had a hard body with a bit of a gut and arms that could twist a full-grown pig like wet wash. I remembered that Marvin had told me he was one of two fat guys. Boy, was he full of it. This John Law was big enough and mean enough looking to use an elephant's ass to store his shoes and make the elephant like it.

"You already talk to my buddy?" I asked.

"No. Thought I'd talk to you. Hear you're more reasonable and you don't have lace on your panties."

"You're right. I am. And that lace remark, not smart. Leonard heard you talk bad about him like that, he might stick you in your hat and piss in it after you."

"Doubt that."

"A man with confidence," I said. "I like that. I know a lot of confident men Leonard has handed their teeth."

"Yeah, I hear you two think you're tough guys. Be that as it may, what I know about you and him and me, I'd say I'm doing some better than either of you."

"Probably. Less graft in the jobs we have."

For the first time he didn't look amused. "All right, let's get formal. My name is Budd Conners. I'm half the law out of No Enterprise."

"Do the two of you count as one lawman?"

He thumped ash from his cigar on the ground. "Let me tell you why I'm here."

"Let me guess. I stuck my dick in your territory."

"Something like that. You can wise off all you want, but I'm here to do you a favor."

"I could use some yard work done."

He leaned forward. "Listen, asshole. Listen good, and tell your partner what I'm going to tell you."

"Should I take notes?"

"You can take notes, or you can just let it whistle through your ears. This way, I came to you and told you and I'm giving you a chance. Those guys you fucked over, shot one in the leg, took that girl from, flushed their dope down the shitter, they didn't like it."

"Well, I hope not."

"They're mad at you, and the more connected guys who work the dope through them, guess what? They're pissed too."

"Get in line. Me and Leonard piss a lot of people off."

"I can believe that. I can believe you two are not going to listen and you're going to wind up with your body parts in separate trash bags in different parts of the county."

"This isn't the first time we've been threatened."

"I don't doubt that, peckerwood. But this has put a little pressure on me. The organization that runs those turds you slapped around, they got folks that run them, and they are bad folks. The Dixie Mafia."

"Do they have Dixie flags and still whine over the South being unionized into the rest of the country? Do they talk about cotton a lot? Get weepy about the Old South? I don't know about you, but nothing—absolutely nothing—touches me less or bores me more than those assholes. I was you, a black man, I'd throw my rag in with someone else."

"It's bigger than any of that. Some of them, they come out of the Aryan Nations, out of the prisons. But they aren't so down on the brothers anymore. They just don't want them to fuck their sisters. They feel they can do business with them, anyone else for that matter. These guys, they don't care about any war but their own little money war. They're all about commerce and respect, ass-wipe."

"Watch your language. I'm sensitive, and I just might go sensitive all over you."

He leaned back in the chair and grinned. "I'm twice your size."

"And I'm twice your mean."

"So you say. Do you want to hear me out or not?"

I looked at my watch. "Might as well. It's still a couple hours till dinner."

"They aren't getting their dope back, so maybe they'll think to make some kind of example out of you. That would be their way. The low guys on the turd totem pole can't take care of you, then they'll bring in the middle guys. That don't work, then the middle guys will bring in the top guys, and those guys will hire someone that'll be meaner than a bucket of rattlesnakes. They won't dirty their hands. They'll bring in real talent. But they probably won't have to go that far. Enough guys with no real talent is still a lot of fuckin' guys."

"So how do they know it's us done all this? Could be two other guys of equal handsomeness and anger management issues."

"You've already admitted it was you."

"I was just playing."

"Sure. Tanedrue figured you were friends of Marvin Hanson, the grandfather, and all he had to do was ask around. You weren't that hard to figure. You could maybe pay back the money they lost."

"Oh yeah, that's gonna happen. If it cost a dollar to fart I'd have to sweat instead. Don't be an idiot. We aren't paying anybody anything, and mostly because we don't want to. And, by the way, how do you, a fine law-abiding police officer, know all this? Could it be because you're in cahoots with them? My God, say it ain't so. Aren't policemen here to protect us? If that isn't true, my world has been turned upside down."

"You know what I make in salary?"

"I could care less."

"Not a lot. Drugs are all over. You think I stop some drug traffic I stop drugs? That I stop people from wanting to use them?"

"No. But it is your job."

"Look, I'm gonna tell you something, 'cause it's just you and me in your crappy yard. Drugs go on. Money is being made. It's like pussy. Someone is always gonna sell it and someone is always gonna buy it, and sometimes, that pussy, it's got a disease and it kills people. You takes your chances. No one makes you buy it, use it. So what if me and my partner, who is a nice fat white guy named Reggie who is like a brother to me and will hate your guts if I hate your guts . . . what if we get a little piece of the action? They're gonna buy from someone. So who the hell does it hurt if they're getting what they want?"

"The people who are paying you not to take a piece of the action. And you might toss in the ones it kills or the ones get addicted. Until it's legalized and they got that stuff in a vending machine, your job is to not make money off of it."

Conners took a big suck on his cigar, blew the smoke toward me. I was so manly I didn't wave it away, just squinted my eyes, trying to look like Clint Eastwood. I probably looked like a guy with smoke in his eyes.

"I've heard some things about you and your boy," Conners said, "and you sound a little self-righteous, considering what I've heard you've done."

"Don't believe everything you've heard, lawman. And let me give you another line, right out of *Billy Jack*. Ever see that movie?"

"No."

"There's a line where he says: 'When policemen break the law there is no law.' After that he beats the crap out of some guys, but that's not the point. It's corny and it's movie crap, but it's right. I don't owe you a fucking thing. You come to warn me and you think I'm supposed to thank you for it, but mostly you want me to stay out of your business, because you are the scum at the bottom of this big old pond and what you're afraid of is that me and Leonard are going to ripple the surface so much that the big frog on the big lily pad is going to hop on your head. You aren't doing me any kind of favor. Now get out of my yard before I take that cigar out of your mouth and shove it up your ass."

He stood up so fast he knocked over the lawn chair. "I ought to kick you into next week."

I stood up carefully. "Start kicking. You're out of your jurisdiction."

He stood there with his fists clenched. A vein vibrated in his neck like the string on a stand-up bass. Provided the string was really big.

I didn't want any part of him, but I didn't want him to know it. I managed not to piss myself, tried to look like I was thinking about something pleasant, like a politician waiting for a free blow job.

He took a deep breath. "All right. I tried. You warn that fart, Hanson, warn him that he's in this too. I was him, I'd take that split-tail you two rescued, pack all of you in a bus and head for the high country, or just some goddamn rabbit hole. Change your names. Change your sex. 'Cause they're comin', smart-mouth. And when they do, you ain't gonna like it. It might be the little fucks first, but they ain't nothin'.

You might take care of them. But then it's the others, and I tell you again, you ain't gonna like it."

"Neither are they," I said.

Conners tossed his cigar on the lawn, gave me a last look that told me there was nothing he'd like better than to reach up my asshole and jerk me inside out. "When it comes down," he said, "remember your old Uncle Conners tried to tell you how it was going to go."

"That'll certainly cheer me," I said. "But I wouldn't count me and Leonard out just yet, Uncle Tom . . . Oh, sorry, that was Conners, wasn't it?"

"You don't know a thing. Ain't no Uncle Toms no more, just a fella trying to do business."

"One way of looking at it, I suppose."

"It'll be a clean sweep," he said. "Not just you and Leonard, but those around you. You have a woman, don't you? That's what I've heard. And Hanson, his family. I don't want to see that, something happening. Truly, I don't."

"Here's a feather for your cap. I ever think you have anything to do with screwing around with me and mine, some morning you just might find yourself dead."

"You threatening a law officer?"

"I don't consider you much of an officer. Besides, you couldn't arrest a fly here. You're nothing but one of a two-man operation in a little town that has its presidential elections in a filling station. You two are so small-time you probably share a dick. So don't come in here and act like the FBI. You are nothing to me. And yeah, that is a goddamn threat, with bells and whistles on it."

"Have it your way, pal. But next time you see me comin', man, you better run."

Conners went out to his car and drove away.

15

"He came here to the house?" Brett said.

I nodded.

We were sitting at the kitchen table, she still in her nurse uniform, me still in my sweaty, filthy work clothes. She was sitting out from the table, had her legs crossed, and the nurse dress was hiked up pretty far. I liked that, and she knew it. I liked the little hat she was wearing too. I'd have liked her without the hat. I'd have liked her without the dress. She could lose those nurse shoes too. I don't have a fetish for stuff like that, but I do have a fetish for her.

I was laying out what had happened with Conners, and I was drinking a cup of coffee. I had fixed some for both of us, and Brett was stirring creamer into hers. She even made me horny doing that. I know. I'm a bad dog.

"He threatened you here in our yard?" she said.

"He threatened that other people were going to do something to me that probably wouldn't pass for a manicure and a haircut. And maybe those same people would do something similar to those around me. He also said next time I saw him I better run."

"And he's a policeman?"

"A big goddamn policeman. One of the two of No Enterprise's finest on-the-take assholes. Actually, don't tell Leonard, but between me and you, he was kind of scary."

"It's okay, pumpkin," she said and patted my hand. "If we're going to be killed, it might as well be together."

"Sorry, hon."

"Don't be. You're my man and you do things others wish they could. I like you just the way you are. Most of the time. Though I do wish you could remember to change the toilet paper, and on top of the hamper is not where your underwear belong. They go inside, dear."

"But you have to lift the lid on the hamper."

"I know. It is a bother."

I gave her a look that I hoped made me look like a big-eyed puppy instead of a startled marmoset. It didn't have the effect I hoped for— deep sympathy and a desire to pat my head. She drank more of her coffee.

I said, "I'm a middle-aged man with a crummy job that's over as of today and you may be a little less thrilled with me if this turns bad."

"It's been bad before. And besides, you're cute and well hung."

Now that was the response I wanted. I said, "That's the first I've heard of that."

"Considering the circumstances, it seemed like a kind thing to say."

"Oh."

"Now don't get pissy. Remember what Bessie Smith sang. It's not the meat, it's the motion."

"Okay. I can live with that. Brett . . . this policeman, I got to tell you, he had a loud voice and a big hat and an ugly cigar and his face was all wrinkled and he had a funny ear and he talked kind of loud and I don't think he's very nice. He uses bad words."

Brett smiled, looked me in the eyes. "Do you think this is really serious, baby? I mean, really?"

"Yeah. I do."

"What do you think will happen?"

"No way to know for sure, but my guess is the little guys, the ones me and Leonard gave a bad time, might think they got to get back at us to save face, so they can point to us and tell their bosses they got those nasty boys who destroyed the dope and made them lose all that money and insulted a perfectly nice pair of Scooby Doo shorts.

"Course, we can flip that and say maybe the guys in the middle don't believe the guys at the bottom. Not all of it anyway. The head dudes might just decide to take it out on the bottom-feeders because they might think they're lying, that they took the dope, made up a story, and are settling other scores with us. All the middle guys know is they didn't get a piece of the profit. And the guys at the top, what they know is they didn't get their slice of it. So instead of them solving the problem, they could want the two layers in the cake below them to solve the problem. Most likely, the top layer gets involved, they'll bring in someone special and skilled. That's the way it usually works. But I wouldn't bet on any one scenario. We might be dealing with all of them."

"So what do we do?" Brett asked.

"First, I'll have Leonard move back in."

"That means more cookies and Dr Peppers and probably a box of shotgun shells."

"Absolutely," I said. "You have some time off coming, don't you?"

She nodded. "Two weeks. Three if I really need it."

"You pack your highly attractive ass up and you and Marvin and his family head for the hills. Go someplace where no one knows you. Stay there until I tell you to come back."

Brett reached out and took my hand. "I don't really have family anymore. My daughter isn't exactly one to keep in touch. You know, the whoring business is so time-consuming, and her plans for college didn't work out, she said."

"Oh yeah," I said. "Something about having to get up early."

"That's right. I love her, but she's grown and made her own way, and I'm here if she needs me. But she doesn't have a family bond, and maybe that's my fault, but it's the way it is. Except for you and Leonard, I'm about tapped out in the family department. I don't want to leave you. I can use a gun, and I'm not afraid."

"Yeah, but I am. Even if I wasn't, I'd want you to go. Someone has to keep telling Marvin he has to stay with his family. He's a great guy, but frankly, he's not at his best right now. Bum leg and all."

"You actually think Marvin will run? That doesn't sound like him to me. Does it to you?"

I waved it aside with my hand. "When I explain things to him he'll be happy to stay out of it," I said.

16

"Absolutely not," Marvin said.

I had Leonard and Brett with me and we had gone over to explain how things were. We were sitting in his living room and Rachel was there, and so were Gadget and JoAnna. The three women looked so much alike it was amazing. All dark and beautiful and soft, T-shirt- and jean-clad. Well, actually, Gadget didn't look so soft. She scratched at her arms constantly and her eyes darted. The dope was calling collect and she wanted to answer. She was still attractive, just itchy and a little hard-looking around the mouth and eyes.

"I got you two in this trouble," Marvin said. "I'm not about to bail on you."

"You're not bailing," Leonard said. "You're running like a spotted-ass ape."

"Oh," I said, turning in my chair to look at Leonard. "That helps. He'll feel better now. You are like one of those, what do they call them . . . diplomats."

"Figure of speech," Leonard said.

"So far," Brett said to me, "your powers of persuasion are not quite up to the standard you presumed."

"Hap should know me better than that," Marvin said.

"I'll tell you what I know," I said. "And let's cut the crap. You did get Leonard and me into this. You didn't tell us the whole gig, about how connected these guys were."

"I didn't know. Completely. I mean, I had an idea. But I didn't know."

"Exactly," I said. "You didn't stop to consider. Me and my brother just thought this was a trailer trash episode. We whipped some ass, threw a dog out of a window, shot a guy, took Gadget and brought her home. We went, we saw, we conquered, we came back. And now our asses are in the soup. We want you and yours, and Brett, out of here. And, no offense to Gadget, but you don't tell her where you're going till you get there. And you have the only cell phone between you. Not that I don't trust mother and daughter," I said, smiling at them. "But one cell phone can be controlled more easily, and you don't want a lot of people calling you anyway. Any little thing might leak out and you might then involve someone else. And I don't trust you, Gadget. The monkey on your back howls the loudest at midnight, when everyone else is sleeping. You might decide to decamp."

"Just let me go back to Tanedrue," Gadget said. "He's not going to bother me."

"Except when he's making a field goal with your head," Leonard said. "There's that, and, oh yeah, about a ton of drugs you can suck up your nose."

"You don't know how it is," Gadget said. "I'm . . . I'm in pain. And Hap hit me too."

"Yes," Leonard said, "but it was swift and beautiful and full of the power of love."

"Ha!" Gadget said. "He still hit me."

"You had it coming," Marvin said. "Never thought I'd say such a thing, but you did."

Gadget's lip went pouty. She said, "You still don't know how it is."

"I don't know how it is," I said. "But I've seen it before."

"Just let me go back," she said.

"Don't be ridiculous," Leonard said. "These guys suck rat bag. And you're on your way to being just like them."

"At this point," I said, "I'm not even sure Tanedrue might not blame you for their situation. There's no future there for you, Gadget."

"There's no future for me anywhere," Gadget said. "Just let them do what they want."

"That's the drug willies talking," I said.

"We're going to get her help," JoAnna said, and she reached out and touched Gadget's shoulder.

Gadget shook her head. "No use, Mama. I'm lost."

"No, you're not, honey," Rachel said, and I saw the fire in her eyes. She had it, always did. I knew what Marvin saw in her first time I met her, and right now I was seeing it again.

"Don't talk that way, baby," JoAnna said. "You're not the first one to make a mistake. I've made a few."

"Yeah, but I made more than a few in less time," Gadget said.

That floated for a moment, then I said, "This business boils down to this: Marvin, you and your family need to pack up some things and hit the road."

"You act like these guys are fucking CIA," Marvin said. "They're a bunch of goobers."

"It's not the original goobers I'm worried about," I said. "It's all them other goobers."

"With me and Hap here, the rest of you gone," Leonard said, "it makes for a smaller target. And we're not an easy target."

"I can vouch for that," Marvin said. "I thought you two would be dead years ago."

"Gee, thanks," Leonard said.

"Actually, that was a kind of a compliment," Brett said.

"Oh," Leonard said. "My bad."

"But this is my mess," Marvin said.

I nodded, said, "Now I'm really going to pour on the juice. You're a cripple and you'll just get in our way. We need you to whip someone's ass with your cane again, we'll call you up. But we're past that. Maybe way past. Way I see it, Tanedrue may just let us out of the picture. He's got nothing to gain. He's not getting his drugs back, and I bet he can figure pretty quick we don't have that kind of money to pay back what it was worth. So he could let us go."

"That's what I think," Marvin said. "That's what I always thought."

"On the other hand," I said, "he lets us go, then he can't even tell his bosses that he avenged the loss, and I think he's the kind of guy that thinks he's some kind of player, wants to look good in front of his posse. Last time he tried that, he got his ass kicked. So he could feel vengeful. Power, control, being in charge, that's all very important to these little sucks, and it's even more important to the middlemen and the men at the top. The other thing"—and I looked at Gadget when I said this— "they may come for Gadget. Not because Tanedrue loves her—"

"He does, you know," Gadget said. "He does."

"Sure he does," Leonard said. "That's why he beats on your ass."

"I get out of line," Gadget said.

"Honey," Brett said, "that is pure-dee ole bullshit. Unless you're trying to kill him and he's fighting back, you aren't out of line enough to warrant any kind of physical beating. You think we're in fucking Afghanistan. Pardon my French."

Gadget put her head on the table. JoAnna put her hand on Gadget's back and looked hard at Brett. Brett looked back equally hard. JoAnna averted her gaze. I could sympathize. When Brett put "that look" on you, you didn't want to mess with her. In her eyes you could see the next world war.

"What Hap was saying," Leonard said, "guy like this, he might come and try and get Gadget. He might even come to kill her."

Gadget lifted her head. "He wouldn't. He loves me."

"There's no way to argue with that," I said. "She believes it and you can't talk her out of it. Not until the drugs are out of her system. And even then, not easily."

"You don't know nothin'," Gadget said, jumping up from the table, running to the back of the house, disappearing into a bedroom, slamming the door.

JoAnna looked at me, said, "No use being hard on her. It doesn't help."

"She shouldn't get off scot-free," Marvin said. "Problem with this world is we've lost the idea of shame and guilt. We need a little of that. No one thinks they ever do bad anymore. They just do different."

"I'm sorry we've disrupted things this morning," I said to Rachel. "I didn't mean to scare you or your family, but this is how it is."

"I'm not so scared," Rachel said. "I once fought a serial killer with a hammer. JoAnna was with me. We aren't shrinking violets."

Marvin nodded. "She did. When I was on the job in Houston."

I had heard the story before, but I didn't let on. Every now and then Marvin brought it up and told it over. About the Houston Hacker. It had been his biggest case as a big-city cop.

"My granddaughter, my family," Rachel said. "I got to do what's right for them. I'll tell you honestly, I don't like you two, never have. And Brett, I just don't like you on sight. You act like you're better than everyone else."

"Well, duh."

"And you're a smart-ass."

"That's all right," Brett said, looking prim and beautiful. "I'm not selling happiness, and when I go to bed at night I have my witty repartee to keep me company. And Hap. And since we're expressing ourselves, you aren't exactly at the top of my love list either."

They locked eyes for a moment, then Rachel looked at me and Leonard. "But I'll say this about you two—you're straight with things. You know how to do what you do. I don't even want to know what it is you do, even if I have a pretty good idea. So me and JoAnna and Gadget, and yes, you, Marvin, we're leaving here tomorrow."

Brett raised her hand. "Don't forget me."

Rachel looked at Brett with those hard eyes of hers. Brett looked back. Neither broke gaze. "And yes," Rachel said. "You too, Brett. We can hate each other politely."

"I ought to stay," Marvin said.

Rachel stuck her finger in Marvin's face. "I've been through a lot of shit with you, baby, and I've held it together. I been through you messin' with another woman. I've been through your cop days in the city and in LaBorde. I've dealt with your accident, your leg, and all manner of hell. I've set by your bedside watching them feed you through a tube, and I've fed you like a baby when you didn't have the strength to lift a finger. You are going, or we're going without you, and don't look for us to come back if you don't go."

Marvin nodded. "All right," he said. "I'm going. We'll pack some things tonight, go to the bank tomorrow morning for some money, then we're gone."

17

Way we figured it, Leonard was going to keep working his security job, which had switched from days to nights. Brett was going to put in for her two weeks the next day, and since my job had played out, I wasn't going to look for anything right away. Truth is, if it wasn't for the money I'd just hang out and not work. I should be ashamed, but I'm not. I'm so lazy Leonard has to call me and remind me to work out, threaten me a little. I actually like the workouts soon as I start them, but it's easy for me to get sidetracked and want to read a book or see a movie or eat a sandwich, or do the bump with Brett.

I drove Brett to the hospital the next morning, very early while it was still dark, and they let her have the two weeks. She said it was an emergency, that she might be back early, before the two weeks were up, but right now her daughter was sick and she had to go check on her.

They grumbled a bit, but they allowed her the time. Brett was a hell of a nurse.

Brett had her suitcase in the pickup, ready to go. I started driving us through town, on my way to drop her off at Marvin's place. It was a very still morning, no traffic except for a beige Cadillac that was going our way. The moon was still up, a silver scimitar in the sky, and we had the heater on low because it was chilly out, though not exactly cold.

Brett was armed, had the little .38 automatic she sometimes wore strapped to the inside of her thigh. That was when she had on a dress. Today she had on jeans and a T-shirt and she had an ankle holster. I was armed too, with the gun that was registered to me and the one I had the conceal/carry papers on. A nine-mil automatic in a clip holster snapped to the back of my belt under my open windbreaker. I had a twelve-gauge pump shotgun in the backseat under a blanket, and of course, a pocketknife for whittling and a clear throat in case I had to resort to vulgar language.

We didn't go around armed normally, so for us the guns weren't fashion accessories. I hated the damn things, but, alas, I ran with a rough crowd from time to time, and of consequence, so did Brett. Way things had been going lately, I thought it best we be prepared.

She sat close to me that morning, like a teenager on a date. She kissed me on the cheek, and when she did, I felt wetness. She had tears.

I turned and looked at her, said, "Come on, baby. It'll be okay."

"I'm not scared," she said, as I turned to look back at the road, check the mirror to make sure the Cadillac behind us wasn't about to run up our asses. "I just don't want to leave you to it by yourself."

"I have Leonard."

"I know. And I'm glad. But that's not what I meant."

"I know what you meant."

"I could stay, Hap."

"I need you with them. Rachel might need an ass whippin', and you're just the gal to do it."

"She's okay," Brett said. "She's just protecting her family, but you know what?"

"What?"

"There's a part of me that would like to throw down with her, just to see how it would come out."

"I know how it would come out. You'd lose a bit of that beautiful red hair and she'd be in the hospital."

"You're just saying that to make a girl feel sexy."

I laughed.

The Cadillac passed us. I gave it a glance. Four guys were in it. No one from Tanedrue's trailer was inside the car. Not even the dog. The car went on ahead, got about three car lengths in front of us. The driver was, as so many drivers are, on the cell phone. Who the hell do you call at this time of the morning? I thought

We crossed Gibbon Street, and as we did, a shiny black crew cab pickup with a big sunroof and tires about the size of a small planet came burning out and swung in behind us. I glanced in my rearview mirror. I recognized the truck's driver. Tanedrue. Beside him I could see the ball-kicked guy and in the backseat the guy who was mad about me tossing his dog, and beside him some red-faced guy I had never seen before. Between them was Gadget.

"It's them," I said. "And Gadget's with them."

Brett turned to look. "That bitch."

"I'm going to try and outrace them," I said. "Call Leonard."

As Brett popped open her cell phone, I hit the gas and started around the Cadillac. The Caddy weaved in front of me.

"Get off the phone, asshole," I yelled at the Cadillac just like the driver could hear me.

I heard Brett say, "Leonard, we got trouble. We're on Main, just crossed Gibbon, about three blocks from our street. Yeah."

Brett clapped the phone shut. "He's on his way."

"This goddamn Cadillac," I said, and weaved the other direction. It weaved with me. I glanced in the rearview mirror. The red-faced guy in the truck had a cell phone to his ear. I glanced at the Caddy. The driver was still on the phone.

"They're in cahoots," I said.

Brett was looking back, she said, "Oh hell."

I looked in the rearview. Red Face was lifting up through the sunroof with a shotgun. It looked as big as a howitzer to me.

I tried to get around the Caddy. No luck. They had us between a patch of houses and trees, no side streets.

I turned quick, bumped over a curb, went through a lawn, bashed a couple of lawn gnomes and a pink flamingo, which might be considered a public service, then bounced through a driveway and clipped the tail of a parked car just enough to knock it out of our way. I weaved between an oak and an elm and took out a yard swing, a birdbath, and a Vote-for-Some-Republican sign. I gave myself an extra two points for that.

The Caddy and the truck ran along beside us on the street. Red Face's shotgun banged and a back side window went out on my truck. Brett let out a yip like a surprised dog.

"You hit?" I asked.

"Just my pride."

I saw an alley between two houses up the way, took a sharp right, and saw it was a screwup immediately. There was a wooden fence at the end of it. I yelled to Brett to hang on and put my foot to the floor. The pickup jumped and I hit the fence and lumber went out in all directions and we roared on through and down a little hill. There was a clump of trees in front of us and a low area I knew was a creek, so I hung a hard left and took out another wooden fence and went through a backyard and made a cocker spaniel jump for cover. I took out a matching fence, whipped hard left through a side yard in time to see our pursuers whisk by on the street, make several car lengths ahead of us.

I started back in the direction we had come, saw people in the yards now, out rubbernecking. I don't know what possessed me, but I waved at a couple of them. In the rearview I saw the truck had turned and so had the Caddy. They were coming down on my ass pretty snappy-damn-quick. I had my foot all the way to the floor when I tried to make a turn, and that's when I lost it. My truck skidded, fishtailed, then got itself together and looked like it was going to be all right. Another shot banged behind us, and this time the back glass of the pickup shattered. I caught some sting in the back of my neck. Brett yelled, "Goddamn it," and flipped over the seat and got the twelve-gauge and brought it up and started pumping. She poked it out the busted window in the back, got off three rounds faster than a buck rabbit can fuck, and their truck spun to the right, went into a yard, right into a house with a sound like a cannon going off. Steam rose up from their hood.

I checked the rearview, saw the Caddy was still behind us. I turned my head and saw the truck rammed up in the house, bricks in the yard. Red Face and Tanedrue were out of the truck, guns in hand. Red Face was moving quickly. Tanedrue was limping toward us, due to his gun-shot, but he looked lively enough and dangerous enough to me.

I said, "Put your seat belt back on, baby."

Brett climbed over the seat like a monkey, snapped the belt around her waist, clutched the shotgun like a life raft.

I hit the brakes. The truck spun almost completely around. I gave it some gas and turned the wheel and we were heading right at the Caddy. I got the nine out from the small of my back and sent my driver's window down with a touch of a button, stuck out my arm and fired left-handed. I starred the glass of the Caddy and it whipped to our right and passed us and swerved and hit the back end of my truck and made us spin like a Tilt-A-Whirl. Then we were rolling over and over. Next thing I knew, we were upside down, hanging by our seat belts. A curious weenie dog was looking in my open window, possibly hoping for blood.

I unsnapped my seat belt and fell in a heap, found my nine on the roof of the truck, reached for it. I could hear Brett cussing like a longshoreman. "Goddamn it, sonsofagoddamndogshittin'bitches."

And then she was loose from her belt. She got hold of the shotgun as I crawled out ahead of her, my head hazy, my vision blurred. The damn weenie dog bit me. I slapped at him with the back of my hand, got on my feet and leaned back against the upside-down truck. The yard and the sky kept jumping around. The dog grabbed my pants leg and tugged and growled and I had to kick him loose.

Brett came out on her hands and knees, dragging the shotgun after her.

"Goddamn it," she said. "Motherfuckin'cocksuckin'dicklickin'ballsuckin'sonsagoddamnshitsuckin'monkeylickin'sonsabitches."

Even I was a little embarrassed.

18

My head cleared enough to see the Caddy had veered off and hit a tree. The ass end of the car was sticking out in the street leaking gasoline and some other fluids; tree bark floated in the liquid. I started walking that way, limping. After a few steps I was walking straight, but my stomach was twisted and sour and my balls had tried to shrink up and hide and had almost succeeded.

I could see that air bags had popped and the driver wasn't moving. Same for the passenger in the front. The back door opened and a guy fell out with a gun in his hand. He crawled on the ground a bit, then stood up. I shot him in the head and he fell down in the pool of gas and a swirl of blood. The sunlight caught the blood and gas and the color they made was not something I could identify. When the shot went off the weenie dog took to his dog paws and tore a path around the back end of my overturned truck, across a lawn and out of view, went away from there so fast he damn near left a vapor trail.

There was another guy moving in the back passenger seat of the Caddy. He opened the door and stepped out. I shot and missed. I grabbed at Brett, who was standing out in the street with the shotgun, her legs spread wide, cussing—"Shiteatin'assholelickin'"—and pulled her around to the side of the truck as a blast peppered the opposite side of it and a shot whistled by my ear like a rocket-propelled bee. Just as we got around to the other side, I heard a sound like someone scalding a cat to my right, glanced that way, saw a dark Chevy flash down the street like something out of Buck Rogers.

It was Leonard.

I peeked around the end of the truck and the guy at the Caddy had moved to the front of it so he could see us. He steadied his gun hand on the hood and fired, and the shot took out my upturned back tire. I opened up on him with three shots, but none of them hit him. I heard the shotgun pump beside me, and then I heard a blast and heard Brett say, "Fuck you."

I fired a shot at the Caddy and broke and ran for it just as the guy raised up for another shot. I fired and he ducked down behind the car. I jumped, planted a foot on the hood, nearly lost my balance, came down on top of him with both feet, knocking his gun flying and losing mine in the process.

We came together like a couple of wild sheep, actually butted heads and knocked each other down. Across the street, moving out of the yard, taking position behind trees, I saw Tanedrue and his posse trying to cross over to us. I saw Gadget lying facedown in the yard beside the pickup, her hands over her head, crying loudly.

I bit the guy I was fighting so hard I took part of his nose away. He let out a bellow and I leaped forward and poked a finger in one of his eyes. As he staggered back, I kicked and caught the inside of his kneecap and it made a pleasant sound like a drover cracking a whip. He fell with one hand on his face, the other clutching at his knee. I picked up my gun and walked over to him and shot him in the head.

I started crossing the street. I had lost my brains. I was crazy. I saw Leonard. He was walking up the street, on my right. Tanedrue was firing at him, and so were the other three, and I knew Leonard was as good as dead.

But he wasn't. I heard his Colt .45 revolver bark and I saw the top of the ball-kicked guy's head tear off and sail across the curb and roll down a ways and spin like a furry hubcap. I shot at Tanedrue and missed and hit the house behind him. He yelled and started firing at me with an automatic pistol, fast as he could. The bullets plucked at my hair and the sleeve of my shirt, and I shot him dead center of his chest. His right leg jumped back behind him and he crumpled back with an expression on his face like he'd just found a kidney stone in his oatmeal. He went to one knee, dropped his gun, said, "Don't shoot."

I walked right up to him and shot him in the face; he'd dug in his shorts for the last time. Another bullet whizzed by me. I should have been dead ten times over. But now I was emboldened by luck and success, and that's the kind of thinking that gets you killed. Leonard, still wearing his security guard uniform, walked up beside me. The two remaining gunmen, including Red Face, fled back to their truck and were trying to get inside of it, maybe start it up and drive out.

My adrenaline rush fell off, and I let out with a deep breath. I felt light-headed. My knees were shaking. I heard Brett behind me.

"Yeahbuddythat'srightyoubunchofpussyassmotherfuckersaren'tso hotnowareyoupigsuckin'goatfuckin' . . ."

The truck's engine was going now, but the truck didn't move. It was hung up good. Gadget didn't move. She was still facedown with her hands over her head, crying. The two came out of the truck firing. I felt something tear at my neck. I fired and missed. Brett cut down with the shotgun. I caught a glimpse of what looked like a splash of red paint and then I saw Brett's shot had torn Red Face almost in half. Leonard walked toward the other guy firing. It took a few shots bouncing off the truck and the brick house, but with bullets whizzing around his head, Leonard finally hit the shooter.

The guy flipped backwards, turned completely over like he was doing a tumbling act. He was lying on his stomach. He raised his head. There was a sound coming from him like a busted manifold.

"Dirtyfuckin'ratshiteatin'dickcheesesuckin'," Brett said, deep into her French.

"What she said," Leonard said and fired, hitting the man on the ground in the mouth, making it the size of a manhole cover, knocking his head so hard on the neck it snapped sideways and teeth tumbled out on the grass.

"Hey," Leonard said, looking over at me, his eyes bright, his mouth in a kind of rictus grin. "How's it hanging?"

I didn't have an answer. I got weak and went to one knee. I turned away from the carnage we had just made. I saw the ball-kicked guy's skull down by the curb. The weenie dog appeared, grabbed it, headed off between a couple of houses, running like he had just caught a touchdown pass.

Leonard and I walked over to the Caddy and looked in at the guys in the front seat, ones pushed back by the air bags. One of them was moving.

"Should I shoot him?" Brett asked. "I want to shoot him. Other one's alive, I'll shoot him too."

"No," I said, pushing the shotgun down. "We're done."

I could hear sirens wailing, coming closer and closer.

"Glad you could make it," I said to Leonard.

"Me too," he said. "Your neck's bleeding."

I put a hand to my neck. I had been grazed. I couldn't believe it. That was the worse I had got, except for a stray shotgun pellet and some broken glass.

Brett handed me the shotgun. "Wait right here. I'm fixin' to slap the shit out of Gadget."

I didn't stop her. She went across the street, jerked Gadget to her feet, and slapped her so hard it knocked her down again. "Get up, bitch," I heard Brett say.

Gadget didn't move.

Brett kicked her in the ribs. "Get up, bitch, or I'll stomp your head in."

Gadget reluctantly got up, and Brett slapped her down again.

People were starting to poke their heads out of their houses, move out into their yards. Four police cars and a medical unit arrived. We dumped our guns on the Caddy's hood, walked out into the street slowly with our hands up.

Brett didn't move. She stood in the yard looking down at Gadget, who was crying louder than before.

"Get up, bitch," I heard Brett say, "and I'll give you something to cry about."

19

They separated us and put me in a poorly lit cell with a burly tattooed guy with greasy hair and a lot of muscles and a way of looking at me that made me feel like a pork chop with a butt hole. At least he had all his teeth and no pustules on his face. We would at worst make healthy if not overly attractive children.

He was sitting on his bunk and I was sitting on mine. My hands were shaking a little bit; they still tingled from all the shooting and I could smell cordite on my clothes, and there was another smell inside my head, a cloud of death and doom.

The cell's walls were as pink as a baboon's ass and we were both wearing pink jumpsuits to match. It was a new jail philosophy. Tough guys didn't want to go back to jail because they'd have to wear pink and sit in pink jail cells. Some thought it was an idea that worked. I didn't believe it. Some redneck decides to shoot his wife over the fact she burned his squirrel potpie, I could hardly believe he'd be considering before the deed: Well, damn. I better hold up on this killing. I stick a broom handle up Bessie's nose, set her on fire and shoot her eye out, I'll have to wear pink and sit in a pink room, and them's girl colors. What if the fellas see me?

I wondered how the fella across from me felt about wearing pink. Maybe he didn't like it, but it certainly hadn't been enough to keep him out of jail, and from the looks of him, he'd been here before, maybe had a pillow with his name stitched on it.

Fuck rehabilitation. Go for the pink to embarrass them.

My partner put an Elvis smile on his face, eyed me for a while, said, "You don't get much pussy in jail."

"That's a natural fact," I said.

"It ain't available."

"You, my man, are like an oracle. You see things the rest of us don't. You are Nostradamus in pink. You are a ripe cherry blossom in an orchard of dullards."

He eyed me for a moment, trying to figure out if what I said was an insult or a compliment. Then he picked up where he'd left off. "Not real pussy."

I was already tired of this guy.

"Sometimes, you got to make your own nookie," he said.

"You got you a theme, don't you, buddy?"

"You hear what I'm sayin'?"

"Are you suggestin' that I'm pretty in pink?"

"Poontang is where you find it, boy."

I saw where this was going, and it was where I'd figured all along. I jumped off my bunk and was across our little gap before he could open his mouth again. I hit him as hard as I could, right across the cheek; it was like I dropped a fucking anvil on him. He fell backwards on his bunk, but his ass was hanging off and the weight of it pulled him onto the floor. He lay beside the bunk twitching like a Pentecostal having a Jesus rigor. There wasn't any blood, but he was going to have a bruise and a headache and his pink jumpsuit was going to have floor nasty on it.

I backed to my bunk and sat down and watched until he quit twitching. Then I turned my attention to how many years I would be behind bars before they put me to death by lethal injection for the shoot-out we had just been in. Maybe they could put me and Brett and Leonard in a room together. We could hold hands from our cots while they put the needles in our arms. I looked at the guy on the floor, the man without pussy.

I sat there and thought on things and tried to figure how I had come to this. Mama always told me to stay away from guns, and though I could use one and I was a good shot, I had never been comfortable with them. Though I agreed that guns didn't kill people, people killed people, guns sure made it a lot easier and far more successful than hunting down victims with a pointed stick.

If I hadn't been armed today, I'd have been deep napping inside my truck amidst broken glass and a bloody car seat with a hole in my head, Brett dead beside me, a yard gnome and a Vote Republican sign still standing. So there had to be something good said for guns, and maybe we could even throw in a few kind words for erratic driving, but if we had all been carrying those pointed sticks it might have been less of a massacre. When you really think about it, humans are a scary branch of evolution, especially the male division. Man can turn anything into a weapon, even his tongue.

Perhaps living in Texas was my problem.

Maybe if I had been born in Connecticut.

Nah. They talked funny and it was cold up there.

I thought about Gadget and Tanedrue and the trailer, and how me and Leonard had whipped those guys' asses. I thought about those birthday and Christmas cards on Tanedrue's mirror; his mother had meant something to him, and he to her, and now she'd have him to grieve over. I thought about the shooting, the way I had acted and felt, about how something had clicked inside of me and turned me hot as the core of the sun, about how the bloodlust had taken me over and wrapped me up tight until I exploded. I thought about how Leonard was, and Brett. I had seen something close to joy on their faces. I figured mine had probably looked the same. Maybe we all deserved execution just because we could do what we did and not blink an eye. It wasn't just self-defense. When it all came down and I felt that click inside of me, I had been scared but exhilarated too, and in the moments of the happening I had felt born to kill. Now I just felt small and sick to my stomach and a little weird. Like it had all happened to someone else and I had watched it from a distant rooftop.

My life had been too full of quick punches, blood, and gun smoke. I wanted to go with Brett to some island and live off coconuts and screw until it killed us. I wanted to never throw a punch again. Never see a gun again, not even from a distance, not even a picture in a magazine. I wanted to never be mad again. I wanted to not have to worry about my code of honor. I wanted it not to matter. I even wanted to get away from Leonard.

I was tired of the whole dirty, bloody thing that was my life. I was beginning to consider heavily that old saying about being careful when you fight monsters so that you do not become one. In that moment, I was feeling pretty monstrous. It was as if I had been born under a violent star.

I wondered what Leonard was thinking about.

He was probably in his cell sleeping on his bunk, dreaming of vanilla cookies and Dr Pepper. Happy in pink. He was alive and had helped keep me and Brett alive. For him, that was enough, and for me it should have been.

The guy on the floor stirred and started to sit up. I thought: Fuck it. In for the snout, in for the tail. I stood up and kicked him in the head as hard as I could under the jaw. He went down again and didn't get up. This time he bled. I sat down on my bunk and watched the blood run out of his mouth.

Hap Collins, you are one walking, talking contradiction. I also decided I didn't deserve execution after all. I probably just needed a spanking. Maybe someone could call me some names and send me home without my supper. I felt myself tremble as if something cold had crawled up my spine.

I watched some shadows advance down the hall. I heard some prisoners yelling and talking. Somewhere someone was watching a television. There was no television in my cell. Not even a deck of cards. Just the man without nookie, lying unconscious on the jailhouse floor.

After a while a big shadow came down the hall. It fell into the cell, and pretty soon there was a guy following it. He was one of the cops who had arrested us. He was a big guy with a belly that was teasing the buttons on his shirt. He was bareheaded and he didn't have much hair. He stood at the door to my cell, looking through the bars. He stared down at my pal on the floor, said, "What happened to him?"

"Faintin' spell," I said. "Saw a mouse."

"A mouse, huh?"

"It was a big mouse."

20

They brought the three of us, wearing handcuffs, into an interrogation room that smelled strongly of Pine-Sol and too much mop soap and more than a sprinkle of urine. The floor was a little slick. A roach lay legs up in the corner.

There was a mirror on the wall, long and narrow, and I figured it was one of those see-through jobs where they could watch into the room from the other side. They couldn't fool me. I had seen TV and movies. The mirror was smeared in places with fingerprints and nose prints, and some stains that were probably not worth knowing about. There was a single fat bulb hanging down from a frayed, dust-covered wire and the dust was so thick and dark it looked like fungus. I half expected the wire to snap and spray the room with sparks and set the place on fire. I saw a video camera in the top corner of the room on metal struts. Boogers were smeared on the wall, and some of them were big enough to use as bricks in construction. I had the uncomfortable feeling that one of the larger ones was looking at me.

They put us on one side of a long table with initials and fuck-you messages carved into it. I looked up. The camera was pointing right at us. I gave it a smile.

They had already talked to us separately, right before tossing us into our individual cells. Now they had us as a trio, the three of us sitting there in all our jail-suited glory, pink roses in a light green booger-dotted room. They brought us there and went away, and we sat alone for a moment, and then the door opened and two men came in. They were not in uniform.

I knew one of them. His name was Drake and he was a detective and we got along all right. We had had reason to meet before. I hadn't shot anyone that time, and he knew Marvin, so he had been nice to me. I got off easy. I hit a man at a Dairy Queen because he hit his wife when she dropped his DQ Dude on the way to their table. I thought this was a bit excessive, even though Dudes are good and inexpensive if you go with the basket, French fries, and a drink. The wife got mad at me and I was the one that went to jail. As the old saying goes, no good deed goes unpunished.

Drake was whip-lean, black as straight coffee, with a soft-looking face and a boxer's flat nose. His shirt was lime-colored. It matched the paint on the walls. He didn't have on a tie. His top button was unbuttoned and his shirttail was pulled out. If he was trying to look any more casual he'd have come in his underwear carrying a teddy bear and a pacifier.

Drake knew Leonard too. Who didn't? Brett he also knew of. I could understand that. A lot of men knew of her and wished they knew more of her.

I had no idea where Gadget was, or the two who had been in the front seat of the Caddy. I wondered if my cell mate was still napping. I wondered if the weenie dog was somewhere hidden, nibbling on his prize.

Drake had another cop with him. A pink-skinned, redheaded guy with freckles and fat lips. Kelso was his name. He was leaning in the corner of the room acting like he couldn't believe what the human condition had come to.

Drake sat on one side of the table and we sat on the other. Brett in the middle. The chairs were shorter on our side of the table. It's an old trick the cops use to make you feel less significant than the interrogator. We didn't give a damn, though. We were tough enough to tear doughnuts in half.

Kelso kept his corner, turning his head to take us in with those disappointed eyes. Drake lit a cigarette and asked if we wanted cigarettes or coffee.

"Have you got those little flavored creamers?" Leonard asked.

"No," Drake said.

"Any cookies?"

"Nothing like that," Drake said. "Some coffee. Standard shitty creamer with some sugar packs. Or Sweet'N Low. But maybe we can bring in some caviar and nice crackers."

"Could you?" Leonard said. "That would be damn nice."

Drake made a point of ignoring Leonard. He looked at me and Brett. We asked for coffee. Drake nodded, turned to Kelso, said, "Is the camera on?"

He knew we knew how it worked, so he wasn't trying to be cagey.

"Nope," Kelso said.

"Good," Drake said. "Leonard, you can go fuck yourself."

"From your lips to God's ear," Leonard said.

"Go on, man," Drake said to Kelso. "Get the coffee."

Kelso left. I guess it was his day to be fetch bitch.

Drake looked us over. "So, you people have had quite a day. Enough dead to put a dent in the population. If only you could have set fire to downtown and shot a busload of orphans, it would have been perfect."

"Hap ran over a yard gnome," Brett said. "That damn sure ought to count for something."

"Yep," Leonard said. "It was a big day, and frankly, I can't speak for everyone, but I'm a little tuckered, and this pink outfit makes me feel like I'm in my jammies. But, just to let you know, I really feel humiliated. This suit, it's got to be the right cure for evil. Wearing this, no one would ever stray again from the straight and narrow. You wouldn't even catch me jackin' off in the men's room if I thought I'd have to wear this fucker again."

"That's a relief," Drake said.

"Thought you'd want to know," Leonard said.

Drake tapped his fingers on the desk, said, "You're going to call it self-defense?"

"Our lawyer will," I said. Of course, we didn't have a lawyer yet, but I wanted to sound like a big-time experienced criminal.

I turned to Leonard, said, "I met a guy in my cell who wanted to fuck me. I knocked him out. Was that anti-gay?"

"Did you write any anti-gay graffiti on him or the wall?"

I shook my head.

"I think it'll be all right," he said.

"No talking amongst yourselves," Drake said. "You know you did a bad thing, you three?"

"Yep," Leonard said.

"What about those guys in the Caddy?" Brett asked.

"They'll live," Drake said.

"Gadget?" I asked.

"She's under arrest."

Kelso came back in, but he didn't have our coffee. He leaned over and whispered in Drake's ear.

"What?" Drake said.

Kelso nodded.

"Goddamn it," Drake said.

Drake got up and went out. Leonard said, "What about that coffee?"

"Fuck the coffee," Kelso said.

"That's some kind of goddamn way for a public servant to talk," Leonard said. "And you with the camera running."

I kicked Leonard gently under the table.

"I saw that," Kelso said. "And that's good policy. You should shut the hell up. And the camera is still off, dick cheese. That way, I wanted to kick your ass it wouldn't get recorded."

Leonard just smiled. Even with handcuffs on, Leonard would be a load and he knew it, and I could tell Kelso knew it too.

Kelso glared at me, said, "The jailer said you hit your cell mate."

"He didn't buy the mouse story?"

"Drake said you two think you're funny."

"There's that insult again," Leonard said. "It could take the edge off our comic timing."

"I think you're funny," Brett said, reached her handcuffs over and patted Leonard's hand.

"Thank you, dear," Leonard said.

"Laugh it up," Kelso said. "We'll see what the jury says."

We were the sort that when we were nervous we couldn't help but run our mouths to show we weren't nervous. It's not a good habit, but it's ours. That comment shut us up, though. We sat there in silence, brooding in our pink jumpsuits, until the door opened and Drake came in and looked at us and sighed. He stood there for a long moment, just studying us, like we were a species formerly thought extinct. I thought any moment the rubber hose would appear, maybe a blowtorch and some pliers and a couple of angry German shepherds. He turned to Kelso. "Take their handcuffs off."

21

After our handcuffs were off, Drake and Kelso went out, leaving us alone. We sat and waited, looking in the mirror that most likely had someone on the other side. At first I counted smears on the glass, boogers on the wall, anything to keep me busy. But that grew boring.

We turned and looked at one another, as if one of us might offer some sort of solution. No great answers unfolded. The nature of the universe was still safe. Stephen Hawking still had the inside track.

We sat there for a long time, then finally began to talk. Brett said, "What's the point of this?"

"They want whoever is on the other side of the glass to take a good look at us," Leonard said.

"Why?" Brett asked.

I patted her knee. "Because you are so pretty."

"Oh. Well, of course," she said, "duh, there *is* that."

"I got a joke," I said.

"Not now," Leonard said.

"It's pretty good."

"Not now," Brett said, and I knew that was the end of that.

"I don't know about you two," I said, "but I miss Kelso already. He had such sweet, if electrified, eyes."

"You'd think they'd wipe these boogers down," Brett said. "I don't know who they think that intimidates. It's just nasty."

"I hear that," Leonard said.

"And that piss smell," she said. "It could hold your coat."

"It could wear it," Leonard said.

The door opened and Drake came in, and there was a guy with him that had a head like a concrete block. His haircut had something to do with that, gold as an Aryan dream, waxed up in front, flared out on the sides. He had a big hooked nose and thin lips and seemed to have more teeth than a human ought to, something a crocodile might envy, only straighter. His eyes were big and dark brown, like two unwiped butt holes. He reminded me of a villain out of those old *Dick Tracy* comics.

Drake went over and leaned against the wall, got a whiff of the piss, moved to another corner. The guy with the square head leaned back against the mirror. He said, "There's nobody on the other side."

"You say," Leonard said.

Drake said, "No. He's right."

"Damn, glad we got your word on that," Leonard said. "That makes it all right, then."

"I locked the door leads into the investigation room," Drake said.

"You got the only key?" I asked.

"No."

"Ah," I said. "No one else would of course use their key and go in there and look at us. . . . But frankly, we don't care. Ask what you want. It was self-defense."

"I know," Drake said.

That sort of stunned us, but lawmen are tricky.

The door opened and two guys came in. One of them was the guy who had been in Tanedrue's trailer, the one who wasn't with the batch we shot up today, the guy whose profile was gone, whose nose was splinted now and taped over good with tape so thick he looked like the Mummy. His forehead looked as if someone had broken in his ball bat on it. A shock of thick hair poked up from the top of the bandages like a rooster's comb. He went over and leaned against the wall and looked at Leonard. It wasn't a look of adoration.

I thought, What the hell?

The other guy was a short fat guy in a black suit with a black tie and some black shoes that needed a shine. He looked like an undertaker in a pet cemetery. He blew some breath out between his fat lips, went over and leaned on the wall next to our friend with the tape and the bruises.

The room was starting to get tight. If one more person came in we'd all be wearing the same suit of clothes, and I was sure I needed to change my underwear.

Brett looked at the two leaning on the mirror, said, "There's boogers on the wall and there's something on the mirror I don't think will pass for mayonnaise. Just a word to the wise."

They stopped leaning.

Leonard glared at the taped-up man, said, "What the hell is the Phantom of the Opera doing here?"

Drake said, "We'll come to that. But first, we got a little deal for you guys."

"A deal?" I said. "Think we're going to rat each other out? There's people saw what happened. We didn't go looking to be shot at. I might run over that yard gnome again I got the chance, but getting shot at like that, trust me, I'd rather pass. And you said it yourself, self-defense."

"You're going to get the charges dropped, or rather they're going to definitely turn into self-defense," Drake said. "No court. No problem."

"No shirt. No shoes. No problem," Leonard said. "What kind of bull is this? There's always court. What's the catch?"

Drake didn't say anything. He crossed his arms.

I said, "There is a catch, isn't there?"

"That's one way of putting it," Square Head said. "It's more like we got your dick in the zipper and we're pulling it up tight. In your case, ma'am, I guess it's your tit we got caught up."

"Then you better have a lot of zipper," Brett said, "'cause I'm serious in the tit department."

No one opposed this opinion.

"Agent Tenson here," Drake said, nodding at the *Dick Tracy* villain, "he's with the FBI, and he and his buddy here, Captain Bandage—"

"Man, that's some funny shit," Captain Bandage, aka the Mummy, aka the Phantom, said.

"They want to talk to you," Drake said. "Me, I'm just a lowly fucking public servant who's always got the raw ass from these fed guys sticking their dicks in it, and I hate them."

"Come on," Tenson said. "There's no need to turn this ugly. You and me, I'm sure we got things in common, Drake."

"Yeah," Drake said. "These guys, that's what we got in common.

May have been self-defense, but it didn't just come out of nowhere, these folks wanting to kill them. There has to be a backstory. I don't like lettin' them off. They shot a lot of people. They ought to at least have a paddling, a night in jail, noses in the corner. This isn't right, man."

"What I want to know," Leonard said, "is why is the fucking Mummy in on this?"

The Mummy's voice sounded snotty, which isn't unusual when your snout is packed with cotton. "It's Milhouse. I was working undercover. Thanks a lot, asshole, you fucked up a real sting operation just to take some whore home."

"Her granddaddy doesn't see her that way," Leonard said.

"Yeah, but me, I've had surgery, and I got to have some more. Thanks."

"You're welcome," Leonard said, and the Mummy came off the wall and Drake stepped over and put a hand against the Mummy's chest.

"After what he done to you," Drake said, "I wouldn't push it. I think he can do it again. And we took the handcuffs off."

"Yeah," Leonard said, still sitting, holding his hands up. "They took the handcuffs off."

"We ought to all just beat him down," the Mummy, aka the Phantom of the Opera, aka Captain Bandage, said.

"We ought to," Drake said, "but we won't."

"You were undercover," Leonard said. "Might have been nice had you warned us Tanedrue and his mutts were going to take a run at us."

"I didn't know," Milhouse said. "Had no idea. I told them I had some family concerns, got out. My figuring was some higher-ups were gonna come down on them, and I didn't want to be there when it happened."

The fat guy said, "Way it was gonna work was we was gonna let Tanedrue and his dopes take care of you guys, then we were gonna come down on them, spread their asses all over Kingdom Come. Guys like them are too stupid to deal dope, and let me tell you from experience, that's putting them in a real stupid place. We got guys working for us that are damn near retards and they do better. One guy in Dallas hasn't got any legs and goes around in the streets on a wheeled board selling dope and peddling ass for us, and he does a better job than those fucks."

"And who are you?" I asked. "My first guess is since you got people selling dope and ass for you, you're not a cop, though these days, hard to say. And though you could be a priest on vacation, I'm doubtful."

"I'm the guy that wanted you two killed," the fat man said.

Leonard shifted in his chair. Drake said, "I got a gun, Leonard."

"I don't like people want to kill me or Hap," Leonard said. "Fact is, it seriously chaps my ass. I don't like you bringing him, whoever he is, in here to lord over us like he's somethin'. What the hell is going on here? Tell us or arrest us or shoot us or do some goddamn thing or another. I'm fed up."

"Hold it a minute," I said. "Didn't someone say something about a deal? I mean, there's some kind of deal, I want to hear it."

"Oh yeah," Drake said. "These guys got deals out the ass."

22

A day after they let us go, after they offered us the deal, Marvin gave us a short-lived holiday. He owned a boat and he took me and Leonard and Brett out to a lake near LaBorde to go fishing. It was a nice lake with a big dam. Marvin had some kind of membership there, and you could only get in with a key to a gate that had a sign on it that said BEWARE OF ALLIGATORS. It was an open boat and had plenty of seats and a lot of room, a place to lay your rods and clamp them down. There was a container in the floor of the boat and we had some cold drinks in there, but it was too cold to want them. We also had a couple thermoses of coffee, some bologna-and-mayonnaise sandwiches, some bags of potato chips that were more inviting.

Marvin steered the boat out to the middle of the calm water, making it less calm as we went. Small, dark birds were in the willow trees across the way and the grass near the trees was tall and still green even in the brisk beginnings of winter; it grew out from beneath the trees, ran across the bank and into the lake like a green tattoo. Once we got settled and the wake of the boat had subsided, the water around us looked like a huge sheet of tin. There was the faint smell of dead fish in the air and there were a number of old logs floating on the lake's surface. After a while one of the logs swam away.

It was an alligator, probably sneaking up on a frog. It had fooled me. I cast my line away from that direction, but watched the alligator, the way it split the water and gave the lake a darker color wherever it swam.

"I certainly got you guys in a mess," Marvin said.

"You did," Brett said, frowning at the little green rubber lizard she had on the end of her line for bait.

"I know, and I regret it. Thanks for having them cut Gadget loose, Hap."

"I didn't have them do anything special," I said. "I just told them they wanted a deal from us she had to be cut loose."

"It's the only way they would have let her go," he said.

"No problem," I said. "How's she doing?"

"She's in rehab, out in Arizona. Rachel and JoAnna are with her. I convinced them, after what you two did, I couldn't go. Had to be here to help you. But Gadget, I guess she's doing all right. Rachel said she's still in a kind of shock. She feels guilty going back to Tanedrue, didn't know they would come after you and take her with them, didn't know it was going to be like that. She doesn't love that dead fuck anymore, sees him for what he is and what he was doing to her. Now, after all that garbage she finally sees. She's as naive as a fresh-born baby sometimes. Said to tell you, Brett, she deserved every slap you gave her, and then some."

"Hell, I know that," Brett said, and cast her line. She looked cute today, in a heavy coat with a tan cap with earflaps and big cream-colored puffy boots full of warm stuffing. Her long hair was tied back in a ponytail, and it was bloodred against her back because of the way the sun was falling on it.

"The FBI sort of got us over a barrel," I said. "That had something to do with us telling them yes, trying to better our situation. We're not all that noble, Marvin."

"Speak for yourself," Leonard said. "I am one noble sonofabitch, and way special. If I weren't so tired I'd walk on water and kick that alligator's ass."

"You'd have got off anyway," Marvin said. "There would have been a trial, and a lot of time taken up, but in the end, they'd have let you three off and fined you for the shotgun. I don't know, might have been some jail time. Witnesses, though, they were on your side. There was one fellow upset about some yard gnomes, another about some pink flamingos, but other than that it came out all right."

"Death to gnomes and flamingos," I said.

"Bottom line," Marvin said, "is I know why you did it, and you can downplay it all you want, but I know why you did it, and I won't ever forget. Already owed you guys, now I really owe you."

"We owed you some too," Leonard said. "For something or another, though I kind of forget what. But after this we'll be even. We can start running tabs on each other again."

We fished all day in the cold, dry weather on the flat gray lake beneath the pearl-colored sky, eating the sandwiches and chips, drinking the coffee and talking a little, but not too much. I cast my line without purpose, and with no real hope of catching anything. I was fishing a wish and nothing more. I reeled my line in time after time, watching it cut the water like the thin edge of a knife. I cast and recast until the sun was falling down behind us and the sky that had been clear and pearl-colored at my back turned red as a whore's lipstick, then was stained with purple like the insides of a plum stretched out. I reeled in my line and turned to take a good look at the sky. I thought it might be the last time I saw a sky like that, or went fishing. Might be the last day and night I saw Brett, because in the morning I was sending her away. It had been a battle, but I had convinced her. She was going out to Arizona too, to join Gadget and Rachel and JoAnna. Secretly, I think events had unnerved her. Not that she was fearful of what might happen to her—well, no more than someone should be reasonably fearful—but because she had enjoyed it all too much; there was something inside of her that had snapped. It was the same thing that had allowed her to set her ex-husband on fire and beat him with a shovel, and pistol-whip a midget. It hadn't frightened her before, but now it had. She had seen its full face and it was gruesome. This time people had died. I didn't question that they needed to die, but they had, and by our hands, in an explosion of blood and urine and feces, a whiff of gun smoke on the air.

I knew how she felt. Problem was, that thing inside of me had clicked loose so many times it was starting to feel normal, like the necessary lancing of a wound. I had looked into the abyss so much it was no longer just looking back at me, it had its arms around me and was puckering to kiss.

I wanted to just let it all go, do the jail time, forget about the FBI deal. But then I thought some more about that jail time, and since I had already done prison some years back and I could remember it as if it were yesterday, I didn't want any more of that.

I cast my line toward the setting sun and the stained sky, and when I started reeling it in a fish hit. I reeled it until it was close enough for me to reach out and take hold of the line just above the fish. It was a moderate-sized perch. I loosened the hook from its mouth and gently tossed it back in the water.

We started ashore then, my fish having been the only one caught. Marvin hadn't driven the boat far toward shore before the night overtook us, collapsed over the water and made it dark as the River Styx. When we got to the boat ramp there was no more light except a thin ray of rising moonlight that was slowly being bagged by some fast-moving clouds. The wind picked up and really turned cold. The weather had changed in a flash. Welcome to East Texas.

We used flashlights and got out at the front of the boat without stepping in the water and fastened the crank line to Marvin's trailer, then used the automatic crank and put it in place. We drove away, along with a rumble of thunder, and soon after, out on the highway, there were thin streaks of lightning, like bright varicose veins cutting across the black sky. We drove to Marvin's place and put the boat in the carport and closed it up, then he drove us home in his big Ford truck, and he and Leonard spent the night at our place.

We put Leonard on the couch and we got a blow-up bed for Marvin, some extra pillows for them from the closet. We weren't supposed to have guns, but Marvin had brought a shotgun for himself and one for Leonard and he gave me and Brett handguns. We talked for a long time in the dark, sitting in the living room, then finally Brett and I went up to bed, placing the handguns on the nightstand.

Brett and I were fiery that night and at first I feared they would hear us downstairs, then after a while I didn't care at all. When we finished, we hugged for a while, then she said, "You're sure Jim Bob's coming?"

"Oh yeah, he said so, so he'll be here. Marvin arranged it. I just wish we could have found Veil. But you know how he is. Locating him is like trying to find a virgin in a whorehouse."

"Jim Bob, he's good."

"Real good," I said. "After Leonard, he's who I would want at my back. Veil, I'd kind of like him there too."

"He's like that character the Shadow."

"He is. Kind of gives me the creeps, but he's a good one to have on your side. Wish we could have found him."

"What about this guy Marvin knows that's comin'? Tonto?"

"Marvin says he's good, so I reckon he is. He's one more, and that's good."

"Yeah," she said, "that's good."

"Marvin said Tonto owes him a big favor. He won't say what the favor is, but he says he'll pay him back."

"Not everyone pays favors back," she said.

"Marvin said Tonto does, so I got to believe him."

We were hugging close and I could feel Brett's warm tears on my cheek. I said, "It'll be all right, baby."

"I feel bad leaving you."

"I don't feel bad you're going," I said. "It's the right thing to do."

"All right, then," she said. "There's nothing else to say, is there?"

I shook my head. "Nothing else."

She pulled her big T-shirt that said SHEN CHAUN, MARTIAL SCIENCE over her head, kissed me, and rolled over and went to sleep with my hand on her hip. She could do that a lot of the time, just go down into dreamland no matter what was on her mind. Wasn't that easy for me, not when I had plans for the next day, especially the kind of plans we had to set in motion.

The rain outside picked up. I sat up and put my pillow behind my head, against the wall, listened to the rain grow savage. Thunder shook the upstairs windows with a sound like dice being rattled in a cup. Lightning was jumping around outside. The rain made a sound like a giant snake hissing, and the roof was taking some serious shots from drops that were hitting like artillery fire.

Brett didn't stir. She was snoring.

I looked at her for a while, taking in everything I could about her, and then I thought about what it was we had agreed to do, me and Leonard. When it was all done, it wouldn't surprise me if what was left of my soul wouldn't fill a thimble.

23

In that booger-lined room with the greasy mirror, the deal they offered us sounded easy, but with all things that sound easy, there is often something at the bottom of it all that makes it stink. It's always something that begins with "All you got to do," or "This won't take much of your time." That should be enough of a cue to make you throw your hands over your head and run the other way. But not us; no one ever said we learned from our mistakes, not me and Leonard. Besides, we sort of had our asses in a crack over this killing a whole bunch of people deal, and our options were thin.

The fat guy in the black suit was from the Dixie Mafia, whatever that was exactly. His name was Hirem Burnett and he was turning state's evidence. In a nutshell he was one of the middle boys in the organization. You had your water carriers like Tanedrue and his buddies, then you had Hirem, and above his fat ass were Satan's Angels.

That's what Hirem called them, Satan's Angels. They sounded like a motorcycle gang, and thing was, there was a connection to some biker gangs in Houston. Some of the guys at the top had been bikers, then prisoners in one or several of our fine institutions, mostly for drug deals and violent acts. Bunch of guys tattooing themselves in cells and doing shank hits in the rec yard, running some dirty work from prison via messengers, a few of them getting out and turning into businessmen, their tattoos hidden under long-sleeve shirts, their formerly greasy hair trimmed and spruced up; sometimes they went as far as to wear a suit and tie and not scratch their nuts in public.

Lot of them were still Aryan Nations guys at heart, worrying that a strain of black blood would make soiled whites want to throw spears and run with watermelons, piss on the Dixie flag, maybe vote Democrat and wish for socialized medicine. Still, as Conners said, they were businessmen and green was their true color, and as time had gone on, they had lost some of their interest in racial purity but none of their interest in crisp folding money.

It was Hirem who told Tanedrue and his posse to hit us. And to bring in a whole bucketload of irony, now me and Leonard were going to have to do him a favor, and all because of Gadget. I rewound the bitch slapping Brett had given her in my head and enjoyed all the details I could remember. I might even have gussied up my memory some. I even quit feeling bad about punching her.

Hirem's son, one Tim Burnett, had bucked Daddy's ideas and had gone to college to be an environmental engineer. He didn't want to grow up to sell dope and run pussy. He ran off with a black girl and about three hundred thousand dollars' worth of drug money in a duffel bag. The guys at the top wanted the money back and they wanted the son to pay. The girl had to go down and not get up. They couldn't let word get around a colored gal had taken up with one of their mid-management fellows' sons and helped swipe a chunk of their money. Just wouldn't do.

She had to be whacked and they had to get all the money back, and the son, well, he had to take it and like it. That way Hirem wouldn't find him in a damp cardboard box inside his garage next to the garbage can. Those were Hirem's words, said it was the exact threat he had gotten from one Cletus Jimson, the upper-level man with a plan.

Hirem knew everyone in the business. He had been there when it was run by old fat guys in Hawaiian shirts wearing needle-nose Italian shoes. Back then, families were left alone. You didn't bother them no matter what a member might do, not unless their family was part of the business. Cops were also left out of the mix. Killing a cop was considered bad form. Business was between those in the group and no one else.

These days they were a lot more freewheeling. They'd kill anyone or do anything to maintain business. That included Hirem's son and girlfriend, and now that he had come forward to help the cops, it included Hirem himself.

The bad guys were also unhappy that a good chunk of their potential earnings had been flushed down the crapper by me, and Leonard had helped me do it. Couple of goons from a nearby town coming in and slapping their lower-level errand boys around, that didn't look good. That's why there had been a hit on us.

In that booger-dotted room Hirem said, "Wasn't nothing personal, you two. It was business."

"What about her?" I said, nodding at Brett. "What did she do to you?"

"Not a thing. And in the old days, she wouldn't have been part of it. But these ain't the old days, and I'm not in command. New guys at the top, they're younger and meaner and more demanding, and they keep me on a tight leash. Most likely, ten years ago this would have just been a business loss and we'd have taken care of Tanedrue and his morons and that would have been the end of it. But that's not the way they play these days."

"Just for the record," the Mummy said, "I wasn't really one of their morons."

"Informer, double agent, whatever you are or were," Hirem said. "In the old days, we figured you were a cop, we might have let you go. And a thing like this, my son getting jungle fever, wanting to ride a porch monkey, taking off with a bag of money, it would have been handled differently. I could have paid it back, made him apologize, sent the shine girl packin', maybe she would have caught a bullet, but no one else. Not like that anymore."

"Shine?" Leonard said. "That word is still in the vocabulary?"

"It's right next to colored," I said. "Just south of porch monkey."

"Oh," Leonard said.

Bottom line was, Hirem was under the gun, literally, and instead of following through with what the Dixie Mafia wanted him to do, he decided he'd had enough and it was time to pull the train out of the station. He had come to the FBI to tell them about the hit on us, that he had been behind it. Came to tell them lots of things, some of those things not yet spoken, and the reason for that was he had to have a deal before he let out all the juice he knew.

But the thing was, he needed some patsies to find his son and the money. Some muscle. And since we had our asses in a crack, self-defense or not, and considering the cops figured they could probably find two more just like us to do Hirem's work if we refused, we got picked and we accepted.

So the FBI, represented by the Mummy and the *Dick Tracy* villain, they said to us, and I paraphrase: You scratch our back, and we'll scratch yours. You help Hirem get his son back in one piece, save that girl, and get us the money, since it isn't exactly earned legal and it could be used by the United States government to continue the war on crime, we will wipe your slate clean. They could do that, they said. No trial, nothing. We would be helping the FBI, 'cause when Hirem got his son back, he was going to sing like a goddamn canary and we would be the recipients of all kinds of goodwill.

Course, on the record, we weren't working for anyone. If the Dixie Mafia punched our tickets, the FBI wouldn't know anything about it. If we said at any point we were working for the FBI, they would deny it. They could always find replacements for us in the wings, other fuckups they could take advantage of. They said just that.

"Yeah," Leonard told them, "but you aren't gonna find any bigger fuckups than us."

No one argued.

We could leave the offer, of course, take our chances at trial, but Flat Top said, "Might not go so good you don't help."

"Isn't that blackmail?" I said.

He said, "Uh-huh."

I looked at Drake. He looked toward the wall.

And so that was how Leonard and I had come to unofficially work for the FBI so they wouldn't have to get their hands dirty. They said if we wanted to, we could get help, but the help was in the same water we were. No one would know them and no one would protect them. It was us and our friends and whatever moxie we might have against the world, and that was it. Oh, and we did get their best wishes, and if we couldn't get the duffel bag back, they'd let that go.

24

About four a.m. I heard a car pull in the drive. I had a good idea who it was, but I wasn't taking any chances. In my pajamas and rabbit slippers, a gun in my hand, I left the bedroom. Brett was still snoring. I went downstairs with the rabbit ears flapping and found Leonard and Marvin in their shorts and T-shirts holding their shotguns.

After a few moments there was a knock on the door, and a voice said, "Ya'll about to shoot, don't. It's me, Jim Bob. I'd like to keep my good-lookin' ass intact."

Leonard opened the door. "Hell, man, knowing it's you is what gives me reason to shoot."

Jim Bob, tall and broad-shouldered, thin but not skinny, came into the house and Leonard shut the door. Jim Bob took off his gray Stetson. The hatband was a thick strip of cloth in a cheetah-skin pattern, and in the band were toothpicks and little feathers. The hat was stained in a lot of spots. Without the hat, Jim Bob looked a little off; it was like seeing a rooster remove his head. He was red-faced and his hair was short, wheat-textured and orange-colored. He had a scar on his face I didn't remember from the time before. He had on a light green snap-pocket Western shirt, blue jeans, and a pair of brown boots that looked as if most of the world had worn them for a while and then given them back. He looked at me, studied my bunny slippers. "You look like an idiot."

"Don't be jealous. I can hop real far."

Jim Bob grinned, said, "Ain't there no coffee?"

"There will be." It was Brett, at the top of the stairs. She had pulled on some men's boxer shorts under her T-shirt and she had on some flip-flops. "You loudmouthed guys don't know how to let a girl get her beauty sleep."

"Well, now," Jim Bob said, looking up as Brett came down, her red hair tousled around her shoulders, her braless breasts bouncing pleasantly, "it's good to see there's still women know how to make coffee."

"I didn't say I was making it," she said when she got to the bottom of the stairs. "I said there will be coffee. Right, Hap?"

"I'm on it," I said.

"You look lovely," Jim Bob said, flashing a grin at Brett that had probably charmed trailer-trash women from LaBorde to Memphis out of their panties and their Beanie Baby collections.

"And you are still full of shit," Brett said.

"Yes, ma'am, I am. And you are still so lovely my back teeth hurt."

"Just your teeth ache?" Brett said. "If that's the case, I'm losing my touch."

"Well," Jim Bob said, "I was trying to be polite."

There was the sound of another car outside, so I put down the coffee makings and went to the living room window for a look.

I peeled back the curtain and had to wipe the frosted pane clear with my arm to get a view. The rain had slacked and there was only a bit of the garage light to see by, but it was all I needed. A big black van was pulled up behind Jim Bob's classic red Cadillac, the one he calls the Red Bitch, and when the driver got out, came around the back of Jim Bob's ride, started for the house, it was as if the great shadow of Armageddon had fallen across the cold winter earth. He was at least six foot seven, with shoulders wide enough to make football players slash their wrists with envy. He had legs like trees and arms like smaller trees, a face that appeared to have been knocked into shape from granite and then beat on with a sledgehammer. His muscles moved under his clothes, like animals trying to escape a sack. He had long black hair tied back in a ponytail and he wore a black denim shirt, black leather jacket, black jeans, and black round-toed boots. He walked swiftly, like he was anxiously leaving a prayer meeting and was on his way to a whorehouse with a wallet full of money and a pack of rubbers.

"I hope this is Tonto," I said. "Otherwise, I'm heading out the back door at a run."

"That must be him," Marvin said, " 'cause that's the usual response. Keep in mind he's a little shy."

When we opened the door, I said, "Hello," and Tonto nodded, stood where he was for a moment, wiped his feet in a slow, methodical manner, like a trained horse trying to count for its master.

When he came in, he ducked a little to go through the door and stood in the center of the room, saw Brett, held that view for a while, then looked over at Marvin.

"You needed me?" he said to Marvin, and it was as if this big man's voice was on vacation and he had borrowed a voice from a child, soft and musical, almost feminine.

"Yeah," Marvin said.

"I pay my debts."

"I know," Marvin said.

"I never thought you'd ask."

"Never planned to."

"Then it's important."

"That's right," Marvin said. "It's important. To me."

"Tell you what," I said. "Let's have some coffee and talk about things. I don't think it's been completely explained."

"I came because Marvin asked," Tonto said. "I don't know anything. There's nothing been explained to me."

"And me," Jim Bob said. "I'm here 'cause my plastic fuck doll ran out of air. Wasn't nothing else to do."

"My guess," Brett said, "is the doll pinpricked herself and committed suicide."

"Now, honey," Jim Bob said, "that's just an ugly thing to say."

25

We pulled some kitchen chairs up and got some folding chairs out of the closet and congregated at the kitchen table with coffee and Leonard's cookies, which from the look on his face I could tell he didn't appreciate. Through the kitchen window I could see the rain had cleared and the almost pink sky with the bone-white clouds above it looked like some kind of strawberry brew topped by foam.

"Curious? We got to kill somebody?" Tonto said. "Not that I mind, but I like to know. Well, sometimes I mind. I got scruples, they're just flexible."

I thought, man, how did I arrive at this place, with a man with flexible scruples? It was bad enough I was suspicious of my own.

He took off his jacket and he had a twin pearl-handled .45 in a shoulder holster under each armpit. He was wearing a crucifix on a chain, and he pulled it out from under his shirt and let it lie on the front of the cloth in line with the buttons. Nothing says I love Jesus like a crucifix and twin .45s. He was sitting in one of the folding chairs and I feared at any moment it would wrap around his big ass and drop him to the floor.

"That's something we want to avoid," I said. "But one never knows. We're not dealing with priests here."

"So," Jim Bob said, "instead of an ass fucking from one of God's finest, we're talking about bullets."

"That would be yes," Leonard said.

I explained, mostly for Tonto, about the kids who had run off, about

Hirem, how we were patsies, and how we could expect zip help from anyone outside of our little group. I told him we had no real idea where the kids were, but that we were supposed to talk to the FBI and Hirem one more time, and then the only time we were to see them or talk to them again was when the mission was over, provided we survived. All nonsurvivors could pretty much count on being buried beside the road in a shallow grave with nothing to mark their passing except a wild-flower or the droppings of the random dog or armadillo.

"And what do we get out of this?" Jim Bob said.

"Well," I said, "me and Leonard get to not go to jail, or maybe just avoid some long, inconvenient court time. You get the pleasure of our company."

"Doesn't sound like much of a deal," Jim Bob said.

"It's not," I said.

"Well," Jim Bob said, "considering that we get nothing out of this, and I'm doing this just because I know you guys and sort of like you better than guys I don't, count me in."

I looked at Tonto.

He nodded, said in his almost sweet little voice, "I owe Marvin one." He glanced at Marvin. "And after this, we're through. Right?"

"Right," Marvin said. "We're even."

"Everyone in?" I said, and held my hand out over the table.

"So we're supposed to put our hand on top of yours?" Jim Bob said. "All for one, and one for all?"

"Yep," I said.

"Too silly," he said.

Leonard put his hand on top of mine. "I'm in."

Brett put her hand on top of his. "Actually, I'm not going to be here, but hey, in spirit, okay?"

Marvin got up carefully from his chair with his cane and edged over and put his hand on top. "I will do what I can, all things considered. Hell, I got all of you into this, so I got to show solidarity, right?"

"Damn right," Leonard said.

"Oh, hell," Jim Bob said, and put his hand on top. "I always was a sucker for that musketeer jive."

Tonto grinned. He even had big teeth. "Hell, why not."

He put his hand on top of Jim Bob's.

"Maybe we could have some kind of saying," Leonard said. "You know, something that's just for us. A slogan. A motto."

"No," Tonto said, removing his hand. "Maybe we won't have that."

"Yeah, that idea sucks," Jim Bob said, pulling his hand back.

"Even I don't like that," Brett said, and picked up her coffee cup.

"Got to vote no," Marvin said.

"Yeah, I'm out on that one too," I said.

Leonard looked hurt. "Spoilsports."

26

After finishing up the coffee and cookies, we had a real breakfast of eggs and toast and bacon, and Brett did the cooking; then I left with her and drove to the bus depot. It was one of the hardest things I had ever done, and I knew then—well, I had known before, but I knew all over again, down deep and tight to the bone, that I loved this woman dearly and that she was a part of me, like a heart or a liver. I had loved my first wife and she had been a shit and I had loved her anyway. Then she betrayed me, got herself killed, and nearly got me and my buddy Leonard killed. I still loved her for a year after that. But not the way I loved Brett. It's only right that when you find the one you care about that you keep that part that's you and not give it all away, but by the same token I'm old-fashioned in that I feel when you do find the right person you are part of a whole, and when the other leaves, a bit of you is no longer there. And when they leave and you think you might never see them again, it's like more than a part of you is gone. It's like being ripped in half and your half has been cast to the wind.

She was dressed in jeans and sneakers and had on a big sweater and a sweater cap that her hair stuck out from under like a flaming water-fall. The bus depot had very few people in it, and we sat down on a bench. A bus depot is one of the loneliest places in the world, and it doesn't help when the bench you're perched on is near the restrooms and they stink of recent trips, and when people walk out, the tile, dampened by urine and bad flushes, makes a sound like someone pulling duct tape off a hairy dog's ass.

We sat for a while, the sun rising higher and eating away at what was left of the darkness, and then we heard a bus come and they called it over the speaker. It was Brett's ride. I walked her out. There were others getting on, and we stepped back and let them. She had a small bag with her. It had a few clothes and her toiletries in it, a book and some magazines. She set it down by her feet like a trained pet.

"Well," she said, "don't get yourself killed."

"I won't."

"Promise? For me?"

"Hell, I promise for me and you."

"Cross your heart?"

"Big-time," I said, and crossed my heart.

"Make sure Leonard doesn't get killed either."

"You got it."

"I guess you can kind of watch out for Jim Bob and Tonto."

"All right."

"It's hard to know about Tonto, isn't it?"

"So far," I said.

"He'll always be hard to know. I can promise you that. You all have screws missing, all of you, but he's like an empty parts house. It's not just the screws that are gone, but all manner of stuff."

"I think you're right," I said.

"Marvin, he'll be all right at home, won't he?"

"Sure. Wherever he ends up, he'll be okay."

I wasn't sure of that, and she knew I wasn't sure, but it was a little game we were playing. I saw a tear in her eye and I took hold of her and we held each other, and finally we kissed, and she took up her bag and gave me a smile and started to get on the bus. I patted her butt. She said, "Why, thank you."

I laughed and she got on the bus.

I stood there until I saw her take her seat, and then I still couldn't go, so I stood there until she turned to smile at me. She looked as if she was about to bust out crying, which was exactly how I felt. I watched until the bus started to move and she lifted a hand, and I waved back. Then with a turn of the corner and a fart of exhaust, the bus and Brett were gone, on their way out to Arizona.

It was solid daylight when I drove over to the cop shop and went inside and asked for Drake. I was lucky. He was in. The dispatcher picked up a line and Drake appeared and gave me a not-so-friendly drag of the hand, indicating I should follow him.

We went along the hall and passed the booger-lined room with the greasy mirror, turned into another room with a long table and some chairs and a counter with a pot of coffee brewing and a couple boxes of doughnuts holding court next to them.

Drake went over and picked up the pot of coffee and poured some into a Styrofoam cup, asked if I wanted any. I looked at the coffee. It was thick and very dark, like sewer sludge.

"No thanks," I said.

Drake got a couple of doughnuts out of one of the boxes and put them on a napkin. He didn't ask me if I wanted a doughnut. He went over to the table and set the doughnut-laden napkin on the table and set the coffee beside it, then put his ass in a chair and crossed his legs. I sat across from him.

"You know," he said, "I'm the unluckiest man in the world. I wasn't supposed to be working this shift. I wasn't working it, I wouldn't have you."

"I don't know," I said. "I thought you and me, there was a kind of spark, you know."

"No spark," he said. "What do you want?"

"I don't know," I said. "These FBI guys, this all on the up-and-up?"

"What do you mean?"

"I mean, they gonna keep their part of the bargain if we help them out?"

"I assume the 'we' you refer to is you and Leonard, 'cause it sure isn't me and it definitely isn't the department. We got nothing to do with this."

"Yeah, that's what I mean."

"I have no idea what they'll do," he said, sipping coffee, pausing to bite into a doughnut. "The FBI, they do their thing and we do ours. Unfortunately, sometimes the things clash."

"Just like sex."

"No. There's no fun in it. Not even a little bit. All I can say is Hirem knows all manner of stuff the FBI would love to know, and it's stuff worth them knowing, but I got no love for them FBI boys. They come in here like we're dog mess on the bottom of their shoes, like they're the goddamn ghosts of J. Edgar Hoover hisself."

"If they were the ghosts of Hoover," I said, "they'd be wearing dresses."

"What?"

"He was supposed to be a transvestite. You know, transvestites put on dresses. I think he was gay too."

"I hadn't heard that."

"Oh yeah. Big-time."

"Huh? I'll be damned."

"Sorry. Didn't mean to interrupt."

"You're sure about that dresses thing?"

"That's the story. I'm not sure about anything."

"I'll be damned. Hadn't heard that."

I let him contemplate. He said, "You know, considering how Hoover was, the way these guys act, that's kind of funny."

"Yep. But about the FBI guys . . ."

Drake shrugged. "What I can tell you is, if they're wanting you to do something like this, it's more than an ask. It's a kind of push, and it might be a lot nastier than you think. It might be worse than a trial and a jury. But if you've come to me to know more about them, more about what they want, you're in the wrong place. I understand you defended yourself, you and Leonard and Brett. But I can't feel good about citizens doing what you done and all you get is a slap on the wrist. I don't buy you were just driving around armed to the teeth and they came out of nowhere and decided to kill you."

"It was still self-defense."

"I guess it was, but some of them were shot in the back of the head."

"They were shooting at me, and I didn't want them to get up again," I said. "Shooting them in the back of the head was a way to assure that."

"I still don't like it, and I don't like the idea of Hirem getting a light sentence by getting you guys to do something I'm pretty sure is against the law but is done in the name of the law. I know that's the game, but it's a game that stinks and I don't have to like it."

I sat there for a moment and said nothing.

"I don't know what you thought I could tell you," Drake said.

"I have no idea," I said. "I guess I was looking for some reassurance."

Drake shook his head. "Can't offer you any. You might call your mother, you want that."

"She's dead," I said.

"There you go, shit out of luck. All I know is these guys want to help Hirem's son out and get some money back, and I got no idea what you'll have to do to make that happen. I don't know what they're asking, and I don't want to know. I'm just a simple cop, one level above working parking tickets and jaywalkers. I come in here and do my job and see some nasty stuff I'd rather not see, then I got to go home to the family and act like it don't bother me and that I didn't bring it home with me. Like there's nothing more I'd like to do than have a picnic or go to a movie. But all the time I'm thinking about murders and dope deals and some penny-ante shit too, and I can't ever let it go. Not really. I'm making love to the wife, I remember having to deal with some rape, or a rape and murder, and that doesn't exactly make me hard as the Rock of Gibraltar, and then I got to fake an orgasm and act like things are cool. 'Cause I tell her what's on my mind, that's worse. We aren't exactly Houston here, but we got our crime and it's a lot more consistent than you think, and there's plenty for me to handle without having to think about you and the FBI. So, again, for you, I got nothing. Not even a doughnut, so quit eyeing them. About all I can give you, and I do it reluctantly, is my most sincere heartfelt go fuck yourself. I got absolutely no sympathy for you or Leonard. You're always into something, and I'm sick of it. Around here, they call you the Disaster Twins, and the way I look at it, you keep coming up with crap on your shoes it's because you keep steppin' where you ought to not be steppin'. I don't care if down deep in your hearts you have good intentions and you're after the same bad guys I'm after. It is not your job, and I don't give a damn if you and Leonard are fucking Francis of Assisi in your souls, I am goddamn sick of all of it."

I sat for a moment not saying anything. Drake gnawed at a doughnut like he was biting my throat out.

"Well," I said, "I'm glad we had this time together, and thanks for nothing." I got up and went out.

27

Tonto's black van was nicer inside than it looked on the outside and it was very large and souped up under the hood and had big wide tires with tread deep enough to lose a quarter in. I wasn't one of those guys who could talk about cars or fix them up or identify everything on the road. I had always been practical about cars. I wanted them to start and drive me around, get me where I was going and start up when I left. It was considered a Southern failing not to know this kind of thing, the insides of cars, all their clicks and sparks and little growls. All the men I knew who were car buffs, and that was most, looked at me as if not knowing about cars was the equal to not knowing about sunrise and sunset. So when Tonto told me about his van and what it had under the hood and what it could do, I forgot it faster than I forgot the combination to my old high school locker. But I remember this: Tonto claimed his van could run a Corvette down and bitch-slap it, which seemed a little much to me, but it did hum down the road with a sound like a hive of bees. The scenery tossed past us in a blur and we zipped past cars like they were nailed down. I had to admit it was some machine. In that van I felt like one of the Scooby Doo gang. I was probably Scooby himself. A big dumb dog without a dick.

The van had three rows of really comfortable seats and a place in the back to put some luggage and gear, and under the floor carpets and beneath sliding floorboards were secret compartments where we put our weapons, except for the ones we were carrying, which in my and Leonard's case was nothing more than a pocketknife (me) and a pack of gum (Leonard) and we both had combs. Mine was green, Leonard's was black. Tonto still had his good-buddy .45s under his armpits, and Jim Bob had a snub-nosed .38 holstered at the small of his back and a clasp knife clipped inside his front pocket and a nut sack packed tight with testosterone.

Marvin had stayed at my house with a shotgun and a cup of coffee. His job was to watch the home front, keep close to the phone in case we needed something he could provide. We gave him directions to where we were going to meet up with the FBI and Hirem, and from there our plan was to keep him informed as we went, because we didn't know what our plan really was, not yet. With Marvin at the house, we always had a home base. It was a good idea, I thought, and a way to keep him a part of things since he couldn't do much else with that bum leg.

The day was clear and cold and the sky had turned a bright polished blue and the sun was a yellow blaze hanging at the ten o'clock position. I was sitting in the passenger seat, Tonto drove, behind me was Jim Bob, and next to him was Leonard. Tonto had a CD cranked up, and we listened to Jerry Lee Lewis's greatest hits as he tooled us along, nodding his head to the music like a bobblehead doll.

When the CD played out, and before he could put in another, I said to Tonto, "That your real name?"

He didn't turn to look at me, said, "Nope."

"Guess you don't want to talk about it."

"Nope."

"Hokeydoke."

I leaned back in the seat and Jim Bob said, "Hap, I had a woman like the one you got, I'd just go to court and take the jail time. You could get your ass killed, and what for?"

"I could ask you a similar question. You could get your ass killed and your hog farm would go to hell," I said.

"Sold all the hogs, and they wouldn't hold a candle to Brett."

"Okay, we agree on that. Brett is better than hogs, and you could get yourself killed easy as any of us."

"Yeah, you're right about that, though I always assume I'm going to come out on top and it's the other guy who'll wind up with the stick in his ass. But you know, lately I'm starting to think maybe it could go the other way. It's a new kind of feeling and I'm not too fond of it. I never feel like I really belong anywhere. I think a lot about a line in a Frank O'Hara poem that goes 'I'm always tying up and then deciding to depart.' Story of my life."

"You read poetry?" Leonard said.

"Just when I'm tired of masturbating," Jim Bob said. "My reading poetry shock you?"

"That you can read shocks me," Leonard said.

"So, if you can read and have a way to while away the hours, why are you doing this?" I asked.

"We got a kind of connection," Jim Bob said. "We're part of a rare kind of club."

"That right?"

"Yeah," Jim Bob said. "It's made up of guys who think the world ought to work smooth and people ought to treat each other right, and when they don't we go out there and try and fix things and every time we do, we change us into them, and yet we keep hoping and we keep trying and maybe one day we'll realize we'll never get it right and we'll just give in. I don't know. I sound like a tired philosopher."

"You sound like I feel," Tonto said.

"I think you're reading your books backwards," Leonard said.

"Again, why are you doing it then?" I asked.

"There aren't many of us left, Hap, and I'm trying to keep you from becoming totally one of us by taking in the slack I don't want you to handle. It's not my job and it shouldn't matter, but Leonard here, he can't do it alone. You aren't a delicate flower, my man, but there's still something of the hopeful in you and I'd hate to see all of that get sucked out. Probably too late for the rest of us."

"You don't know me," Tonto said.

"Oh, yes I do," Jim Bob said.

Tonto didn't argue back. Jim Bob said, "Hap, you ought to be a social worker, not a tough guy. You're tough enough, but your heart isn't in it. Soiled as you are, underneath the dirt there's pretty good linen."

"I keep telling him that," Leonard said. "That he's soiled, I mean. I don't know about the linen part."

"And you," Jim Bob said to Leonard. "Shouldn't you be home too? Ain't you got you a boyfriend? You're a little farther gone on the scale, but at least you've got some sense of normalcy going on, got a relation-ship going."

Leonard sighed. "Actually, it's on the fence."

"That's a shame."

"Why do you really do it?" I said to Jim Bob. "I think you're dodging the question."

"Man, this is like getting in touch with our feelings, isn't it?" Jim Bob said. "I told you why."

"It isn't about me, and you know it," I said. "I see you only now and then. What about the rest of the time? Why do you damn near get yourself killed on a regular basis? Private gun for hire, that kind of thing. Let's expand that question beyond you, my good man. What the fuck is wrong with all of us? And it's got to be more than just wanting to set the world right."

"Too many cowboy movies," Leonard said.

"All right," Jim Bob said. "Here it is. I do it because if I don't I've got nothing but myself, and though I dearly love myself, I'm a little tired of being me right now. Sometimes I feel like I'm laughing in the dark all by my goddamn self, because I am, and what I got to show for it is a paid-off house with no one in it, not even a dog, because I'm gone too much and when I'm gone I can't see a whole lot of reason to race back. I had a woman like you got, Hap, I'd hold on to her until the crack of goddamn doom. Can you understand that?"

"I wish life was that simple," I said.

"I'd just like to come home and have John there," Leonard said. The words sprang from his mouth like an escaped prisoner.

"You've talked to him?" Jim Bob said, pushing his hat back on his head.

"I've tried."

"Leonard's idea of talking," I said, "is telling people how it is. Not the same thing as a true discussion. The signal of his love for John was that he climbed up in the bed and shit in it."

"Yuck," Jim Bob said. "I wouldn't like that."

"Yeah, he took it hard," Leonard said. "I'm just not a talker about some things, you know. Not like you share-your-feelings guys."

"So you go straight to shitting in the bed?" Jim Bob said.

"It's a statement," Leonard said. "And I'll have you know, at the bottom of it all I'm a sensitive motherfucker."

Tonto, who had been listening quietly, watching the road, said, "Hey, Leonard, were you saying you're queer?"

"The queerest," Leonard said. "You got a problem with that?"

"Where's the dick go?"

"Anywhere I can put it."

"Oh," Tonto said. "No problem. Just curious. Hap, you're pussy-whipped."

"I know."

"That's all right," Tonto said, his voice growing higher than before. "I wish I was pussy-whipped. What about you, Jim Bob?"

"Well, currently, I don't have a pussy in this fight."

"You know," Tonto said, "I think we are bonding like some righteous cocksuckers, don't you?"

"I assume," said Leonard, "that you are speaking symbolically, because to the best of my knowledge I am the only cocksucker present."

"Righteous sonsabitches then," Tonto said.

28

We bonded righteous sonsabitches stopped at a McDonald's on the other side of Tyler about two hours later. We went in and got some drinks and Tonto got a couple of burgers and then he gave me the keys to the van.

"Something happens to us," I said, "you may be a long time with Ronald McDonald."

"This one still has a playground," Jim Bob said, as he and Tonto took a seat in one of the plastic booths.

"Well, in that case," I said, "you boys play pretty."

I drove Leonard and myself over to our meeting place with the FBI. They didn't know about Jim Bob and Tonto, which was all right. We had agreed to do what they wanted, try to find those kids and get the money back so Hirem would tell all he knew about the Dixie Mafia organization, but we hadn't said how we were going to do what we had agreed to do and we hadn't said with whom.

The FBI guys gave us directions to a house at Lake Tyler where they said they were keeping Hirem secluded like a rare animal on the endangered species list. Before we went out there we drove to a place nearby and stopped and used a screwdriver Tonto had given us to take off the plates and put on some others that I think he had had made special. It was a precaution. We didn't want them to know where we got the van or who it belonged to, so if they ran the plates, they'd come up belonging to someone Tonto made up.

Finished with the plates, we got in and drove. It had turned windy and the blue had gone out of the sky because gray clouds had come in, hiding the sun. The lake house wasn't on the good side of the lake where there were fine homes and the grass was always freshly mown and there were nice boats docked up close to shore. It was down a precarious red clay road with ruts deeper than the ass crack of time, and the road just kept winding around the evergreens and barren oaks until it died out near the lake. Then you had to park and get out and walk across a messy clay clearing toward a cabin nestled near some pines and beneath a couple of massive cyprus trees from which moss draped like feather boas. The wind whipped the boas and it whipped at us.

It wasn't much of a cabin. Pretty small and made of logs. The logs had been treated poorly and they were starting to rot, and the cabin leaned downhill toward the lake, which was visible like a blue patch through the boughs of the trees and the mossy boas. The porch was caved in near the steps and there was a window missing and a slab of Sheetrock had been nailed over it from the inside and the Sheetrock was obviously damp and all it would take to knock it loose was a strong cough or foul language.

When we were close up on the cabin I stopped and hollered out, "Hello, the house."

Some time passed and then the door cracked and I heard Tenson's voice call out, "Come on up, but you got guns, you need to lose them."

We had already left them in the van, under the floorboards, so we walked straight to the cabin, wiped the caked clay off our shoes on a stone near the steps, and went inside. Soon as we did I saw Hirem sitting in a rickety chair at a card table, and then I saw Tenson standing in the corner with his gun drawn, dangling by his side. Hirem had lost the suit. He had on casual clothes and a light jacket. Tenson was wearing a dark shirt and jeans and sneakers.

The Mummy was still well wrapped and he stood in a spot on the other side of the room without his gun drawn. There was a humming sound in the room, and it came from small rectangular plug-in heaters on either side of the place. The coils in the heaters glowed red and there was just enough heat to make you glad you were inside instead of out.

The Mummy came over and told us to turn around and put our hands on the wall and spread our legs. We did. Leonard turned his head and looked at the Mummy, said, "You are so butch."

"Fuck you," the Mummy said.

"See," Leonard said. "Told you."

The Mummy patted us down and took away our combs and my pocketknife and Leonard's gum.

Tenson said, "All right, relax."

"We want our combs and I want my pocketknife back," I said.

"Don't forget the gum," Leonard said.

The Mummy gave them back. There were only three chairs. Hirem was in one and the Mummy and Tenson occupied the other two. That left us leaning our backs against the wall. Tenson never put his gun up. He sat with it on his knee.

Leonard looked at the Mummy, said, "How long you got to wear that getup?"

"Too long," the Mummy said. "I wasn't even one of them, you dumb ass."

"How was I to know?" Leonard said. "Wrong place, wrong time, both of us."

The Mummy didn't look appeased, or so I thought. Actually, you couldn't tell much about how he looked. You mostly got what you got from him in the way he moved his eyes or his busted mouth, the way he shrugged his shoulders.

"Hirem here," Tenson said, waving the gun like a pointer, "he's got something to tell you, maybe will lead to his boy, but he's not telling us. He tells you, you take the lead and go after the boy and his poke and bring the money back. FBI gets the drug money, Hirem gets his kid back, the girl doesn't get shot, and Hirem tells us what he knows and we make all kinds of arrests and you guys go free, no trial, and everyone's happy, or mostly. You following this scenario?"

"A few dance numbers might liven it up," I said, "but for the most part, we're following."

"Now," Tenson said, "here's what we do. You two go outside with Hirem, and we're gonna stand on the porch so we can see you, and you're going to walk out a ways and Hirem is going to tell you something he won't tell us, and that's okay. That's how he wants it and we can live with that. We'll get our results. You hear what I'm saying?"

We nodded, Hirem pulled a heavy coat over his lighter one, and we went outside, across the porch and down a little trail that led into the woods. The wind was picking up and it was carrying a lot more cold with it now, and it hit us like ice picks. I tugged the collar up on my coat and put my hands in my pockets as I walked.

After we were out a ways, Hirem said, "I got to see you guys are wearing a wire or not."

"You saw him pat us down," I said.

"Wearing a wire for them," he said. "They could pat you down all they liked and not find it."

"All right," I said and we stopped walking and I held up my arms. Hirem patted me down, then did the same to Leonard.

"Good," he said. "Now, let's walk a bit more."

29

As we started to walk, Tenson yelled from the porch, "Don't go too far. We start to worry you aren't so we can see you, Hirem. And you don't want us worried, do you?"

Hirem didn't answer, but he turned to us, said, "They know I'm not going anywhere. I want my boy back and I'll do what I got to do until that's done. They just like to harass me. Hell, I came to them, wasn't like they brought me in. They been trying to nail my ass for years. I finally had to hold the nail for them."

"You got some idea how to find your son," I said, "but you're telling us, not the FBI?"

"That's right," Hirem said. "I don't trust those guys. I don't trust the law. I don't trust my mother-in-law all that much, and she's dead some ten years now."

"But you trust us?" Leonard said. "Didn't you send those bozos to kill us?"

"It was business, but I can tell about you guys, and I can trust you."

"Say you can?" I said.

"I think I can. You're like the old guys in the organization, you got a sense of honor."

I didn't believe the organization, as Hirem referred to it, ever had a sense of honor, but I listened.

"Bottom line is I like you better than them," he said. "Let's put it that way and call it close enough. What I think is I'm gonna get a better shot with you than them."

"You're the one gonna sing to them," Leonard said. "You're gonna tell them everything, so why not tell them this?"

"Get my kid back safe, I'll tell them whatever they want to know. After that, it don't matter for me. I should've been a barber. My daddy was a barber and he offered me into the business, but I didn't take it."

"There's still time to hone up your skills," I said. "But you do, you'll be giving prison haircuts."

"Listen now," Hirem said. "I'm gonna tell you guys some things I need you to know, so you got some idea who might get in your way."

"Sort of figured this might not just be a bring the kid home kind of thing," Leonard said. "It never is."

"What I know some others can figure out," Hirem said, "and the people I worked for, they can figure better sometimes than the FBI. These feds may have our phones tapped, and they may have all kinds of law on their side, but these guys I work for, they been around awhile now, and they got people more expendable than the feds got. You hear me?"

"We're all ears," I said.

"First and foremost, get my boy back."

"And the girl?" I said.

"She ain't nothing to me," Hirem said. "But it makes Tim feel all right to have her around, I can get over her being coated in chocolate."

"So that's what this is," Leonard said, holding out his hands, looking astonished. "I just thought I was dirty, and it's been chocolate all the while."

"Not now, Leonard," I said.

"Ain't got nothing against your people," Hirem said, looking at Leonard. "Just never figured I'd have a boy fuckin' one of them."

"Now that makes me really feel tight with you," Leonard said.

"I'm not used to all the changes in things," Hirem said.

"Civil rights happened . . . let me see," Leonard said, "about mid-sixties, right? And the Civil War, it was over some one hundred years before that. Good to see you're catching up."

"My boy never did cotton to what I do, the way I think. And maybe that's good. I'm not so sure about things I was sure about just a few months ago."

"Death threats and prison terms can change a man's perspective," I said. "We know."

Hirem nodded. "Thing is, I don't really know where my boy is, but I have a maybe. He was a little kid, we were close. His mother was dead and it was just me and some hired help. We had a place we went to, rented a cabin by the lake and fished. He mentioned it from time to time, though we quit going there some years ago. It had good memories for him, back when he thought I was just a businessman and his daddy. We went there and fished and talked, and from the way he talked, I knew then he wasn't like me, that there was something different about him. I'd had any sense I'd have gotten out of the business and gone into the barbering."

"Shoulda, coulda, woulda," Leonard said. "Ain't nothing in that story matter to me except where you think he is. I want to get this done and go home."

"You'll keep him from being hurt?" Hirem said. "He's only nineteen."

"That's the plan," I said. "We'll do everything in our power to make sure he is protected. We'll protect the girl too."

"She's your choice," Hirem said. "Something happens to him, you got to make sure whoever did it gets theirs."

"That's not our business," I said. "Not part of our agreement."

"All right," Hirem said. "Just protect him if you find him. Place we used to go, place I think he may have went because I noticed a couple of his rods and reels were gone—I don't think he understands the deep doo-doo he's in. Him and that girl, they don't got a clue. They've run off with dirty money and they took some fishing poles with them."

"I'm sure they don't know what they're into," I said. "I'm beginning to suspect that neither do we. Where's the place, Hirem?"

"Lake O' the Pines. There's a series of cabins up there, fella named Bill Jordan rents them, or used to. They're on the east side of the lake. Ain't much. And there's no guarantee my boy's there, but he might be. He's not there, maybe I can think of something else. But right now that's all I got."

"That's it?" Leonard said. "Man, you got a con on these feds, don't you?"

"Not if he's there," Hirem said. "He is, it's no con."

"Guess that'll have to do," I said.

"Let me give you a word to the wise," Hirem said. "The organization has done had me try and hit you guys, and you're harder to kill than anyone would have thought. But they got other people. They may send some of the regular toughs one more time, some tougher and smarter than Tanedrue. Couple of those boys with Tanedrue, they were real professionals, and you handed them their asses, so they'll be more careful next time. They might just pass GO and jump to the big time."

"Big time?" Leonard said.

Hirem nodded. "That's right. They got people don't work for them directly. Freelancers. Hitters. And they're a whole 'nuther ball game, fellas. These people they hire, one or two in particular, bad sonsabitches. There's no one quite like them. They're like those, whatchacallits, the Jap guys in black."

"Ninjas," I said.

"I know, sounds like some kind of movie, but they're for real. I know their work, but I don't know them, and I don't know anyone that's ever seen them. They get a call through some kind of contact, the job gets done, and they get paid. So keep your eyes peeled and your ears open."

"I got a question," I said. "Conners, the cop. He have anything to do with the hit?"

"Conners helped put it together," Hirem said. "He didn't like the way you talked to him, Hap. He thought he'd go over there and show his big ass and that would be enough. You'd start some kind of payment plan on the dope you flushed. Or go to work for them, something like that. When you didn't, well, he came to me. And I've told you how it is these days with the upper management. They ain't much on compromise or negotiation. It's all about respect. They learned that in prison. You don't get respect there, you either wind up with a shank in your gut or a dick in your ass. They come out of prison, they're still the same. And you two, you disrespected them big-time by beating up their hired help. But Conners—he has to get permission, but he's the contact for the hits. He knows all the hitters, and the management likes it that way. Something comes to him direct instead of them, that's all right with them. It's more distance from the deed, and as long as things get done, they're happy. And now you've killed off some of their help. It's not that they care about them, it's that they don't like that disrespect part, the loss of that dope money, and they can't have you two dropping their soldiers like cigarette butts."

That must have reminded him, because he reached inside his coat pocket and found a pack of cigarettes and put one in his mouth. He patted around on his pockets for a moment, said, "Goddamn it, they took away my lighter. You guys got anything?"

We shook our heads.

I said, "Your kid. What was he driving?"

"He took my Escalade. It's black."

"Anything else?" Leonard said.

"Guess not," Hirem said.

Hirem put the cigarette pack back in his pocket but kept the cigarette in his mouth. He wagged it in his lips when he said, "I just got one thing for you. A bit of fatherly advice from a fella tried to have you killed. You guys are pretty confident guys. You think you got the world by the tail, even if you're just day laborers with an attitude. And you may be tough as you think you are, hard to kill. Like a cockroach you can't step on right, keeps running out from under your shoe. But remember, now and again even cockroaches get crunched."

30

After we walked Hirem up to the cabin, the Mummy came out with us. He walked us to our van. I kept expecting a scarab beetle to come out from under his bandages. He said, "It would be a lot easier you just told us what he had to say right now."

"It would be for you," I said.

"For you too. Your job would be done. We'd go get the boy and the girl and the money, and everyone would be happy."

"We kind of gave our word," I said.

"To him?"

"That's who we were talking to," Leonard said.

"You're yankin' me?"

"I don't think so," Leonard said.

"You gave your word to a guy tried to kill you, and you won't tell the FBI what he said?"

"That's pretty much it," Leonard said. "Hey, remember back at the cop shop? He said it wasn't personal, so why should we be mad?"

The Mummy shook his head. "I don't get you guys. We're doing you the favor. We could call this whole thing off right now, have you locked up. Might even take Hirem out back and see what he thinks about having his ass kicked until he talks."

"He won't talk and you know it," I said. "Otherwise, you'd have already done it. And you do that, find the kid, you won't get all the other information you want to get out of him. All the inner clock workings of the Dixie Mafia."

The Mummy looked at us. His eyes peeking out of the mask were dark and narrow, his lips had turned beet red from the cold. It made him look pretty damn creepy. "You go get that boy and girl and that goddamn money, and you go get it quick."

"Gee," Leonard said, "can we stop for dinner, take a pee?"

"You do what you got to do," the Mummy said. "But you make it quick as you can. Today would be good."

"It might take a few days," I said. "I don't know exactly. Things may not fall in line just the way we like it."

"I can tell you this," the Mummy said. "We're tired of hanging out in this shit hole. We want to go home, be warm, not have to hang around with Hirem. You hear me?"

"If you'll reinforce your words with sign language," Leonard said, "we might get a clear message."

The Mummy shot Leonard the finger.

"There," Leonard said. "I understand that. See, I get you now."

"Make it quick," the Mummy said and walked back toward the cabin.

In the van, driving away, I said, "From one cockroach to another, I don't think the Mummy likes you very much."

"I think it's because I beat his ass."

"Think?" I said.

"Uh-huh. You know, odd how the Mummy and his buddy think we ought to believe them just because they're from the government."

"It's like religion," I said. "You accept it on faith."

"Well, that's stupid."

"I said it was like religion, didn't I?"

"Oh yeah, so you did. What you think about that Conners guy?"

"I think he doesn't get out of this business unscathed," I said.

Leonard nodded. "I was thinking pretty much the same thing, and I've put him on the list."

"Okay, but put a couple of stars by his name," I said.

31

Hadn't gone far before we stopped and switched the license plates, hid the ones we had used under the floorboards again, then drove back to McDonald's. When we came in, the table where Jim Bob and Tonto were sitting was piled high with food bags and drink cups.

"So," Jim Bob said, "you're back and hopefully without bullet holes or the clap."

"Yep," I said.

We ordered some food for ourselves, then slid into the booth and told them what we had been told.

Tonto said, "That's pretty thin, that the kid went fishing some spot where he went when he was little. That's damn thin."

"He took fishing rods," I said.

"That makes it absolute," Tonto said. "Why didn't you say that in the first place? You know, he could be jackin' with the old man, 'cause he thought Dad would come after him because of the girl, and of course the money, and maybe he's just wanting the old man to show him how much he cares."

"He's nineteen," I said, "and I don't think he's that smart. Anyone who would steal that much money from a bunch of cutthroats and know they're cutthroats can't be all that bright."

"Naive, anyway," Leonard said.

"My goodness," Jim Bob said. "Was that a positive comment on a member of the human race? What in the world have you been drinking, Leonard?"

"Yeah, you're right," Leonard said. "That was oddly optimistic. I'm giving up Dr Pep . . . I'm giving up Diet Coke as of this moment."

"You don't drink Diet Coke," I said.

"See how it's working?" Leonard said.

I said, "Thing is, it's what we got, and the way I figure it, Hirem knows his son, or at least thinks he does. Most sons in one way or another want to please their fathers, or at least capture some good moment in time they had with them."

"Speaking from experience?" Jim Bob said.

"Yeah," I said. "I am."

"I don't have those feelings," Tonto said. "If I went somewhere and was waiting on my father to find me, waiting on him to care or even miss me, I'd have been waiting one long goddamn time."

"You're the one said that might be what he's doing," Jim Bob said. "So maybe you know more about this kind of thing than you think."

"Maybe," Tonto said. "Guess I'm not all that big on parents of any stripe."

"It's not always that way," Jim Bob said. "There are even parents who like their kids. Mine liked me, in spite of myself."

"Way I look at it, between the pussy and the asshole is no-man's-land," Tonto said. "You either come out a baby or a turd, and I think I came out of the wrong hole. Nobody much cared I was around."

"Who lives in No Man's Land?" Leonard said.

"I'm uncertain," Tonto said. "It wasn't a very good example."

"All right," I said, "all turds aside, here it is again. It's what we got, and that's why we check it out. They're there, we bring them home if we have to tie them up and toss them in the back of the van. Or at least the boy, and more importantly, the money. I think they get the money back, lots of feelings are gonna be less hurt."

"I been thinking about that," Tonto said, sipping a soft drink through a straw, then pausing as if he were seeing something far away. "What say we find the money and split it and go home?"

"That wouldn't help mine and Leonard's situation any."

"No," Tonto said, "it wouldn't. But it would help our billfolds big-time. Split four ways, that's not so bad. And there's also this: the boy and the girl, they could end up dead. They end up that way and no one knows me and Jim Bob was in with you, we can just say, hey, the bad guys, they got there first and all the money was gone. They must have got it back."

"That still wouldn't help us," I said, "and I wouldn't do that. You don't know me, Tonto, but I wouldn't do that. Neither would Leonard."

"Absolutely not," Leonard said.

"I know that," Tonto said. "Hell, I know that, but it's something I could do, and I had to try it out, see how it fit."

"It doesn't fit," I said.

"I wouldn't do that either," Jim Bob said. "Maybe we aren't exactly on the same team after all, and we are not self-righteous cocksuckers together."

"That was changed to sonsabitches," Leonard said. "Remember, we established that."

"In fact we did," Jim Bob said.

"I'm not as pure as you guys," Tonto said. "I'm here because I owe Marvin Hanson a favor."

"Doing it that way wouldn't be much of a favor," I said.

"No," Tonto said, "it wouldn't. Forget I brought it up."

32

Doing something like we were doing can make a man paranoid. I thought I saw the same car two or three times that day, and wondered if it had followed us out of LaBorde, wondered if it had followed us to the McDonald's, and then followed Leonard and me on out to the cabin in the woods and back again. I thought about that a lot, then decided I was starting to see things. The car was an old brown Ford, and I had seen a lot of them that day, and when I finally started noticing the drivers, I realized they were all different, and the Fords were all over the place, and that was a popular color that year for that make and model.

When I told the boys about it, Tonto said, "I been followed by the best, and I always knew they were there. I been watchin' too, and I've seen some brown Fords. I've also seen some green Chevys and all manner of cars, but I haven't seen anyone I thought was following us."

"You ever been wrong about being followed?" I asked.

"Not yet," Tonto said.

"Could there be a first time?"

"Unlikely," he said.

"I ain't someone easily followed either," Jim Bob said, "but then again, I haven't been paying any attention."

"Then you can be easily followed," I said.

"Not when I don't want to be. Being followed wasn't something I expected or was looking out for. I was too busy daydreaming about what I'm gonna be when I grow up, and I was countin' on your guys. If we're being followed, then you sonofabitches have let me down."

"Whatever it is you're gonna be when you grow up," Leonard said, "I hope it pays better than this."

"Me too," Jim Bob said.

When we neared Lake O' the Pines, I convinced the others we ought to pull in somewhere for the night and get some rest and make sure we weren't being followed, make sure it was just my paranoia, and that tomorrow we could check out the cabins by the lake.

Just outside Lake O' the Pines the woods grew thicker and we could see dark water between the trees and on the water were spots that looked like blue oil slicks and the sun made parts of it shine like a mirror. In the woods were lots of vines and moss, and they were twisted up thick as Brer Rabbit's briar patch, and in some spots the water had run out of the woods and onto the road and we had to splash our tires through it. We found some old-fashioned cabins not far from a dark patch of deep woods and a big worn-out peeling sign with a fat preacher on it holding a Bible and pointing his finger in the air. The sign said: JESUS IS COMING. I thought he ought to hurry some, because it had already been over two thousand years.

The place we came to is called a motel these days, but once upon a time they were called tourist courts, and the original ones, of which this was a survivor, were small and simple and close together. This one was a row of brown-red buildings that were starting to strip paint and shed shingles.

Leonard and I rented a room from a guy that seemed surprised to see us, or most anyone for that matter. He was a bald little guy seated on a tall stool behind a counter, and there was a little brown and white dog sitting on the floor by the stool. The bald guy looked us in the eye and the dog looked up at us, its mouth wadded up, as if it was angry or missing teeth.

Tonto and Jim Bob rented a room too, all of it paid for with Marvin's money. He had given us a thousand dollars, and anything over that Leonard and I had vowed to pay, which meant we were trying to keep it cheap and keep it real.

The tourist court was cheap and the rooms were small. There were two narrow beds with worn bedcovers and a desk with a mirror and two chairs and a little TV on a wall mount. It didn't have a remote so you had to change channels by hand and all it got was three stations and some static. There was dust on the windowsills and the tub in the bathroom had a creaky-looking shower; there was a rim around the drain in the tub that was either rust or dried blood from when the last depressed occupant had slashed their wrists. Home Sweet Home.

The room Tonto and Jim Bob got was next door to us and it was the same as ours, except they had a microwave that didn't work and the inside of it housed the remains of an exploded burrito. We visited with them briefly and left.

In our room I peeled back the dusty curtains and looked out the window to see if I saw a brown Ford, but I didn't see one. I watched the old cracked highway from the window for a while. A lot of cars went by. Some were Fords, but none of them were brown.

"Hap," Leonard called from the bathroom, "will you come hold my dick while I pee?"

"Go to hell, Leonard."

"Will you wipe my ass? I'm tired."

"Fuck off."

"I'm gonna shower. Will you come wash my back?"

"Die," I said.

I kept looking out the window all the while the shower was running, and I kept getting the same non-results. I gave it up and sat on the bed and got the paperback Western novel out of my bag and put one of my guns next to me and read for a while. When Leonard finished his shower, I took one. There was no soap and no shampoo and the water was almost hot.

We dressed and joined up with our pals next door, and with directions from the bald guy behind the tourist court counter, we drove a few miles to a small town and a little cafe that was doing brisk business. The waitress was slightly overweight but cute. She walked like she had just had horseshoes removed. She gave us a booth with a table that was still sticky from having just been wiped. We sat with our hands in our laps while it dried, waiting on the menus she forgot to give us.

When the menus came we studied them and got coffee first. I said, "Way I figure it, instead of a whole pack of us going to look at the cabins where Hirem said his son was, me and Leonard will go, and call you when we need you."

"You need us," Tonto said, "you won't have time to call."

"If you're right," I said, "and no one's following us, we'll be fine because we're not up against anything but two kids and some fishing rods and about three hundred thousand dollars, minus pay for some gas and a meal or two."

"I could be wrong, though," Tonto said. "Been having a feeling things aren't right."

"What's it based on?" Jim Bob said.

"My gut," Tonto said.

"I don't believe in that sort of thing," Jim Bob said. "I believe you feel that way, it's because you've noticed something, something that hasn't registered consciously but it's there. Something has struck you. Seen something, thought someone didn't look right. It may have been on some deeper level, but you know something because there's something to know—or you're just fucking paranoid."

"That's a lot of somethings," Tonto said.

"Doing this kind of work can make you paranoid," I said.

"I believe in premonitions," Tonto said, "and I believe in my gut. My gut's telling me this isn't going to be a cakewalk, and that it's going to turn ugly, and that we're already into it and we don't know it yet."

"My brown Ford," I said.

"Haven't seen any brown Ford," Tonto said. "I tell you simple, it's my gut telling me things."

"Right now," Leonard said, "my gut is telling me I'm going to order some fried chicken and some mashed potatoes with gravy, and maybe afterward, a slice of some kind of pie. And then, if I'm feeling really rowdy, I might wipe my hands on my pants."

"You are such a tough guy," I said.

"And don't you forget it."

33

On the way back to the tourist courts, Tonto stopped and got a six-pack of beer and Jim Bob bought some Jack Daniel's. Leonard bought a bottle of malt liquor, to keep up stereotypes, he said, and I bought a six-pack of Diet Coke and a peanut pattie, also to keep up stereotypes. I almost got an RC to go with it. That would have been even more perfect. Maybe a couple of MoonPies too.

In Tonto and Jim Bob's room, we all drank our poison and talked. After three beers, Tonto began to talk. It just sort of flowed out of him like sweet maple sap in the springtime.

"You know, I grew up in Louisiana, not really all that far from here," he said.

"No shit?" Jim Bob said.

"No shit," Tonto said. "My dad, he worked offshore on an oil rig, and one time there was a big storm. They say it was so big the waves climbed up high enough to look like the walls of the world. That's what the survivors said. See, they were supposed to have a helicopter fly them out, 'cause they got word of the storm, but the helicopter got delayed, and then when it finally got out to the rig, the storm was swirling up the sea and swallowing up that big rig like it was made of pipe cleaners and a whore's best wishes. My dad, he went down with all that steel. They never found his body, so I guess it's still down there, or is all ate up from the fishes and such. I think about him nonetheless, and here's the thing. I didn't even like him.

"When he wasn't beating me he was calling me stupid, and this went along with what they called me at school, and that's where they started calling me Tonto, on account of I look like I'm an Indian."

"You're not?" Leonard said.

"Nope. Greek. Full-blood. But they called me that so much I started going by it. Got so it didn't hurt if it was my name. See what I'm saying? You can't call me a thing and make it bad if that's the name I got. So, in time, that's what everyone knew me by, and soon enough my real name was forgotten. I even almost forgot. My dad was dead, that left me with my stepmom and some nuns at school, and I want to tell you now, I got the Lord beat into me and he's in my skin and in my blood and down in my bones. I love the Lord and I disobey him every day. My stepmother, she was lonely like, and I was a pretty big boy, and pretty soon she's greasing my weasel, and my little brother finds out, and then it gets around to the nuns at school, because my brother, Jimmy, he's jealous, 'cause my stepmom, Trish, she's a looker, and he's wanting to get him some of that too. She was that kind of woman, went around the house half naked. She was askin' for it, and I gave her what she was askin', and at the time it seemed like pretty good stuff. Now, all these years later, I feel dirty about the whole thing, but you see, it was like I was fucking what my father fucked, and I was showing him, even if the old bastard was turning round and round at the bottom of the sea. Showing him I could take his piece of tail and be as good or better than him. That fucking asshole beat me with a big leather belt that he kept hung on a nail by the door. He hit us, me and my little brother, with it so much that when it was laid across the nail it hung flat. It was damn near worn out from slapping ass.

"When I got into Trish I told myself I was a man from then on and wasn't nobody going to use a belt on me. No one was going to lay a hand on me. And then one morning I got up and she was gone and I never saw her again. I took to doing push-ups, by the hours. I got so I could do hundreds, and I got stronger and I grew bigger, able to bend a tire iron over my thigh. You don't believe that, I can show you."

"I'll take you at your word," Jim Bob said.

"Not me," Leonard said. "I want to see it."

"Later," Tonto said, and took a deep drink of beer and crushed the can. "One day my brother, Jimmy, he run off because the nuns were rapping his knuckles and a whole bunch of people at school were calling him names, and like I said, it was known at school about me and

Trish, and I was getting called stuff too. Guess Jimmy couldn't take it no more. I never did see Jimmy again, at least I don't know for a fact if I did, though one time in the Houston airport I saw a fellow I thought was Jimmy. He was with a woman and a baby. I studied him for a long time, and he looked over at me a time or two, and I got this feeling he knew me and that it was Jimmy. But I just walked on by and never knew for sure, and didn't want to. Not really. I had gotten used to him being gone and not having a brother. I liked it that way.

"But after Jimmy run off, the meanness that was divided on me and Jimmy all turned on me. Even the nuns got worse. I think maybe they thought they could beat the evil out of me, and one of the worst was a younger nun who I always thought was looking me up, trying to think if she could figure some way to get her a little of what I was toting between the legs. It could have just been my thinking, 'cause I always did want to fuck a nun. Anyway, I don't know that for a fact, but it could have been true, and she maybe thought about it so much and got so much a feeling of being a sinner that she took it out on me with that ruler. One day I took it away from her and broke it and threatened to stick it up her ass and break it off again. I was a pretty big boy then, even if I was young, and it scared her. I got sent home for a few days, but when I went back she never did hit me with that ruler no more. But it didn't change the way the kids talked, especially this one fella, Danny Sonier. He wouldn't let it go, and he went around saying I was fucking my mother. Well, she wasn't my mother. She was my stepmother, and I don't even think she and Daddy were married. I think she was just some whore he brought home from Shreveport.

"Anyway, one day this Sonier boy followed me home with a couple of his buddies, and as they got closer to my house, walking behind me, calling me names, saying things, I finally got fed up and stopped in the middle of the road, grabbed up some rocks and threw them. They bolted. But when I got to the house, which wasn't much of a house, by the way, I was going up on the porch and turned around and there was Danny Sonier, standing in the yard. His buddies were gone. It was just him.

"He was calling me names and acting all tough, and I came off that porch like a rocket. We went together hard at it, fists flying, and all I remember was everything turned red, and when it wasn't red anymore, I was looking down at Danny and his head was like a big squash that had dried out and been broken open, only it was leaking blood, and I had a big stone in my hand. I had pulled it out of the ground and beat him like a snake, and I didn't even remember it. He was dead. I dragged his body off out to the swamp, where I knew there were alligators, and I dropped him in. I sat there on the bank the rest of the day, and the body floated. It didn't sink like I thought it would. It floated. And it was just about night when a big old gator came up and grabbed the body by its mashed head and took it down. Happened so sudden it made me jump to my feet. And when I did, I heard a scuttling, and behind me was two more gators. I made a run for it, but they went straight into the water. I saw this when I got to a tree and went up in it. Those gators went in the water where the other gator had taken Danny down and there was all kind of rolling around in the water, a flashing of gator tails, a glimpse of big teeth, and it went on like that for some time. And then just when I was fixin' to come down from that tree, I see that an old bull gator had crawled up under it, this old cypress, and he was just waiting there, his head lifted, and his mouth open, like he was expectin' me to drop into it.

"Well, I stayed up there in the tree, and fell asleep between two limbs. When I woke up and looked down the next mornin', the gator was gone. I climbed down and went home. When I was able to go back to school, I did, but with Jimmy gone they sent out some social workers and discovered the stepmom was gone too, and I got put in foster care for a while, but I didn't get along with nobody, so ended up in an orphanage until I run off at sixteen.

"Course, before that, Danny was missed and he was looked for, and his buddies said he followed me home. I told the nuns and the cops I had thrown rocks at them, and they had run off, and that was the last I had seen of Danny. They didn't believe me, but that was my story and I stuck the fuck to it. In time they gave up on me, and that's when I went to those foster homes, and then the orphanage, and then I run off. They brought me back twice, but finally I was old enough to get emancipated, and that's what I did. Then, one night, in Houston, in a bar, I was sitting on a stool, minding my own business, which was drinking a beer and chattin' up a good-looking brunette with a set of titties you could use as a water float, when in comes this fellow all pissed off. I had just put my hand on her thigh, and she was wearing a dress so short, when she moved, her skimpy underpants looked like something crawling. This fellow, he had a knife and he meant to use it, and did. He cut my arm with a slash, and then I took it away from him, and in the commotion the girl ran off and the guy ended up with the blade in his throat, and when it was over, I looked up and the bar was empty except for the bartender and four guys in Hawaiian shirts, and one of them, a big guy with a nose that spread over his face like it was some kind of animal, says to me: 'That was pretty nifty, Injun. You want a job?'

"And so they cleaned up the place and threw away that dead guy like he was trash, and when the cops came I was gone and no one left there remembered a thing, 'cause they all worked for the big man who had spoken to me and this made their memories bad. Well, there was the bartender. But he said he hadn't seen a thing either, and all them other people had run off, including the good-looking brunette with the good tits and the crawling undies. I found out all this from the flat-nosed guy, 'cause I made a deal to meet him somewhere and go to work for him, and the work was to my liking. I killed people for money."

Tonto paused and opened a can of beer and drank a big sip. "And I been at it ever since, except for a time when I was an investment banker."

"That's a joke, right?" I said.

"Big-time," he said.

"You don't mind my asking," I said, "how come you owe Marvin a favor? Why are you here?"

"Simple thing," he said. "I ended up with this gal who was better for me than I was for her, and she didn't have any idea the job I had. She thought I was an insurance salesman. We had this boy. Good-lookin' kid, and I loved him, and I thought I might go straight. Planned on it. Just couldn't quite get out of the business. Like a drunk looking for the next drink, you know. Wantin' to quit, but getting too much out of it.

"So when my boy, Kevin, was twelve a guy talked him into a car and did things to him, and my boy, he didn't live. They found his body beside the road, and my wife, she cut her wrists, and if there was any chance of me being the Christian I thought I'd grow up to be, be anything like the nuns said I ought to be, that was it, it was over. I was already fucked, but this was the big fuck. I believe, and I'm loyal to the faith in my heart, but in my hands and in my mind and in my deeds I'm not. But the guy did it, he got caught and he was tried, and they couldn't prove it. And when he got loose he got drunk and admitted he did it, and the guy he told at a bar, he told the papers, and then it was all over the place, and this guy, he said, 'Yeah, I did it, but there's no second bite at the apple.'

"Even child molesters usually have enough sense to know what they do shouldn't be admitted to, but not this guy. He was proud, and it was his philosophy, the whole man/boy love bit. This guy lived for little pink boy butt holes. So I wait a few months, and I go over to his house and I kick in the back door and I find him in bed with a bunch of lit candles and some child pornography, and he's naked and probably pulling his rope, but he won't never pull it again, 'cause I get hold of him and twisted his neck so far around ain't nobody could sneak up on him from behind, provided he hadn't died from it.

"So, Marvin Hanson, he's a cop in Houston, and he figures it's me right away. He didn't have nothing on me, but he knew who I was and what I did, and he had a pretty good idea I'd do just what I done. So they found some fingerprints there, and though I had been careful, I was so mad, when I got hold of that fucker's head and twisted it, the gloves I was wearing ripped, and I left a fingerprint on his neck. Can you believe that? On his fuckin' neck?

"Lieutenant Hanson, he came to me at my house, and he has the evidence with him, and he says something like, 'I don't cotton to what you're doin', Tonto, and if this was some other thing, some other mur-der, I'd crawl so far up your ass every time you took a shit my life would play before your eyes instead of yours.' And he took a match and he lit the evidence and he tossed it in the kitchen sink and leaned his back against it and looked at me. He said, 'Got nothing for child molesters. Especially proud ones.' And he started out, and I said, 'Look here, man. You ever need anything, anything I can do, all you got to do is call and it's done.' And he said, 'Not likely.' But the other day, I got the call. And here I am. I owe him. Got to tell you, it was a joy to twist that cocksucker's head in my hands and hear his neck snap like a goddamn chicken bone. I liked the way he looked at me and the way he tried to yell when I twisted his goozle. Liked the way the light went out of his eyes. I've seen a fish on the dock do that. You catch him and he flops and he flops, and then slowly the eyes slick over. Only with this chicken fucker, it was quick. Real quick. I just wish he had been there to feel that rolled magazine I shoved up his ass. I couldn't help myself. And I didn't grease him none. Had he been alive, the paper cuts alone would have made him bleed out. Or so I like to think. Anyway, that's who I am, and I ought not to have told any of that. Haven't ever told anybody about it, and didn't intend to ever, and it's probably a mistake. But there it is, on my sixth beer and having sucked down four or five shots of Jack Daniel's, and I'm with guys I like, and because there ain't many guys I like, I've talked my ass off, and that's the whole thing downloaded like a fuckin' movie off the Internet."

We all sat silently for a while.

Jim Bob said, "So, Tonto, you've had a fairly uneventful life, have you not?"

Tonto slowly grinned.

34

I was in my bed and Leonard was coming out of the bathroom buttoning up his pajama top. It was an ugly set of pajamas. White cloth with anchors on it; matching shirt and pants. No footsies.

"So," I said, "where did the pajamas come from?"

"John."

"Were they a gag gift?"

"No."

"He think you're a sailor?"

"No. He thought they were cute."

"Trust me," I said. "They aren't cute."

"I have a little red teddy I could wear, you prefer."

"Most definitely not . . . you don't, do you?"

"Now what do you think?"

"I don't know what to think about much of anything anymore. I was actually thinking about Brett. And I was thinking about that story Tonto told us."

"You believe it?"

"I do."

"Me too. Do you think he can bend a tire iron?"

"I do."

"Yeah, me too."

"He scares you a little, doesn't he, Leonard?"

"Me? Hell no."

"He scares me."

"Really?"

"Yep."

"Well, all right. He scares me a little. I think he made me pee-pee some in my pants."

"Is that fear or sexuality?"

"I do kind of find him attractive," Leonard said, "but, alas, he's not my type. He's heterosexual. That always puts a damper on things. And another thing—he's a killer."

"So are we."

"Not for money. Not for any reason that isn't self-defense or the defense of someone else."

"So we're noble?"

"Nope," Leonard said. "We're two guys trying to be like heroes, and the problem is, we're just two guys. Though I, of course, am highly attractive and hung like an elephant and have nifty pajamas and smooth black skin."

"I have bunny shoes."

"Yep, but you didn't bring them."

"There is that. . . . How about John? How's things? Have you called home since we been on the road?"

"I have. He told me to eat shit."

"Not good."

"Nope. Not good. These days he doesn't find me that attractive, which is something I can't quite wrap my mind around. I look in the mirror, I'm pretty satisfied."

"So what did he say?"

"He said don't call anymore, he has things to work out."

"That stinks."

"He thinks Jesus is pulling his ear, trying to get him over there on the good side with the straights. Thinks suddenly he's gonna lose interest in the rod and go to the hole punch."

"Maybe it's the devil pulling his ear."

"Whatever it is, I don't like it. We had a good thing going."

"Sucks."

"He used to suck, and I liked it. Now he doesn't suck. I don't like being without him, Hap. I don't like someone's mythology getting in the way of my romance."

"I know."

"It's like you being without Brett."

"I know that too. And I miss her."

"We should really give up on the adventures and stay home."

"Yep. But we didn't really have a choice here."

"We could have gone to trial. I think we'd have been no-billed. It was self-defense."

"But it was nasty self-defense."

"This is Texas," Leonard said.

"There is that. Let's go to sleep."

"Hap?"

"Yep."

"Will you tell me a story?"

"All right. There were four bears."

"Four?"

"This is my story. There were four bears. Two of them were not as smart as the other two because they were really at heart nicer bears, and they kept getting themselves into rotten situations, and eventually two of the bears, the ones that weren't so smart but were nicer, they got themselves killed."

"Those two dead bears? That us?"

"Yep," I said.

"I don't like that story."

"Me either. You want to hear a joke?"

"Hell no. Not one of your jokes. Go to sleep."

"Spoilsport. . . . There was this dog—"

"I said I didn't want to hear it."

"—and he came limping into this Western town—"

"You've told this one."

"And he held up his injured foot, said, 'I'm here to get the man who shot my paw' . . . get it?"

"I get it. You tell this to me at least once a month."

"You see, paw and pa, like the old Westerns. Guy comes into town—"

"Hap. I get it. It stinks. It stunk the first time and it stinks this time."

"Brett laughed."

"I don't believe that. You're lying. You made that up. I'll call her."

"There's no need to call her."

"Aha."

"Well. She smiled."

"She was embarrassed."

"Maybe."

"Good night, Hap."

"Good night, Leonard."

35

Lake O' the Pines is a big lake, man-made, like all the lakes in Texas except Caddo Lake. It was made a long time ago and on this cold morning the water was looking blue as a Patsy Cline song. I thought that by midday, we didn't get any cloud cover, the cold could burn off a little and it might be a fairly warm day. But if the clouds came in, it could turn damn cold damn quick because a wind was starting up, and as we drove by the lake, I could see through the trees along the bank that the water was rippling the way coffee will ripple when you blow on it to cool it.

We drove around, trying to follow the directions Hirem gave us, but there were a lot of little cabins. Finally, about lunchtime we came out from around the lake and stopped at a gas station and mini-mart and got some gas. There was a couple there with a break-down cage that you could put up easy and dismantle easy and haul away, and in the cage was a bear. It was a pretty good-sized bear. They had a deal where you could get your picture taken with the bear, Cindy. Of course, Leonard had to do it and I had to do it with him. When we went inside the cage and were introduced to Cindy, she was sitting on a stool like a human being, as if on break. I half expected her to be smoking a cigarette. She saw us, got up, waddled over, and stretched out her arms and put them over our shoulders. She had done this before and it was a livin'. The muscles in her arms felt like steel cables.

Jim Bob and Tonto, being smarter, didn't have their picture taken. They stood outside the cage and looked at us as if they soon expected to see us eaten. When the photo was taken, Cindy moved her arms and went back and sat on her stool. It was a double cage, two rooms if you will, and part of it had photographs of Cindy the Bear swimming in her pond on her owner's property. They told us all about it. The bear was a Russian bear.

"Is she a vodka-drinking commie?" Leonard asked.

"The Soviet Union is no more," said the lady owner. She was a blond woman with a nice build and the attitude of someone who had never met a sense of humor. Her old man was skinny and he grinned. I don't know if he thought what Leonard said was funny. I think he just grinned a lot.

We got our photograph of us with the bear, which they put between two pieces of cardboard, and then we went inside the station. As we did, Jim Bob said, "You guys are pretty weird, you know."

The station had a little stove and grill, and there was a glass cover where you could see what they had cooked. There was some fried chicken on greasy white paper and hot links and there was a place where you could get some slices of bread and put mustard and relish on it if you wanted, make a sandwich with the links. There were also a few sides, like some suspicious-looking baked potatoes and a Crock-Pot of red beans in a congealed soup that looked as if you might need a pickax to crack the surface.

We got a little of this and a little of that, picking potato chips and some candy bars and sodas to go with the chicken and links, and went to the back of the place, where there were a few tables, and had our lunch. There was enough grease in the chicken to lube up a whorehouse on a sailor's Saturday night, but it tasted really good and so did the links. We ate not only because we were hungry but because we were bored. Where I was sitting I could look out the big window at the pumps, and I could see the van parked up front near the door. And I could also see something else. A brown Ford. It slowed out on the highway, and as it did, I stuck an elbow in Leonard and he turned to look.

"Brown Ford," I said.

"Yep," he said.

Jim Bob and Tonto looked too. The Ford pulled up at a pump and a guy about the size of Tonto, and then Tonto again, got out. It wasn't just that he was tall. He was no taller than Tonto, but he was wide as a truck and had a chest big enough to store a winter's worth of corn in it. His legs were bigger around than my waist and his head looked like someone had anchored a medicine ball to his neck. He had blond hair and a little goatee and the kind of tan that comes from solar lamps. I figured he had fallen off Jack's beanstalk and was learning to make his way in our world.

There was another guy in the front of the Ford, and two in the back, and they just sat. After a while, when the gas was done, the others got out and they all came in.

We watched them carefully. The big guy who had been driving and who put in the gas looked back at us and nodded. Just a regular guy, bigger than most regular guys, seeing some other regular guys, acknowledging us. We nodded back.

We kind of huddled over our food and whispered.

"They might not be anything," Leonard said.

"Maybe not," I said.

"Lots of brown Fords," Jim Bob said.

"Yep," I said.

"Bullshit," Tonto said. "They're somebody. They got guns. I can see the bulges under their shirts."

"Maybe those are cell phone cases," Jim Bob said.

Tonto looked at Jim Bob. They both smiled.

"But," Jim Bob said, "probably not."

"If they've been following us without me seeing them," Tonto said, "they're good. And Hap, you're good. You spotted them and I didn't."

"They want us to know they're following now," Jim Bob said. "They want us to know they're tired of playing."

"I didn't know we were playing," Tonto said, "but now that I do, I'm ready to get out the toys. Ah, here they come."

They came back and sat at the table next to us. My side of the bench was closer to the big guy, and on the other side of our table was Tonto, and he shifted a little so that one of his hands was under the table and the other was lying on top of it next to a gnawed chicken leg.

They were all big guys. Only the driver, the guy on my side, was as big as Tonto, but the others were easily bigger than the rest of us. I got to thinking we weren't nearly as nifty as we thought. These guys had been on us for a while, and though I had gotten glimpses of them, they were good, damn good, at least as far as sneaking went. Thing I was wondering was when exactly did they get on us, and were they FBI guys or guys from the Dixie Mafia. I was voting pretty heavily on the latter.

The big guy had some chicken and was about to eat it. I said, "That chicken isn't nearly as nasty as it looks."

The big guy paused with the chicken close to his mouth. "Yeah. That's good to hear. I was worried."

"The links, they're not bad either. You guys, you don't look like fishermen."

"Neither do you," said the big guy.

"We're just riding around," I said.

"That's a coincidence," the big guy said. "So are we." He bit into the chicken and chewed, then looked at me and nodded. "You're right. That's pretty damn good."

He paused and wiped his hands on some paper towels that were on a roller in the center of the table. He shifted on the bench and turned toward me, said, "We're more the hunter type."

"Now that," Jim Bob said, "is one big goddamn fucking coincidence. So are we."

"Really?" said the big guy.

"Oh, yeah," Jim Bob said. "Big fucking time."

"What do you hunt?"

"Skunks mostly," Jim Bob said.

"Oh," the big guy said. "I don't believe there's a season for that."

"What makes it thrilling," Jim Bob said. "Ain't nothing better than sneaking up on a skunk, or a weasel, and blowing them right out from over their ass."

"I can see that," said the big man, and he pushed the paper plate with the chicken on it away from him. "It sure was good to chat with you boys. You know, the weather looks as if it's going to turn bad."

"Yeah?" Leonard said.

"Oh yeah, big-time. I think I heard it on the radio. Thing is, I wanted to share that because you don't want to get caught up in a big old storm that might blow you away. That would suck."

"Yeah, and it would mess up our hair," I said.

He gave me a smile thin as the edge of a razor blade. "You got any information for us? You might know where we can find a good place to stop for the day, and get some things we need, and then maybe the storm won't come."

"And what kind of place is that?" I said.

"Someplace with a couple of dumb kids with lots of money who aren't any of your business."

"Shit," I said, "you know what another big coincidence is?"

"What's that?" the big guy said.

"We're in the same business," I said.

"Are we?" he said.

"Sounds like it. We too are looking for two sweet kids with lots of money that could be a port in the storm, and we think of them as our business, all the way."

"Huh," he said. "Well, we wouldn't want to cross up, would we?"

"It could happen, though, couldn't it?" Jim Bob said. "I mean, us both looking for two sweet kids and some money and a nice place to ride out the storm."

"Storm like the one that's coming," the big guy said, "it could blow your little port flat out of existence."

"We've ridden a lot of storms," Jim Bob said.

"Hell," Leonard said, "we're like storm chasers. We're like *the* storm chasers."

"I think you're a bunch of amateurs," the big guy said. "I think a good wind comes along, might just blow you completely out of the ball game."

"You know," Jim Bob said, "you were going pretty good there with the storm analogies, and then you got to go and screw it up with the ball game thing. That doesn't scan."

The big guy looked at Tonto, said, "What about the Indian? He talk?"

"Just smoke signals," Jim Bob said. "And you know what, none of your buddies are talking, so I don't think that's fair to ask."

"My buddies aren't my buddies, and they say what I tell them to say and when I say it," the big guy said. "And before I go, just so we stay with the storm analogy, you best not go out without your slickers and your hip boots, and maybe an umbrella."

"We got umbrellas out the ass," Jim Bob said.

Big Guy studied us for a moment, said to his boys, "Wrap this shit up, and let's go."

The big guy and his bunch wrapped their chicken and links, put them back in the sacks, and carried them out.

I watched them through the glass as they walked toward the Ford. I said, "Just so I'm certain, when he said slickers, boots, and umbrellas, he was talking about guns, right?"

"Yep," Leonard said. "That was my take."

"And they're the storm?"

"Bingo."

Tonto, who had just taken a bite of a link wrapped in bread, said, "This would be a lot better with hot sauce, some of that fancy mustard that's got a tang."

36

Full as ticks, we drove to another store near the lake where they sold fishing supplies and rented boats, and parked in front of it and sat in the van. Out front was a rack with T-shirts on it with Lake O' the Pines logos. The wind moved them about.

The place was doing pretty brisk business for the time of the year. There were cars parked to the left and the right of us and people got out and went in and came out carrying fishing supplies, coolers, snacks, and items like caps and bait. One of the people who parked and got out was a blond woman in jogging pants with a tight top and a baseball cap with her long hair tied up in a ponytail hanging over the stretch band at the back of her cap. The jogging pants were tight and I worried a little about her circulation and watched her out of biological interest until she went into the store. I didn't see her face, but she had the kind of body, hair, and walk that assured you she looked good and knew it.

Over the top of the joint the sky was losing its blue and turning the color of polished silver and there were starting to be dark puffs of clouds. The lake could be seen on either side of the building and the water was growing choppy; little white waves like nightcaps rose up and fell down. Jim Bob opened up the flooring and got out some hand-guns. I took a .38 automatic with a clip holster and put it on under my coat. I preferred revolvers—more dependable—but, alas, the times were a-changin' and nearly everyone these days carried an automatic for more firepower. Leonard took a nine with clip holster and Jim Bob clipped on a .38 automatic similar to mine under his coat. Tonto had never stopped being armed. He still had his twin .45s.

"What makes me nervous," I said, "is the fact we weren't armed back there, unless you count a chicken leg and a link sausage."

"I was," Tonto said.

"Yeah, but what about the rest of us?" I said.

"You had my best wishes," Tonto said.

Leonard said, "Here's my question. They're so goddamn sneaky, how come they decided to come to us like that?"

"Way we were wandering around," Jim Bob said, "my figure is they thought we knew they were following us. They didn't know we didn't know what the hell we were doing, so they thought we were giving them a hard time, being clever. And I think they thought they'd be all scary and we'd tell them what they wanted to know, then they'd run us off and they'd find the boy and the girl and all that money."

"They obviously didn't know me and Hap had our picture taken with a bear," Leonard said. "They ain't so tough. You see me give that bear a bad look, Hap?"

"No."

"I haven't been followed like that in a long time," Tonto said. "Thought I was being careful, and I'm pretty damn careful, and still, they were following. That takes some chops. I mean, I haven't never been followed before where I didn't know."

"You said it couldn't happen," I said.

"I was wrong," Tonto said. "Those guys are good."

"The big guy," Jim Bob said, "he knows what he's doing, all right."

"You think they'll take a run at us?" I said.

"I think they still hope we'll lead them to something," Jim Bob said.

"How did they get onto us so quick?" Leonard said.

"Someone somewhere told them something," Tonto said. "You got to wonder who and when, but the thing that matters is, time comes they'll stop fucking around and come for us. They'll maybe think they can make us talk by pulling out fingernails or cutting off eyelids or some such thing, sticking a stick up our dicks."

"That eyelid part," I said. "I want to be up front and go on record right now. I'll talk like you haven't never heard anyone talk before if that's done to me. I'll be like a whole flock of canaries. They won't have enough paper to write down what I got to say. And they start threatening my dick, I'll start making stuff up to go along with it."

We had tried to do it the easy way, which was drive over to the side of the lake where Hirem said the cabins were, but the easy way turned out hard, so we were going to cut to the chase and ask directions. We waited until the traffic at the store played out, then I went inside and found the owner behind a counter that contained whoopee cushions, fake dog shit, and all manner of redneck yuks. An older woman with gray hair and a face only a blind, prideless mother could love was behind the counter arranging a stack of little Texas flags on sticks in a large decorative coffee cup.

She said, "What can I do you for, honey?"

I gave her my winning smile, though I couldn't remember the last time it had won me anything. "Me and some buddies, we were supposed to meet a friend here on the lake, but we're kind of confused."

"Lake's out back of here. How confusing is that?"

I grinned like that was the best I had heard since my joke about the dog with the shot-up paw. Come to think of it, Leonard was right. That joke sucked.

"This buddy of ours said he was gonna meet us at a cabin on the east side of the lake—"

She pointed. "That's east."

"Yes, ma'am, we been over there. But the problem is, we can't find where we're supposed to meet him. He said a fellow named Bill Jordan had some cabins—"

"Bill Jordan. That old fart is in the ground, some three years now. He don't own them anymore."

"Oh, well, that puts a damper on things."

"A crippled fella with a funny haircut owns them now, but he don't rent out much. Got a pension."

"I see. Well, I'm pretty sure my friend is meeting us there. That's what he said anyway. He hasn't been here in a while, so he probably rented from the other fella."

"It's kind of hard to get to actually," she said. "Road is near washed out and it winds up in the pines. Good hunting up there, though. I know a fellow killed a wild hog there big enough to tussle with an elephant."

"That a fact?"

"Of course not. Ain't no hogs big as elephants. But it was big."

"I see. So, you go around on the east side, but where do you turn? We were all over that place, and we couldn't find what we were looking for."

She got a piece of paper and a pencil and drew me a map, explaining as she did. Pushing it across the counter, she said, "Now, you got to watch all the ruts and potholes, and it's narrow and there's limbs all grown up around it. I was up there last year taking the crippled fella with a funny haircut some supplies. He calls up and I deliver. For a little extra fee, of course."

"Of course."

"Anyway, it's like the goddamn Amazon up there."

"Well, thanks."

I started to go out. She said, "You know, you wanted to, there's an easier way. It'll take a little longer, but it's still easier, and you'd have to get going before the storm comes up, 'cause one is coming."

"So we were told."

"You could rent one of my boats, take it straight across the lake, and you could just dock at the place."

"How long would that take?"

"About an hour, maybe two if you get some tough wind and you ain't no hand with a boat. You go now, you got to rent the boat for overnight. Or you can rent if for a few days if you'd rather be over there awhile."

"How much is the boat?" I asked.

37

In the van I explained about the map and the boat. I said, "Me and Leonard can take the boat across, and you guys can follow the map. Thing is, I think you don't want to go over there right away, because you do, they might follow."

"They won't fool me again," Tonto said.

"Just in case they do, however," I said, "we could go across by boat, which they may not expect, see if we can find Hirem's boy, the girl, and the money. It might even be a sneakier way to come up on them if they're there. We can maybe call you when we get there and you can come around."

"Checked my phone a little while ago," Jim Bob said. "No signal out here."

"All right," I said. "Go do something that will give us two hours before you arrive, and we'll take the boat across. We get there early we'll hold our own until you show up. I think we can handle two kids and a pile of money."

"But if that big fellow and his pals show up before we do," Jim Bob said, "you might have your hands full."

"They been full before," Leonard said.

We spent some of our money on fishing poles and a bucket of minnows for show, a can of gas, bought a couple of sandwiches and a bag of vanilla wafers and a six-pack of Dr Pepper. The owner of the store, who told us her name was Annie, took us down to the boat and gave us instructions, and we set out.

It was really choppy and the boat rode high and dropped low. It was making my stomach queasy. The motor churned the water behind us and I pointed the bow due east, like Annie had suggested. There was a big stump in the middle of the lake she had directed us to, and when we got to that, she said we ought to start following a line of orange buoys and then those would go away and we had to hold due east until we saw a strip of land. She said it would be a lot farther away than we thought it was. Thing then was, when we got closer, we'd see a rise of pine trees and a dock out front of them, and there was a little trail that led up from the dock to the cabins.

For the moment, that stump in the distance was my bearing.

When we were out a ways, we overturned the minnow bucket into the lake and let all our guys go. Leonard said, "Swim, little fishes. Go, make your way in this big wet world. Make us proud."

The stump showed up and then the orange buoys. We followed those until they played out, but we couldn't see a strip of land. Not yet. It was a big lake. All we could see was water, and the sky had darkened and it had started to rain, and we didn't so much as have an umbrella.

The rain grew thick, and then I got nervous because the boat was holding water. Leonard took the minnow bucket and started bailing. I kept hold of the motor throttle and thought maybe I might regain some religion, because the water was jumping now and the rain had gotten so wild I could hardly see my hand in front of my face, let alone a distant strip of land sporting pine trees.

I decided keeping my hand on the throttle and using my wits would probably do me better than religion, and I kept at it. The rain kept at it too. We bounced up and down, and at one point the boat listed to port and water splashed in heavily, and Leonard was really working that bucket.

"That damn rain is cold," he said.

"What, you think I haven't noticed?"

We went on like that for a while, and I feared we had gone off point and were traveling in the wrong direction, maybe even boating in circles. But then the rain slacked and I saw a strip of land and some pines rising up. I glanced at my watch, putting it close to my face. We had been at it for an hour and a half.

The wind was really whistling now and the boat was struggling. Leonard was bailing like a maniac.

"Almost there," I said.

The engine sputtered and died. We were out of gas.

"Now," Leonard said, "if a goddamn whale will swallow us, it will be a perfect day."

38

The gas can was under one of the seats, and I pulled it out and went about trying to pour some of it in the outboard tank. Way the water made the boat hump up and down it was hard work, and some of the gas went into the lake.

I finally finished with the can, but by that time we had drifted a considerable distance. I didn't care. It didn't matter to me right then if we got to where we were going or if we just made land, any land, and because of that, when I saw a glimpse of shoreline, I took the boat in that direction. I hoped we wouldn't bring the boat up against a stump, 'cause at the speed we were going if we hit one, we'd be flung into the cold deep churning water, and that wouldn't be good. Still, I couldn't seem to slow the throttle down. The rain was slamming us and it was cold and I wanted off the lake.

Something went wrong, and we went into the water, the grateful minnows we had released would save us. Like Aquaman, we would call to them and they would come and lift us out of the water on their shiny backs and carry us ashore.

But I wasn't counting on it.

Most likely, we'd drown like rats.

I saw it just before we hit it. I thought it was a log, but it was an alligator, and when we struck it the boat jumped and I went out of it as if shot from a catapult. I caught a glimpse of Leonard, still clinging to the handle of the minnow bucket, go up and over and make a nice little flip into the water and disappear under the waves.

I swam and my arm hit the gator and I screamed like a little girl. The rest of the gator sailed on past me and I could smell a rotten odor, realized the big bastard was dead, and had been awhile. He might have died up in the reeds along the bank and the storm had stirred him loose. He sailed past and the waves rolled over him and took him under and then I went under. When I came up the minnow bucket was floating past me. I grabbed at it like it was a life raft.

Holding on to it, I kicked toward shore, but shore had moved away. Or so it seemed. The water had carried me out farther and quicker than I could imagine. The lake was so cold I could hardly get a breath. I looked around for Leonard and didn't see him. I looked around for the boat, didn't see it either. Annie was going to be pissed.

I kicked toward what looked like shore and hoped a live alligator didn't find me, hoped in this weather they would be somewhere cozy. Then again, I wasn't sure if alligators liked it cozy. Maybe they liked the rain.

I called out for Leonard, but the wind took my voice and carried it away and all I got out of my yelling was a hoarse throat.

And then my feet were touching ground. Not well, but they were touching. I pushed on toward some reeds, and after what seemed like enough time for the Big Bang to have happened and all the species on the planet to have developed and moved on out to the stars, I made it to some waving grass and reeds and stumbled into that, went down a few times, came up with a mouthful of muddy water. As I tromped through, barely able to stand, hardly able to see, I came across a long four-foot-wide fragment of our boat. On his back in the water, hanging on to the fragment, was a big black guy.

"Leonard," I said.

He let go of the board and sat up in the water and said, "Well, Ahab, that boat trip was sure a good idea."

I checked for my .38. I still had it.

Leonard checked for his automatic. Still there. Well, at least we had that going for us. We were in a position to add to the worst nature of man and the final downfall of the world. By God, we had our guns.

Leonard stood up slowly and looked around. The minnow bucket had floated up into the tall grass and was hung there. He focused on it, said, "I guess the cookies and the Dr Pepper didn't make it."

"Missing in action," I said.

"Now that's a blow," Leonard said.

Slogging along the shoreline through the rain, we saw a boathouse and made our way over there. It was wide open and we went inside. There was a boat floating in a stall and there was fishing tackle in the boat, and on one wall were some croaker sacks for hunting and some nasty-looking towels that were probably used to wipe the boat down after fishing. There were four rain slickers on nails. A fairly large dead fish floated belly-up near the boat and the waves washed at it until it went under the flooring, out of sight.

We used the towels to dry off and to dry our weapons, hoping they'd still shoot. The towels made us dry enough, but they left us smelling like fish. We sat on the edge of the boathouse dock with the heavy damp towels over our shoulders and looked out at the boat that was docked there. There were paddles in the bottom of the boat and no motor. The boat was bouncing up and down and we could see the lake from where we sat, and the rain was furious. Everything was gray. It was as if the sky and the lake had joined together.

I pulled my cell phone out of my pants pocket, shook the water out of it. It was still working, but there wasn't any signal, like Jim Bob had said. I put it away.

"I saw a dead alligator," I said.

"Yeah, well, I think I saw him too," Leonard said.

"Was he big and dark?"

"Yep."

"That was him, all right."

"Say he was dead?"

"Very."

"Thank goodness for small favors."

We waited for the downpour to slack off, but it didn't. Freezing, we toweled off again and took a couple of slickers off the wall and put them on and went to where we had come in and stood in the open doorway and looked out at the rain.

"I don't want to," Leonard said.

"Me neither," I said.

"But, alas . . ." Leonard said, and we went out into the rain.

39

I had no idea where we had ended up, but my guess was near where we wanted to be. But that didn't change the fact that near was not the same as being there, and every tree looked pretty much like the other, and I didn't see any trails. We wandered around in the rain, damp inside our slickers but better off now with the hoods pulled up and the cold rain not coming right down on us.

Ending up again where the boat had come apart, or at least where part of it had been in the tall grass with Leonard, we again saw the foam minnow bucket caught up in the grass, and floating in the water where it hadn't been before, pushed up in the shallows, was our six-pack of Dr Pepper.

Leonard waded out in the water and got the six-pack, carried it by its plastic holder onto the shore. He set it down on the ground and pulled one of the Dr Peppers off one of the plastic rings, pulled the tab, and nearly drank the whole thing with one big gulp.

He peeled off another and handed it to me, and then got another for himself. We both drank. When he was finished he dropped the can on the ground with the other one and said, "I'm tough enough today to litter."

Even under the circumstances, anal as I am about such things, I wanted to find a trash can but figured it might be best in this situation to be able to draw the .38 more than be an environmentalist and tote an empty can around. Reluctantly, we left the three remaining Dr Peppers there and wandered around like a couple of geese.

I saw a narrow trail and pointed it out, and Leonard said, "Who the hell knows? Let's try it."

The trail went up a steep hill, through some pines. The pines were close together and the soil there was sandy and had turned the color of milk-and-flour gravy. The rain ran down the hill and into ruts that tires had made, and the whole thing was just wide enough for a car. After we had walked halfway up the hill, the trees got thick enough to cut the rain a bit, and finally we broke out at the top of a hill into a clearing, and there was a line of little cabins that made our tourist court digs look like the Taj Mahal. There was one cabin that wasn't in a row, and it was a little off to the side. I presumed that would belong to the owner, the fellow Annie had called The Crippled Fellow With A Funny Haircut.

There was a car in front of one of the cabins. It was the only car present. It was a black Escalade.

"Dat dere, Brer Bear," Leonard said, "be duh goddamn car we be lookin' for, and in dat dere cabin—"

"Leonard. That's enough."

"Okay. I figure they're inside, with the money. Or what's left of it."

"So what do we do?"

"Well, I don't see any brown Fords, and I don't see our guys yet, so my suggestion is we waltz ourselves over to yon cabin and knock on the door and stick guns in their faces."

"That'll work," I said. "And if it doesn't, we'll improvise."

Observing the cabin briefly, we decided Leonard would go around front and I'd go around back. I ducked under a low window and looked toward the big cabin to see if anyone was watching me from there. If they were, they were very clever. I wondered too if anyone was in any of the other cabins. I thought not. No cars. But they could be gone for a bowl of chili. Perhaps they were all over at Annie's, chatting and laughing it up about some plastic dog shit and a whoopee cushion.

Around back, I pulled the .38 and pressed up against the door, pushing my ear tight. I listened. The rain was so loud I couldn't hear myself think. I pushed against the door to see how sturdy it was, decided it wasn't that sturdy.

I heard the front door budge, and I knew Leonard was in. I hit the back door with my shoulder and was in, stumbling. There really wasn't anywhere to go. The back door led through a little kitchen and right into the bedroom/living room, where our two lovebirds were sacked out in a bedraggled bed. The boy reached for an automatic lying at the bedside, but Leonard was already there and he grabbed it and pulled it back. He now had a gun in either hand.

The boy sat up in bed, and when he did the sheet fell back from the young lady. She was wearing a thin white bra. It was cold in the room, and the tips of her breasts punched at it like ice picks. Leonard said, "Don't panic, kid. We don't want to hurt you."

"We'll give the money back," the boy, Tim, said. "We don't want it."

"You wanted it when you took it," I said.

"I didn't think it would matter then," the boy said.

"So why does it matter now?" I said, pushing back the hood on the rain slicker.

"I guess I knew better, but we been thinking it over. We want to give it back. Just let us go and take the money."

"Looks like to me," Leonard said, "you been doing more than thinking."

"Please don't hurt us," Tim said.

"We don't want to hurt you," Leonard said, closing the front door he had knocked open, cutting back the cold wind. "We're on a mission from your dad . . . sort of. We're also working for the law and for ourselves."

"You're not . . . with the organization?" Tim asked.

"Organization?" I said. "You mean the Dixie Mafia?"

Tim nodded.

"Nope. We are freelancers."

The girl, who had not spoken, said, "You want the money for yourselves?"

"That would be nice," I said, "but no. That isn't the deal."

I studied her closely. She was worth running off with. Her hair was cut short, almost man style, but she was a fine-looking girl with a long, sleek neck and deep eyes you'd like to fall into, especially if you were a young man, and from what I could see of her body she wasn't going to make anyone turn their eyes away in disgust.

We lowered our guns. Leonard pushed back his rain hood and sat on the windowsill. I went and shut the back door to the kitchen, came back and found a chair. I said, "You two just stay there for a minute. What we're gonna do is we're gonna wait for some friends of ours, and then we're going to load you, along with the money—where is it, by the way?"

"Under the bed," Tim said.

"Under the bed?" Leonard said. "That's as sneaky as you get? You put it under the bed? They put it under the bed, Hap."

"You're not very good criminals," I said. "But you're lucky we're the ones found you, and we found you for your dad, and we're taking you and the money back and things are maybe going to be okay, except for the part where your dad squeals about his business and you all have to go into witness protection. Maybe your dad does some prison. Up in the air right now."

"Oh hell," Tim said.

"Yep," I said. "Oh hell."

I looked at Leonard. He was turned slightly so he could see out the window. Rivulets of rain ran down the window and it was clouded over. Leonard used the palm of his hand to wipe the inside a bit, and then he said, "It just keeps on coming." He looked at me, said, "Brown Ford."

40

"Drop your cock and grab your socks," I said, looking at Tim. "In fact, forget the socks. Nab some drawers pronto, 'cause it's about to get interesting in here."

"Oh hell," Tim said, threw back the covers, and scrambled out naked, grabbing some pants off the floor. The girl, whose name I had yet to know, came out of the bed on the other side, pulling on jeans.

Leonard said, "You know what's really swell, both the goddamn doors are already broken in."

I went over to the window and looked out. The big guy we had met over chicken and links was wearing a raincoat with a hood and he was standing by the Escalade, looking it over like a prospective buyer. He had an automatic with a silencer in his right hand. The other three guys were out of the car now and one of them had a double-barrel shotgun and the other two had handguns. I felt my asshole pucker, and in that instant every good meal, hot fuck, blue sky I had ever experienced jumped through my head.

I didn't know how they had found us—hit or miss, or maybe they had talked to Annie, bought some whoopee cushions and a box of fake dog shit in exchange for information about what it was some guys might be asking her about.

It didn't really matter now.

Big Guy looked up at the house, and Leonard and I moved away from the window.

"There's nothing left but for you two to get under the bed with the money," I said. "And hope things go better than I think they will."

They did as I suggested. When Leonard and I were dead, it would be easy pickings for Big Guy and his posse. Pop these two and take the dough, stop off for photos with the bear and a couple of hot links, then home.

"Hey, hey, hey," Leonard said. "The cavalry has arrived. Sort of."

I looked.

Tonto's van had pulled up and he and Jim Bob were out of the car. They weren't wearing rain gear. Tonto had his coat pushed back and the .45 holsters were empty; the guns were in his hands. Jim Bob was carrying a pump twelve-gauge with a shortened barrel. They were walking toward the Ford and the four guys as if they were meeting for tea.

Big Guy said something, and then two of his guys, one with the shotgun, the other with a pistol, went back toward where they had parked the Ford. Big Guy eased toward us slowly, and one of the other guys started around the cabin, toward the back.

"Who you want?" I said.

"The big motherfucker," Leonard said.

"Good."

I hurried into the kitchen and stepped up on the counter that was near the door and pointed my weapon, waited. There was a slight sound at the back door, and then it was pushed back gently. I saw a hand with an automatic poke in, and then I heard a shot from the front of the cabin, Leonard's or Big Guy's weapon. I didn't know for sure. And then the guy at the kitchen door, perhaps smelling blood in the water, charged in and I shot him above the ear and he fell back against the wall and his head stayed propped against it while the rest of him spread out in that relaxed manner only the dead have. There was blood on the wall.

I jumped down and charged into the other room. Big Guy had Leonard by the neck and was lifting him off the floor with both hands. Leonard's gun was on the floor between Big Guy's legs, and Big Guy's weapon was thrown up against the wall. I wasn't sure how things had got that way, who had fired and who was hit, but before I could blow Big Guy's brains out, I heard a shotgun blast outside, and then another, and then Leonard went sailing across the room, slammed onto the bed hard enough for the slats to break and the girl to scream from under there, and then Leonard was up and the kids were crawling out from under the bed, cowering in the corner.

I lifted up my .38 and shot Big Guy directly in the chest. He stepped across the room quickly and grabbed my gun hand, and slapped the hell out of me with the back of his other hand. I did a nice backwards roll, and when I got it together, Big Guy was firing at me with my .38.

Leonard leaped like a panther and hit Big Guy above the knees with the side of his body, trying to clip him. Didn't work. He bounced off.

I got the gun from the dead guy in the kitchen, a nine-mil, and went back to help Leonard. Leonard was grabbed again, and Big Guy was slinging him around like wet laundry. I couldn't get a good aim.

All of this was going on at the same time there was a lot of racket outside. Gunfire, cursing, screams.

Finally Big Guy tired enough, that Leonard, still hanging high while this guy choked him, was able to slap his hands over Big Guy's ears. Big Guy dropped him. I tried to shoot Big Guy as he came rushing toward me, but the gun jammed.

Typical.

He grabbed me around the waist and pushed me backwards and slammed me into the wall so that the back of my neck hit a bookshelf and the shelf came loose and fell and the one above it fell too, hitting me on top of the head dead center. At least the owner wasn't a reader; no books fell on my head.

Next thing I knew I was pitched against the far wall next to the open front door. I got up and saw Leonard throw a right hook into Big Guy's body and jerk back his hand with a sour look on his face.

I knew then why my bullet hadn't hurt Big Guy. He was wearing a bulletproof vest.

The kids, both barefoot and Tim bare-chested, yanked a duffel bag out from under the ruins of the bed. They headed out the door before I could get off my ass, and when I did, the cabin felt as if it was moving.

I started to go after them, but when I looked back, Leonard was being slammed by a punch that might have killed a steer. My head was mostly back together, so I rushed Big Guy and threw a hard round kick into his thigh. It was a perfect kick, hitting right on the nerve in the outer thigh, and I had used it before, dropping the leg right out from under strong men, but if it bothered Big Guy his expression didn't show it. He came rushing at me, and without really knowing I was going to do it, I started backpedaling and went right out the front door.

A gun barked to my left and I saw one of Big Guy's team on the ground and Jim Bob walking over. I got a glimpse of Tonto, but I didn't see the other bad guy. The two kids and their duffel bag had disappeared.

Big Guy came charging out into the open, practically foaming at the mouth.

I'm a little ashamed to say I turned and bolted. I thought I was running like a goddamn deer on steroids, but Big Guy was tight on my ass as a dingleberry, and the next thing I knew he had me and we're tumbling down the trail, rolling like a couple of doodlebugs. When we came to the bottom of the hill, I got hold of his ear with my teeth and bit it as hard as I could, taking off a chunk big enough for a small sandwich.

He jerked his head up and came to his knees and let out a bellow. I tried to make a quick exit, stage right, spitting out the chunk of ear as I went, but he got hold of my rain slicker with one hand and hit me so hard with the other I thought I had accidentally stepped onto train tracks and been hit by a locomotive.

He was about to hit me again when I heard a grunt, and Leonard, doing a Superman, flew down the hill and hit Big Guy. The two of them went tumbling down some more, covered in mud, and ended up near the water's edge. Big Guy came up on top and he was giving Leonard a pounding.

I ran down there and kicked Big Guy in the head. It was a pretty good shot, and it did more damage than the kick to the thigh. He was knocked over and into the water. He tried to get up and I kicked him again, but because I had to step out into the water to do it, it wasn't as good a kick, and it only knocked him back. And then Leonard got hold of the minnow bucket and slammed it over Big Guy's head. It was a tight fit. Leonard chopped Big Guy across the throat, twice in rapid succession. Big Guy stood up. Leonard slipped behind him with one smooth motion and tried to choke him with his forearm. The guy's neck was like a tree, and Leonard might as well have been squeezing one. The guy shook like a dog and Leonard went into the water, scrambled up and out of it and onto the shore to meet me. We both stood there looking at the monster with the minnow bucket on his head. Big Guy clawed at the bucket, started pulling it loose. Leonard said, "Run like a motherfucker."

And we did. We ran. We were like little children being chased by the Big Bad Wolf.

Leonard said as we ran, "Where the fuck is that guy from?"

"Hell," I said.

We were coming up on the boathouse. I said, "Goddamn it. Let's take the boat and get away from that sonofabitch."

Looking back, I saw Big Guy minus his bucket, and he was really coming. When we got in the boathouse the kids were there with the bag of money. They had the other rain slickers on and the towels over their shoulders. They were just standing on the platform looking at the boat as if they thought they might be magically transported into it. The rain was really coming down outside the boathouse, and it could be seen through the big opening at the back where the boats went out and came in, peppering the water like buckshot.

"What the hell are you waiting on?" Leonard said to the couple. "Get in the boat."

"I'm scared of water," the girl said.

"Something comin' through that door you're gonna be a lot more scared of," Leonard said, and at that moment Big Guy came in, flinging the door back so hard it slammed against the wall.

The girl was in the boat faster than a jackrabbit. Tim just froze. Leonard and I crouched. Leonard said, "This time, we got to get him."

Big Guy, who seemed to have lost his wits, came charging along the planks and Leonard and I, as if through some mind-meld of knowledge, went for his legs, went low and lifted high. It wasn't quite perfect. Big Guy went a little to the right, out over the platform and hit headfirst in the boat. The boat cracked, rolled, sent the girl into the water with a scream. Tim, who was standing behind us and had caught some of Big Guy's body as it was thrown, was knocked the length of the platform.

The boat righted itself, and there was Big Guy, hanging on to the side of it. The girl, who was crying loudly, was clinging to the bow. I got down on my belly on the platform and grabbed one of the paddles floating in the water and stood up and cracked Big Guy over the head with it. It took about three licks before he went under.

There was movement at the door. I turned my head. Tonto came through, followed by Jim Bob. Somehow, Tonto had ended up with the double-barrel shotgun.

Big Guy was back, clinging to the side of the boat, trying to climb inside. Tonto came over quick and stepped off the platform and onto the boat. It was a graceful move and the boat only rocked a little. He got Big Guy by the hair and stuck the double barrel in his open mouth and pulled the trigger. The back of Big Guy's head jumped out onto the water, and something, pellets, skull shrapnel, rattled against the clapboard wall across the way.

Big Guy, missing most of his head, went under, except for one hand that clung to the side of the boat. Tonto squatted and took hold of the fingers and peeled one of them off and then they all came loose.

Leonard said, "You better find that sonofabitch and drive a stake through his heart. I don't want him coming back."

Tonto made his way to the bow of the little boat and pulled the girl out of the water, then handed her up to me. I set her on the platform. She was shivering with the cold, just like me and Leonard and Tim. Tonto climbed up on the platform and took a deep breath. He smelled like the shotgun blast.

"The others?" I asked.

"They're napping," Tonto said. "Deep napping."

"Yeah," I said. "There's one in the cabin, and he's kind of sleepy too."

41

At the top of the hill, with me carrying the bag of money, and it was a big bag and pretty damn heavy, we discovered that the two thugs were indeed napping by the Ford. While they were napping some red stuff had run out of them and onto the ground and had been mixed up and thinned by the rain so that it looked like spilled strawberry Kool-Aid. They were lying on their backs and they had some holes in them and their open mouths were filling with rain.

We grabbed the stuff from the cabin that belonged to the kids, got the guns, and wiped the place down of blood and fingerprints as best we could, hauling the dead guy out of the kitchen, putting him and the other two in the Ford. Jim Bob drove the Ford, Tonto drove his van, and Leonard took the keys of the Escalade from Tim and drove the rest of us out of there, me in the back with the boy, the girl beside Leonard. The windshield wipers beat methodically as he drove and the heater made it cozy. It was hard to believe that a moment before we had been in a gunfight, a fistfight, a wrestling match, and the like. It seemed surreal, though my ears were still ringing from the gunfire in the small cabin and I hurt all over.

We followed Jim Bob down a narrow clay road with trash thrown out on both sides. He parked the Ford and left it and joined Tonto in the van. Tonto and Leonard found places to turn around and got us back on the main road, which was a strip of aging blacktop.

We followed along behind the van. No one in our car had said a word. And then: "That man," the girl said. "He . . . he was so strong."

"Tell me about it," Leonard said. "And he had a bulletproof vest on to boot."

"You noticed that too," I said.

"I did," Leonard said. "For a moment I thought Superman had gone bad, and it was a real relief to discover he was just a man."

"He was just plenty of man," I said.

"I hurt all over," Leonard said. "I feel like I been chewed up by a wolf and shit off a cliff and my pile got stepped on by an elephant."

"I hear you," I said. "I'm dizzy and I got a headache and I want my teddy bear. Bastard must have taken something. Some kind of drug. Damned if I know. But I'm going to dream about him, and I'm not going to like it."

"I used to have a teddy bear," the girl said out of nowhere. "His name was Lew. I think my momma still has him."

We let that sail around the car for a moment, then, "Figure guy owns the cabins has already called the law," Leonard said.

"No," Tim said. "He said he would be gone a few days. Went off somewhere with his brother. We paid in advance."

"I hope you left a dead body deposit," I said.

"We didn't give our real names. He wrote down our plates, but they're false. I switched them."

"Normally, I wouldn't want to encourage such criminal enterprise as license-plate switching in the young, but let me, at this moment in time, give to you a symbolic high five."

It was entirely symbolic. Neither of us moved.

Tim said, "So . . . are you going to hurt us?"

"Nope," I said. "We already would have if we were. But you got to go back."

"My dad . . . he turned himself in."

"For you. And he's going to talk to the feds. Putting himself in danger from the Dixie Mafia for one reason and one reason only. You."

Tim was quiet for a moment, then said, "He's done some bad things."

"He has, and I suppose he's actually going to get away with having done a lot of them if he tells the feds the right things, things they want to know. But there is this. He loves you pretty damn strong to do what he's doing. Putting himself in danger, maybe going to jail, or having to be in the witness protection program. Something you may have to do too. Thing is, he's doing what he's doing for you so you can maybe do something a lot better than he's done with his life."

"You think so?"

"I think so."

"What about me?" the girl said.

"I don't know yet," I said. "We'll figure something out."

"He just couldn't stand we were together, her being black."

"He got over it," I said. "He only wants you happy."

"He said that?"

"Yep."

"Are you friends of his?"

"Nope," I said. "Not even close."

"Then why are you doing this?"

"We sort of have our asses over a barrel and we got picked because we were expendable."

Leonard said, "Girl, what's your name?"

"Katie," she said.

"All right," Leonard said. "That's good to know in case I want to call you to supper. Hap, are you okay back there?"

"A little traumatized. Not every day you meet Dracula and live."

"Ain't that the truth? We owe Tonto one."

"We owe that shotgun one. Maybe we can take it to lunch."

42

Leonard wheeled us away from the lake, and Tonto, who was driving in front of us, pulled the van to the side of the road and parked. We pulled up beside him, real close, lowered the window on the girl's side. Tonto lowered his window, said, "Now what?"

"I think we ought to think this over before we do anything," Leonard said.

"What's that mean?" Tonto asked.

Leonard looked back at me. I leaned forward in the seat and spoke loud enough for them to hear. "I'm with Leonard. I think now we've done the deed, we should regroup a little. Gonna hand these kids off, I want to make sure I'm not dropping them in the lion's den. We maybe hole them up somewhere, then me and Leonard see how the lay of the land is, figure what to do next."

"I'm just along for the ride," Tonto said.

"Me too," Jim Bob said.

"All right, then," I said. "Let's drive over to Shreveport, put the kids in a hotel, and we stay there with them. Maybe we'll take a day or two and consider what we ought to do next."

Leonard turned, looked at Tim in the backseat, then at Katie. "You're not going to give us shit, are you?"

"I just want to go home," she said. She turned and looked at Tim. "I just want to go home, baby."

Tim reached over the seat and patted her shoulder. "I know. It was a dumb idea. I don't know why I had to take the money. That was stupid."

"Thing is," Leonard said, "we want to make sure it's okay you two go home, that you're safe. So we'll do it the way we're talkin' about, and we'll use some of the money you stole to pay for it. We'll tell the feds we had to use some to get the bulk of it back. Expenses. I think they'll go for that."

"Got a feeling," I said, "Dixie Mafia might hold a grudge, we spend their money."

"Not like we're giving it back to them," Leonard said. "Once we give it to the feds, we're out of this deal and the organization is still out the money."

"I don't think we'll be out of hot water that easy," I said.

"Me neither," Jim Bob said from across the way. "It's not just about the money with these guys. For them, they get it back or they don't, they aren't going to like us much either way. Especially you guys. They know who you two are. Me and Tonto, maybe we can just go home, put our feet up."

"But you won't," Leonard said.

"Of course not," Jim Bob said. "Well, speaking for me, anyway."

"My favor isn't done till the job is done," Tonto said. "And it's not like I got kids waiting at the house. So count me in too."

The Louisiana border wasn't far, and neither was Shreveport, so that's the way we went after we found a quiet place to switch license plates on the Escalade and the van again, doing it out in the rain.

I thought about what would happen if we were pulled over and for some reason a cop wanted to take a look and found the stuff under the flooring; the van was packed with enough weapons and license plates that the four of us could go up for about three thousand years wearing thumbscrews and without possibility of parole.

We drove into Louisiana, and not much longer after that, made Shreveport. Stopping at a filling station we got some gas, then we went to a nice hotel and spent some of the Dixie Mafia's money to put us in a connecting room with the kids, and to put Jim Bob and Tonto in a room together.

We had our clothes in overnight bags that we had left in the van, and we carried those into the elevator, and the kids carried their two suitcases, one of which, the girl's, was on rollers. Leonard carried the heavy duffel bag of money over his shoulder. When we got to the room, which was on a high floor in the hotel, Leonard and I pulled off our slickers, and then the four of us took turns taking showers in the two bathrooms and dressing in clean clothes. The way the suite was set up, there was a bedroom on either end with a bathroom in it, and in the middle was a big room with a couch and television set and chairs, and there was a kitchenette. Through sliding doors was a covered deck surrounded by Plexiglas. It gave us a good view of the city and the casinos and hotels.

After looking at a menu, we ordered up some bowls of chili and a pot of coffee, which seemed like a pretty damn good idea after the cold and the rain, and we went out on the protected deck to sit at the table there while we waited. A short time later, a waiter arrived pushing a wheeled table and we had him take it out on the deck, where the four of us sat and ate and drank our coffee with very little to say.

The day was dark and the lights turning on inside and outside the hotels and casinos on the strip made everything look surreal and strange through the rain. As we sat and ate, and gathered our thoughts, and let the food seep into us and renew us, night dropped down over the city and the multicolored lights appeared brighter than before and almost Christmas-like through the deluge.

I guess we sat there for nearly a half hour before I felt like I was actually going to live. Still, my back hurt where I had been slammed into the wall, and my head hurt where the shelf had cracked me, and when I had taken a shower and looked in the mirror, I was no longer surprised at the way people had looked at me in the lobby, the way the little guy behind the hotel desk had stared at me. I thought it was the old rain slicker that smelled like fish, and that most certainly was part of it, but my face looked like it had been through a buzz saw. Leonard, being darker of skin, didn't look so wounded if you didn't look right at him, but by the time we finished our meal one of his eyes had swollen near shut, and he was starting to look like an ebony Cabbage Patch doll with an attitude. I had found some aspirin in my shaving kit and took four of them, shaved while I was in there, and it was a tender job. When I looked at my hand, I noticed it was trembling slightly. I managed to cut myself only a little, brushed my teeth and went out and got a look at everyone else.

Spruced up, Tim was a pretty good-looking kid, and Katie was the sort of girl that if she told you she was a model for a clean-cut catalog like JCPenney's, you'd believe her. Even with her hair cut close like that, she was a knockout. Coltish in white shorts, with long legs and that long neck and a way of moving that made you wish you were young and single and cool and had a pocketful of money. Maybe enough to steal money and a car from your dad.

Out on the deck, I sat down and said, "We can tie you two up, or you can act like you got some sense and get a good night's sleep. Thing is, you'll be better off with us than out there on your own."

"We'll do what you say," Katie said, and looked at Tim. He nodded.

"It's for your own good," I said. "We don't want anything to happen to you. You're kind of our calling card for better treatment concerning a problem we have. You and the money. Just listen to us and do what we say, and everything will be all right."

"You won't let anything happen to us?" Katie asked.

"No, we won't."

"You promise?" she said.

"Yep," I said. "I promise."

She looked at Leonard. He smiled. "When he promises, or I promise, baby girl, we're promising together."

43

The kids got one bedroom, and Leonard won the other due to a coin toss. I got the couch. It was a good way to make sure the kids didn't get a wild hair up their asses and want to sneak out in the middle of the night. I doubted that would be the case, but insurance seemed like a good idea.

Leonard helped me move the couch close to the front door, which was the only way out of the room, and then I picked up the phone and called over to Jim Bob and Tonto's room to see how they were doing. Jim Bob was watching TV and he said Tonto had gone over to one of the casinos.

We bantered a little, but neither of us was really up for it. After I hung up the phone, Leonard and I took some time to clean and oil the guns we had with a little kit I carried in my overnight bag.

After that, Leonard went to bed and I got a pillow and blanket and turned out the lights and lay on the couch and went to sleep immediately. It was a deep sleep, but there were bad things down there in the deep with me, and so I came awake about three a.m. I lay there for a while, then finally sat up, and saw that Tim was out on the deck, sitting at the table looking at all the lights, which were clearer now, because the rain had stopped at last.

Pulling on my pants, not bothering to turn on the light, I went out there barefoot, and when I pulled the sliding door back, he turned in a kind of panic.

"It's me," I said.

"I don't know who I was expecting."

"Probably the guy you saw killed today. I keep thinking he's going to come back from the dead."

"Tough guy like you thinks that, I don't feel so bad."

"Don't fool yourself, kid. I'm not that tough."

"You look tough."

"I look tired, that's what I look."

I sat down at the table, and Tim said, "I couldn't sleep. Katie, she can sleep anytime. No matter what's happened, she can sleep. I wonder why that is?"

"I'm like you," I said. "Brett, my girlfriend, she's like Katie. We can have an argument, or something can go wrong that will stress me out and I won't be able to sleep, but she can lay down and hibernate like a bear."

Tim nodded. He said, "I really didn't mean to cause trouble."

"You know what your father does for a living."

"You know I do. For some time now."

"You know he has people to answer to."

"Sure. I just didn't think it would amount to this. I thought they'd be mad and he'd be mad at me, and what I did was a kind of vengeance."

"For the work he does?"

"It's not work. It's drugs and whores."

"I agree with you. It's not work and it's not good. You should have just run off with the girl. That said, my bet is her parents are worried sick about her."

"I'm sure they got the cops out after her," he said.

"The cops, the FBI, and us."

"What happens to the money?"

"The FBI gets it."

"And what do they do with it?"

"Good question. Three hundred thousand dollars is lot to do with."

"Three hundred thousand?" Tim said. "It's more than that."

I went into the living room with Tim trailing along behind me. I got the duffel bag with the money out of the closet and dragged it out and opened it up and poured the money on the floor. It was a mixture of hundred-dollar bills and twenties, some tens and fives.

I said, "Get down on the floor there with me, and let's count it."

We did that, and when we had it counted and in stacks, I said, "Just short of five hundred thousand dollars. That the way you had it figured?"

"Sure. I've counted it a few times. It was five hundred thousand when we started. We been living on some of it."

"But your dad is saying three hundred thousand is missing."

Tim shook his head. "I don't understand."

"I don't know either, but I tell you what. Let's put it back in the bag and put it away and go to sleep. Tomorrow we'll see if something comes to us."

Lying on the couch I thought about the money, and I thought about what we had been asked to do, and I thought about Hirem. Something was niggling at the back of my mind, but I wasn't able to grasp what it was. I'd feel as if I almost had hold of it, and then it would move away from my grasp. I fell asleep dreaming of Big Guy coming out of the water with most of his head missing, climbing into the boat and onto the platform and chasing Leonard and me along the lake shore, and when I'd look back at him, he'd be wearing that minnow bucket over his head.

44

Next morning, Jim Bob joined us in our room for breakfast. Tonto was still out on the town. He hadn't come in last night. We ate out on the deck. It was fun spending someone else's money.

The lights were no longer on and the rain had gone, but the day was gray and the air was misty. Everything that had looked bright and amazing the night before now looked grim and sad, sort of sordid, like a used condom tossed in the gutter. Tim and Katie finished up eating and went back to the bedroom. They looked as glum as a couple of coffin carriers.

"Dumb kids," Jim Bob said.

"Love is dumb," I said, "and sometimes that's what I like about it."

Leonard tossed a thumb at me. "He's so cute."

"So Tonto's out on the town?"

Jim Bob grinned, said, "Funny guy, that Tonto."

"Yeah, ha, ha," I said.

"He kills people and then goes gambling," Jim Bob said. "Of course, I haven't lost my appetite."

"None of us have," I said, and then I told everyone about the money.

"That's a lot more money than your man said was missing," Jim Bob said.

"Yep," I said, "and I smell a rat about the size of a possum covered in slime."

Jim Bob poured himself some coffee and looked out at the misty morning. "You know, I got a kind of idea about what's going on here."

"There's a little something coming to me too," Leonard said. "A guy tells us there's three hundred thousand dollars and there's more than that, you got to wonder if it's that big of a miscount on his part—about what's missing, I mean—or he's just a goddamn liar."

"Yeah," Jim Bob said. "I think the thing is your man, Hirem, he made a special side deal with two FBI agents that doesn't involve the agency. You two go out and do the dirty work, bring the money back, not having counted it, and they slice them off a nice piece, turn in the three hundred thousand Hirem said was missing, and they get as good a deal as they can find for him in the system, witness protection, and they promise to protect the kid, and you two get out from under your charges. If you two decide to keep the money, then you're fugitives and you got this charge hanging over your head they could manipulate out of being self-defense and into being murder. You could go up for a long time."

"They could pull that trick anyway," Leonard said.

"Yeah," Jim Bob said, "but the way they see it is it'd be better for everyone all around if they got their money and Hirem got his deal and you two went back to being you two, which is kind of a full-time job."

Leonard and I touched fists. "Yeah, baby," Leonard said.

About an hour later there was a knock at the door, and being paranoid, I carried my pistol with me and looked out the peephole. It was Tonto.

When I let him in he looked as fresh as he had the day before, and he was carrying a newspaper under his arm. He followed me out to the deck and sat in a chair and put the paper on the table, and poured himself a cup of coffee. He said, "You know that woman you rented the boat from?"

"Yeah," I said.

"You won't have to pay for that boat sinking. She's dead."

He reached over and flipped the paper open, scanned it briefly, put his finger on an article. I picked it up and read it. It said the woman had been found dead in her store, shot through the forehead. One of her fingers had been amputated.

I read this aloud, and when I finished, Leonard said, "Damn. I think somehow this is our fault."

"I think someone wanted to know where we went," I said, "and she didn't want to tell, and whoever wanted to know cut off a finger to show they were serious, and then when they got the information, they shot her as a cleanup procedure."

"What I don't understand," Leonard said, "is why didn't she just tell them? She didn't owe us a thing."

"Her own ethics, I suppose," I said. "You can't just let anyone come into a novelty shop and push you around. Next thing you know, you'll be giving the plastic dog crap away because bullies want you to."

"Damn," Leonard said.

"I guess our friends in the brown Ford were watching us when we rented the boat," I said.

"Hell," Tonto said, "I'm glad those guys are dead. They were kind of spooky. I thought I was kind of spooky, but those guys—"

"You are spooky," I said.

"But sweet around the eyes," Leonard said.

"Thing is, boys, there might be another player," Jim Bob said. "Reason we didn't see a brown Ford all the time was because it wasn't just a brown Ford following us."

"You mean we were being double-teamed," Leonard said. "That's why they could keep up with us, why they could watch us and we didn't see them. They decided to let us know about the Ford, put all our thinking there, but there was someone else watching."

"Why didn't they join with the Ford at the cabin?" I asked.

"Maybe they got their wires crossed, something as simple as that. Whatever, it didn't go according to plan."

"So whoever was the backup is on our tail now," Leonard said. "Maybe the ninja Hirem warned us about."

"There will be someone else," Tonto said, "and maybe someone beyond that, but it won't be quite so James Bond as all that. I'm going to get some sleep. I suggest we take another night to get it together, maybe go out and get a steak and have a little entertainment, find some poontang that don't cost more than an arm and a leg and won't give us the ball rot, then we head back."

"Since the poontang isn't USDA-inspected, I'll pass on that," Jim Bob said. "Come to think of it, these days, not so sure that inspection would mean much."

"Brett doesn't let me date," I said.

"Battin' for a different team," Leonard said.

"Whatever," Tonto said. "Me, I'm going to get some sleep."

Tonto finished off his coffee and went out.

"He's even more confident than me," Jim Bob said, "and that's a scary thing. I've been around, and I've seen some things too, just like you boys, and what I've learned the hard way is confidence is a lovely thing, but too much of it will get you cut a new asshole."

45

It wasn't that hard to convince Leonard and me to stay another day. We weren't the type that got to spend nights in good hotels and eat hotel food on murdering scumbags' money. I was also stiff and sore from our encounter with Big Guy and not exactly in the mood to deal with much.

That next night Tonto talked us into going to a karaoke bar he had found, and it wasn't far from the strip and it was pretty nice, and purposely ill lit, except for the stage where karaoke took place. We all went: Tonto, Jim Bob, Tim and Katie, and Leonard and I. They had alcoholic drinks, and I had one Diet Coke after another. I had long ago given up liquor, at least for the most part, and felt better having done so. Still, on this night I was thinking maybe I might have a whiskey, but the closest I got to one was thinking about it.

We were in the front row near the stage and the karaoke was as painful as it usually is.

And then one fine-looking blond woman came up and set her little white purse on the stage in front of her. She wasn't very big, looked to weigh about one-twenty, but was probably a little heavier because she was muscled in a lean sort of way that certainly gave her more weight, but it was weight carried in all the right places. She was young-looking, mid-twenties maybe, wearing white pedal pushers with white shoes with thick elevated heels, and she had on a white top. Her hair was gold as fresh wheat and she had a very fine face, and even from where we sat, we could see that her eyes were bright blue and she had a killer smile, and in the lights from the stage she looked as if all she needed was wings on her back and a message from Zeus.

Way it worked was the singers picked their tunes, and they were supposed to get two songs if they wanted it, and she got up and sang, and the thing was, she was good, very good. The first song was "Driving Wheel," and she did it justice. Her voice was strong and it kind of surprised some of the drinkers, who actually shut up and listened. A few couples began to dance, including Tim and Katie. When the song ended there was a lot of applause, and we, out there in the front row, were giving up a lot of it ourselves. While she had been singing, she had been looking at Tonto, and I glanced to see if he had noticed, and he had. He looked like a little kid that had just gotten attention from the best-looking girl in class.

The second song was Dion's "The Wanderer," and she knocked it out of the park, changing certain words to fit a woman's point of view, which made it clear to me she had done the song before and had given it thought. She moved a little as she sang, not much but a little, and with this girl not much was plenty. There was a seductive quality to her moves without them being overdone, and she had her eyes locked on Tonto.

Jim Bob leaned over to me, said, "Lucky sonofabitch."

"What's he got that I haven't got?" I said.

"No girlfriend that will kill him, and from the size of him, about two extra inches on his dick."

"Oh yeah, there's that," I said.

When the song was over there was applause again, and she ended up doing a third song, "Jim Dandy," and then she stepped down and a guy about half in the bag got up and sang a bad version of some tune I didn't recognize. The girl walked by Tonto and smiled at him. He said, "Buy you a drink?"

"Come to my table?" she said.

He did just that, and though I was happy for him, and wouldn't have bothered with her had she been interested in me because I loved Brett, I was also a little jealous. A woman like that could make a Baptist preacher kill his wife and set fire to his church. I glanced over and saw Tonto with her. He was helping her into a brown leather coat, and the way she stood she was out of the light and cloaked in shadow, and the light from the back door was on Tonto, and his dark face seemed oddly cherubic. I turned away and looked out at the dance floor.

Tim and Katie were still dancing, and the way they looked at each other, held each other tight, made me miss Brett something terrible. I was thinking about this when Leonard said, "I'm thinking of getting up there and singing."

"Now or never," I said.

Leonard caught a turn and got up and sang Charley Pride's "Is Anybody Goin' to San Antone," and he was good. He got some applause, and when he climbed down, we exchanged a few words, and then I looked where Tonto and the girl had been. Gone.

I said to Leonard and Jim Bob, "I think Tonto is trying to round up the cattle, and here we sit. If he goes off all night and drags in tomorrow about noon, I'm going to be pissed. He said we were leaving in the morning."

"Women will make you do crazy things," Jim Bob said, pushing his hat back on his head. "You got a sane guy, goes about his business, and then that gets wagged in his face, sanity and business go out the window. And for all his professionalism, I get the feeling Tonto can be pulled around by his ying-yang."

"But not us," I said.

"No sir, not us," Jim Bob said.

"Ha!" Leonard said.

"You know," Jim Bob said, "maybe it's a small thing, but the money, it's hidden under the floorboard of the van, and Tonto decides he's going to go off with missy, I don't like the idea of it being there. No biggie, but I'm going to see if I can catch him. I'll pretend it's laundry or something so the gal won't know."

"Let's all see if we can catch him," I said. "I'm ready to go back to the hotel."

Leonard went out on the floor and got the dancing kids, and as we were starting out, Jim Bob said, "You know, Tonto would probably have said something to us, he was leaving."

"Maybe," I said. "But we got two vehicles. He's probably thinking we could ride tight we had to. In fact, he's probably not thinking that much. Not with the good head."

"Point," Jim Bob said.

We were parked out back, so we went out the back way. The Escalade was next to the van in the lot, and when I looked at the van, I saw the interior light was on, but I didn't see Tonto or the girl. The air was chilly, and our breath came out in clouds.

Jim Bob said, "This whole deal smells funny all of a sudden."

We looked around the lot and didn't see anybody, just cars. Pulling our guns, we put them by our sides and walked out to the van. Jim Bob went around the front and I stayed on the right-hand side, and Leonard went around back. I told the kids, "Stand back."

They went over and stood on the other side of the Escalade.

I looked in the side window and saw Tonto lying facedown across the backseat. He looked as if he had just stretched out. His pants were down and his ass was like a big moon. I took a deep breath. Leonard opened the door on the other side the rest of the way—that's why the interior light was on, the door was partially open.

Jim Bob and I went around and joined Leonard and we looked down at Tonto. His face was turned to one side and his ear was full of blood. Jim Bob leaned in and looked and said, "Ah, goddamn it to hell. The woman."

Leonard leaned in and looked. "Something sharp, right in the ear. Ice pick maybe."

"Where the hell did she keep it?" I said.

"Purse," Jim Bob said.

Leonard checked Tonto's pulse, looked at us, shook his head. Blood was now running out of Tonto's ear and down his cheek, collecting on the seat.

"Just happened," Jim Bob said, turning to look around the parking lot. "Seconds ago. Damn."

We had put the duffel bag with the money in the back under one of the traps in the floor. We went around and looked. The trap was open. The money was gone.

"Knew where to look," Jim Bob said. "Guesswork, maybe, but good guesswork."

We closed the door, cutting the interior light, put our guns away, and all of us went over and got in the Escalade, Leonard behind the wheel. Jim Bob, sitting next to him, said, "I was just starting to like that asshole."

"He lived this long," Leonard said, "and then he decided to throw in with me and Hap. That was his mistake."

"I can't disagree with that," Jim Bob said. "Look, you guys, you go back to the hotel and get the bags, and I'll meet up with you later. Don't worry about me. I'm going to drive the van and take Tonto somewhere."

"And where will that be?" I said.

"I don't know. But I'm not just leaving him. He's part of the team. He's got someplace, or I'll find someplace. Marvin will know something. He was our connection to Tonto."

"We should have gone home," Leonard said.

"We should have done a lot of things," Jim Bob said. "You guys, you take the kids back, the money. Don't go back to your place, Hap. Call me at some point. I'll meet up with you."

"We—we have a blanket in the back," Tim said, "you want to cover him."

"Yeah," I said, "that's a good idea."

"We ought to look for her," I said.

"No point in that," Jim Bob said. "She's a pro. That little darling is cool as an ice tray. She let him think he was about to throw the spear in the bull's-eye, and then she got him. Had to have practice at it. One good shot with something sharp in the ear, and he never knew what hit him."

Me and Leonard and Jim Bob got out and I had the blanket. Leonard gave the car keys to Tim, said, "We're going to cover him up, you hear? Stay in the car."

Tim nodded. Katie took Tim's arm. "Cold," she said. "I feel so cold."

"You want," Leonard said, "warm the car up."

We went back to the van, and when we were sure no one was in the lot, we opened the door and pulled Tonto's pants up, got the van keys out of his pocket, and left him facedown with the blanket over him. Jim Bob shook the keys, said, "I'm going to take him now."

Jim Bob got in behind the wheel and pulled away. We watched him go.

When he was out of the lot, Leonard turned to me, said, "Hey, I didn't unlock the Escalade. It was already unlocked."

A chill went over me that wasn't due to the weather. We had been so distracted by Tonto, we hadn't really noticed, not then, and that meant she had jacked the car open, and then got out of there fast. Maybe when we came out the back we surprised her, came out and didn't give her time to lock things back.

I turned toward the Escalade. Tim had climbed behind the wheel and Katie was sitting up front with him. We started walking that way quickly, and then I saw Tim move slightly, and though I couldn't see what he was doing, I knew he was about to start the car, get some warmth from the heater.

I started to run, but then the car came apart in what seemed like slow motion and the parking lot turned red and there was a hot wind that picked me up and carried me away.

I was lying on my stomach, had the feeling I had been out for a moment. I rose up on my hands. My ears were ringing. I looked at where the Escalade had been sitting. It was a gutted wreck and flames were licking at it and I could see two dark shapes in what had been the front seat, burning. There was nothing to be done there.

Glancing around, I saw Leonard. He was lying on his face and he wasn't moving, not making a sound. The back of his coat was feeding a little blaze. I tried to get up, but didn't have the ability. Crawling toward him, I got there and slapped at his back with my hands, putting out the flames on his coat. Reaching out, I touched his pulse. He had one. Grateful for that, I put my face down on the cold parking lot cement and passed out.

46

The air was a little chill and my ears were ringing and throbbing and I didn't feel so good. I turned my head. It was a chore equal to the labors of Hercules. It was a hospital bed. I tried to call out, but my mouth was so dry I could only croak. I closed my eyes and went back to sleep.

When I awoke this time there was a man in a chair by my bed, and I knew him. Drake. He looked at me like he really wanted to be somewhere else. He said, "When you two boys fuck up, you like to compound it, don't you?"

I didn't answer. I thought about nodding, but was afraid my head would fall off. Overall, I felt as if I had been rode hard and put up wet, and then shot for having bad ankles.

Drake got up and poured some water from a pitcher into a plastic glass with a straw. He brought it over and took hold of a little control on a cable and touched it. The head of the bed raised up, and when it was positioned, he stopped it and held the water for me to sip.

It was the best water I had ever had. I was convinced it was the best water anyone ever had. When my throat was wet enough, I managed to say, "Leonard?"

"They have to dig some more car shrapnel out of his thighs, but he's pretty much in the same condition you are, which is burned a little and banged up a lot."

"How bad?" I said.

"Not that bad. Not so bad the two of you won't recover and retain your native good looks."

"What are you doing here?"

"I'm asking myself that," Drake said. "Thing is, they found you boys in the parking lot, and whoever was in the car. That would be Hirem's boy and the girlfriend, right?"

I nodded.

"That's all I know about the deal," Drake said. "You were supposed to find them and find some money."

"Batting zero," I said.

"I figured."

"Again, how come you're here?"

"Your license, Leonard's. Had your address on it. My town. So they called me, see if I could find out who you were, what you were doing here. I knew both of you, of course."

"And you bothered to come?"

"I'm trying to figure why. I was thinking you two got off easy, and then they call, tell me what happened, and I'm thinking maybe not so easy. So I call a contact I got in the FBI, and he says you two are off their charts, officially anyway. But some things have changed, and they're feeling kindly."

"What's changed?" I said.

"Someone popped those two FBI agents, and that same someone didn't do Hirem any good. Tortured him."

"They wanted to know where we were searching."

"That's right, and it looks like they found out. And any information he would have given the FBI, any money might have been recovered from illicit business, they aren't getting that now. But the main thing was the names Hirem would have named didn't get named, and now there's nothing but his corpse. Done deal."

"I think the bad guys killed a lady named Annie too," I said, and told Drake about it.

He said, "The FBI has decided not to forget you. They've decided your heart was in the right place. They're going to make sure there are no charges."

"If there were charges," I said, "what would they be for?"

"They have no idea, and neither do I, but we figure you did something. And they figure the something you did was to their benefit. And they figure it was a good thing they found these four guys in a Ford over near Lake O' the Pines, and they were good and dead and they all had records, and somehow, they think it just might be possible they are connected to problems they have, and it just might be possible you and Leonard solved those problems. As for the explosion, and the guns they found on you, you guys are getting a clean slate soon as you're able to get out of here. There's local cops watching your rooms. FBI is sponsoring that indirectly. Directly, they aren't doing squat, and everything I told you they would deny. They found out you had a room in a hotel, that there were two rooms. One for the kids?"

I lied. "Yep."

"They had your bags sent over, after they went through them. Oh, by the way. The local newspaper, it read that four people had died in that blast. That would include you and Leonard. So there are some bad people think you're dead. At least for the moment. Best just to take this as a freebie and not ask any questions."

"How long have we been here?"

"Three days."

"Damn," I said.

"What about Brett?" Drake said.

"She doesn't know what happened," I said. "I'd like to keep it that way for now. She's out of sight and maybe out of mind of these tin-pot gangsters. She knew I was hurt, or Leonard, she'd be here. I don't want that. Not now."

"I can understand that."

"This isn't exactly your jurisdiction," I said.

"Yeah, I got no authority, but I got concern for my citizens, and that includes you two jackasses. And my friend in the FBI, I'm sort of his and the agency's unofficial mouthpiece. What they want you to do is be finished."

"All right," I said.

"And mean it."

"You know, the person who blew up the car, they got the money."

"It wouldn't be stashed away somewhere, would it?" Drake said.

"Not by us."

"That person blew up the car, you know who it is?"

"No," I said, and I didn't mention Jim Bob or Tonto. I was hoping he didn't know about them, and I was hoping the FBI didn't either. I didn't mention the woman who had killed Tonto. She was mine. I didn't mention the money had been in the van, figured Drake would logically think it had been taken from the Escalade, maybe our hotel room.

"These cops watching you, they're only going to be here one more day. So you got to get well quick or hope nobody from the bad side of life is hunting you two down."

"I'm feeling perky already," I said, and this was true.

"Another thing, no charge for the hospital stay. FBI, they're giving you a gift out of some funds they don't have and didn't give you. Understand?"

I agreed that I did. I said, "I'm surprised the FBI even cared."

"Covering their ass is all," Drake said, standing up. "Well, I've had it with you two. I'm going home. And next time I see you, if it's just a parking ticket, I'm going to see there's some way to throw you under the jail."

He was almost to the door when I said, "Drake."

He turned.

"Thanks, man."

He nodded and went out.

I lay there and tried to put it together. Jim Bob had been right. There had been someone else in on the deal. Maybe an accomplice to our Dracula, Big Guy, or maybe as hired backup. Could have even been someone Big Guy didn't know about. Someone to watch the watchers. Did that watcher do the torturing of Annie and Hirem and the FBI folks, or was it Big Guy and his pals? Probably never figure that one out.

Bottom line, the she devil was on our ass when we left Lake O' the Pines, and Tonto was not quite the super ace he thought. Or he'd just gotten tired and, in the end, horny. She lured him out there and killed him and took the money. She had seen the kids and me and Leonard in the Escalade, and we were the hired hits. Anyone else got in the way, like Tonto, they had to go. But she figured one bomb would take Tim and Katie and me and Leonard out. And if she was lucky, it would take the van too, Jim Bob, or anyone else in that wrong place at the wrong time.

She had made one error. Leaving the door on the Escalade unlocked. Probably because we came out more quickly than she expected and she had to get away, forgot the door. Had seen us come out and was gone like a ghost before we knew it. Bottom line was she had succeeded with the bomb. Set it so when the engine cranked, or when the heater was turned on, it would blow. It was just luck Leonard and I had survived.

I really hated that bitch.

Good-looking as all get-out, but still a bitch.

47

A little over two weeks later and out of the hospital we joined Marvin, and we all went out to Arizona. Leonard had tried to patch things up with John again, but John had got religion, and when that happens, common sense, logic, and the obvious fly out the window of the brain like a horde of bees.

Jim Bob we had talked to, and he had taken care of the van and Tonto. Turned out there was no real home where Tonto lived, just a cell phone number that wouldn't be answered again and a post office box where any mail he might get would pile up. Marvin told Jim Bob all of this, and Jim Bob took Tonto in his van and drove the van off to a place run by people he knew who owned an auto farm, old cars with a car crusher that made them flat. They used the crusher with Tonto in the van and then they put the cube of metal in the back of a truck and it was dumped in a deep wet place not far from Houston. Jim Bob said the people did it for him were longtime friends and that there were other crushed cars with crushed people in them in the deep waters nearby. He said he was on call if we needed him again, and we might, but I didn't want him now; didn't want to put anyone else into what we had created. It was our mess to fix.

There was one other thing. He said he had found the photograph of me and Leonard and Cindy the Bear in the van before he had it crushed with Tonto in it, and he mailed the photo to us.

Leonard and I, and Brett, we were all in Arizona now, but we weren't all in the same place. Marvin and his family were together with relatives, and we had been there to visit but the atmosphere was not warm. Gadget couldn't look us in the eye, and her mother and grandmother and great-grandmother made us feel as though we were only begrudgingly welcome. We didn't stay long. Brett, who had been there, was glad to leave; her ass whipping of Gadget hung over the household like a little dark cloud. We were given a rental the family owned that was empty. It was a condo with a little backyard next to other little backyards. There was limited furniture in the joint, just a bed, a couch, a table, and some chairs, and Leonard slept on the couch. On this day we were all sitting outside and the weather was cool but not too cold. We were wearing coats and sitting at a table, Brett and I close together holding hands. On the table were some empty plates that had recently held tuna fish sandwiches with apple cut up in them, heavy on mayonnaise, and there had been potato chips and coffee. I was sitting there enjoying the thought of what I had eaten, simple but good, and thinking about some of the vanilla wafers we had in the house.

"So, this hit person, she thinks you're dead?" Brett said.

"For now. But before word gets out, we thought we might go see her in person."

"You think you could hurt a woman, Hap . . . on purpose?"

"Hey, he punched Gadget," Leonard said.

"You're talking about killing her, though," Brett said.

"Woman, man, shemale, they come after me with a gun, a knife, a pointed stick, I don't like it. And I don't want her coming around again. Thing is, she's the best they've sent after us, and it's only luck I'm here to hold your lovely hand."

"And you didn't get your dick blown off," Brett said.

"That too," I said.

"I consider that an important part of our relationship," she said.

"As do I," I said.

"You got it blown off," Leonard said, "you'd be holding hands with a plastic love doll. Brett would be out of here."

"Not true," Brett said. "He's still got a tongue."

"That's a little too much from the instructional manual," Leonard said.

"Yeah, since when are you grossed out by anything?" I said.

"Since I've had a tragic near-death experience. Did you know, when

I was knocked out on the ground out there, shrapnel in my shapely loins and lower stomach, I saw a white light, and I wanted to go to it, because when I got there, and if God was there, I was gonna whip his ass for what he'd let happen to us."

Me and Leonard touched fists.

Brett leaned over and kissed me. Her eyes were misty. I said, "I'm fine."

"We could stay here," she said. "I could get a nurse job, you could find work. Arizona is nice."

"Need those East Texas trees," I said. "And besides, I couldn't live with myself I didn't find that bitch and put a bullet in her head. And yeah, I can do it, woman or no woman. I don't want to live under the umbrella of her coming back. She thinks she's safe and we're dead, but I'm going to find her."

"Ditto to that," Leonard said.

"Can I go back with you?" Brett said.

"You do whatever you want to do, as always, but I'd rather you not. I think it'll be easier you don't. Leonard and I have been in this kind of thing before."

"Maybe not just like this," Leonard said.

"All right," I said. "Not just like this, but we can handle ourselves, now that we know what we're up against."

"That didn't sound all that convincing," Brett said.

"Well," I said, "I guess I'm not all that convinced. But I'd prefer you stay here, let us go after her."

"What was she like?" Brett asked.

"We don't know. All we know is what we told you, but when it comes to getting the job done, she's something. The whole thing with Tonto, that probably happened so quick he was still getting his hard-on. And the way she wired that bomb up, she's experienced."

"Didn't look that old, either," Leonard said.

"No, she didn't."

"You have some idea how to find her?" Brett said.

"Yep," I said, "I do. Let me ask you something—how's Gadget?"

"You could feel the cold air back at their place, couldn't you?"

"Yep."

"Marvin, he tried to make me feel welcome, but it got so I expected the women of the household to jump me. Except for Gadget. She had

had her butt whipped soundly. I tell you, I was ready to take them all on, do a little head knocking."

"You're just the woman to do it," I said.

"Damn right," she said.

"You can stay here, alone?"

"Better than at their place. The atmosphere there is poisonous."

"Good. And now, Leonard and I, and because you are one of us by proxy, should celebrate our survival from a big car bomb with some vanilla wafers."

"Nope," Leonard said. "Ain't gonna happen. I got hungry last night, and I felt I needed a personal celebration."

"You ate them all?" Brett said.

"Everything but the sack, and I licked that."

"You turd," Brett said.

"And there are no more Dr Peppers. I had a kind of festival of life."

48

Marvin wanted to go back with us, but we made him feel bad about his leg and told him what a burden he would be and it was best he stayed out of action; it was true, of course. We did get some information we needed from him, though, and then we were in Leonard's car and he drove us back to East Texas in a two-and-a-half-day run, except for a four-hour stop in Cross Plains, Texas, where we slept a couple hours in a motel, and then we had to go over and see the Robert E. Howard house because Leonard liked his Conan stories and wouldn't hear of passing it up. I tried to explain to him that we were in a hurry because we had to find and shoot someone, but he wasn't moved, so we did a tour there and then got back on the road.

In the car Leonard said, "I get killed, I know I've seen where one of my favorite authors lived and shot himself to death."

"You get killed, what you saw isn't going to matter."

"Good point," Leonard said.

With the information we had gotten from Marvin, we drove to my place briefly to get a few things, including a sawed-off shotgun, handguns, and a deer rifle. Then we drove over to No Enterprise in the dead of night, on out to where Marvin told us Conners lived. As Marvin had explained, it was out in the country some, and you could take a road that went up a hill, and you could look down on Conners' place, which was on a few acres with a little pond and a lot of junked cars that in the night looked like huge insects. We drove up there behind a little clutch of pines and some gnarly persimmon trees and sat. There were no lights in the house, which meant Conners could be asleep, but there wasn't a cop car in the yard, so we figured he wasn't home yet. Probably out doing something corrupt.

Being true professionals, and having driven really far, we both fell asleep.

When we awoke the day was bright and the sun was high. I looked out the windshield between the trees and saw the house looked the same. Still no cop car. We got out and crapped in the bushes and wiped on napkins we had in the car, and a little later on we took pee breaks and drank some bottled water and peed some more. That's the trouble when you're an over-forty tough guy. You have to pee a lot.

We got out of the car and washed our hands with some of the bottled water, and washed our faces, and tried to figure if we were well hid up on the hill, and decided as long as no one came up the little hunting road, we were snug as bugs in a rug. From down there, Conners' house, the only way we could be seen was if someone was looking for us.

We had some vanilla cookies with us, and a couple of cold burritos, and we ate those for lunch and drank some more of the water. If our guy didn't show soon, we'd be out of food, water, and napkins on which to wipe our asses.

A hawk flew into a tree above us, and we looked up at it and it looked down at us. We didn't worry it any. It was a large hawk and it cast a big shadow in the cold, bright day. Bored with us, it flew off.

We took turns taking walks along the hunting road to keep our circulation up, and then we took turns sleeping in the backseat of the car while the other watched the house below.

After a couple of hour naps, I felt pretty good, and got a paperback of an Andrew Vachss novel Leonard had in the car and read from that, and then it was his turn, and he read from it, losing my place in the process.

The sun dipped down and the night soaked in, and it got cold. I had slipped out of my jacket during the day, but now I was in it again, and we climbed out of the car and eased down among the trees, closer to the edge of the hill, and looked at the house and waited for some kind of revelation.

Leonard pulled his jacket around him and hunched his shoulders. He reached into his coat pocket and took out a blackjack and gave it to me. He said, "I got one, now you got one."

"We are same alike," I said.

"Only I am a handsome black color, and you are white of skin and small of dick."

"Except for that, we're same alike."

Another hour or so passed, and then we saw headlights on the road below, coming toward the house. The road ran past the house, but it didn't go far before it dead-ended, so we figured this had to be our man.

Sure enough, the car was a cop car and it pulled in the drive, and two men got out, dressed in cop clothes and holstered guns. One of them was Conners. He had looked big to me before, but recently I had seen Big Guy and he made everyone look small, even Conners. The guy with him was short and fat, but he had broad shoulders and carried himself in a manner that gave the impression he might be a load if you messed with him.

We, of course, were going to mess with both of them.

The fat guy was carrying a six-pack. They went inside the house.

Leonard said, "Ain't that a shame. Man of the law buying beer, carrying it around in his patrol car."

"Let's go down and see can we have a little talk with them, maybe set them right on their civic duty."

"All right."

"But we don't shoot anybody. I'm all worn out on shooting. At least until we get to our gal."

"I will do my best," Leonard said.

Lights came on in the house as we walked down the hill and the lights were all concentrated in one place, and there was a thin white curtain at the window in the lighted room. We could see their shadows moving across the back of the curtain and eased up close to the house with our guns in hand.

I crept up to the window and looked. I could see through a crack in the curtain. They were sitting at a table and Conners was saying something that was making the fat man laugh.

Leonard slipped away from the window and went around back. I ducked under the window and slid over to the front porch and went up on it and nudged back the screen door and touched the knob, seeing if it was locked. It wasn't.

I took a deep breath, carefully turned the knob, and gently pressed the door back and edged in and then closed it without really pushing it all the way shut. Now I could hear them talking and I could see a slit of light that let me know there was a doorway and hallway and that the hallway led into the kitchen. I looked across the room, letting my eyes adjust, then made my approach through the opening across the way and down the hall. When I got to the lighted door I saw that the back door was at the far end of the hall, and that's where Leonard was. If it had been unlocked, he would have already been in.

With the gun held ready, I peeked around the corner and saw the fat man had his back to me and Conners was crossing to the refrigerator. I walked across the open doorway with my eyes on them, but made it all the way across without being seen. I tiptoed to the back door and figured out the lock by touch, and was able to twist it so that the sound it made was hardly noticeable. Then I opened the door and Leonard came in.

We went down the hall, and then with me in front, we stepped into the kitchen. When we did, Conners, who was coming back from the fridge, saw us and started to draw his gun. I said, "I wouldn't, unless you want a hole in your belly."

The fat man with his back to us dropped his hand to his holster. Leonard said, "That goes for you too, fat boy."

49

Leonard switched his gun to his other hand and reached in his pocket and pulled out the little blackjack and hit fat boy across the back of the neck hard enough to make him fall out of his chair and land on one knee.

"Goddamn," the fat man said, holding the back of his neck. "That hurt."

"No joke," Leonard said. "That's to show we mean business. We been shot at, beat on, nearly drowned, and had the shit scared out of us by some guns and Big Guy and a dead alligator, so we're in no mood to screw around."

Conners was still standing. I had my gun pointed at him. Leonard reached from behind and took Fat Boy's pistol away.

I said to Conners, "Unfasten your gun belt and let it drop."

While he did that, I kept my pistol pointed at him. When the belt hit the floor, I said, "Kick it my way."

He did and I picked it up and slung the belt over my shoulder, his gun at my back.

"Sit down, Conners," I said.

"Get up, fat man," Leonard said. "Find the chair."

When they were both seated, I went over and leaned on the refrigerator, said, "You know we heard you kind of set things up for shooters for the Dixie Mafia."

"They don't call themselves that," Conners said.

"I don't care if they call themselves the Dixie Bowling League. You know what I mean."

"You say," Conners said.

"Don't he love to talk?" Leonard said. "Hey, fat boy, ain't you got nothin' to say?"

"I don't know a thing," the fat man said. "I did, I wouldn't tell you."

"I think you would," Leonard said, and swung the blackjack again, hitting Fat Boy on the neck, knocking him out of the chair.

"You just stay on the floor," Leonard said. "It'll save you the trouble of getting up."

"You're tough with that sap in your hand," Conners said. "You wouldn't be so tough without it."

Leonard put the sap in his coat pocket and took off his coat. "We can see."

"Nope," I said. "I know you can whip him."

"Yeah, but he don't," Leonard said.

The fat man on the ground said, "Conners would tie you in a knot."

"See," Leonard said. "He don't know it either. Get up, Conners. Let's you and me dance."

"Not a good idea," I said. "Having a macho queer moment. Don't do it."

Conners got up and I decided I wouldn't shoot him. I pointed the gun at the fat man on the ground. "You crawl over this way a piece."

Conners came around the table. Leonard moved a little to the side of the table, and then they were facing each other, six feet apart. Conners hulked over Leonard, though Leonard's shoulders were easily as broad as his.

Conners had his hands up. So did Leonard. They stood that way for a long moment. Leonard said, "You waitin' on an engraved invitation?"

Conners moved then, swung. Leonard ducked under it and hit Conners in the nuts with a right uppercut, then he swiveled and kicked at the inside of Conners' leg, catching him just above the ankle. It brought him down.

Conners did a push-up and Leonard let him. When Conners was up, he said, "Them chink tricks ain't gonna help you none."

"They seem to be working all right," Leonard said.

Conners came again, throwing a right cross that was so slow you could have gone out and bought a paper and been back in time to dodge it. It went over Leonard's right shoulder, and Leonard kicked out and caught Conners on the side of the leg, mid-thigh. The nerve cluster there lit up and Conners went down with a yelp. When he hit the floor, Leonard kicked him in the jaw. Conners fell on his back and groaned.

"You can get up if you want to," Leonard said.

I will say this, Conners could have just lain there, but he didn't. He got up and came again, and this time Leonard moved to the right and jabbed right-handed and caught Conners over the eye enough to make him step back, and then it was like a wolf at the slaughter. Leonard hooked Conners in the belly with a left, and then it was a double right jab to the face, and finally Leonard kicked out with his front leg and caught Conners in the lower abdomen and sent him flailing back against the table, which crashed underneath his weight, causing the fat man to slide on the floor and out of the way.

Conners lay in the wreckage of the table, bleeding from the mouth.

Leonard looked at Fat Boy. "Now, how about you?"

The fat man shook his head.

"Damn skippy," Leonard said, then looked at me. "That's what I meant to do to that big guy."

"Me too," I said, "but it didn't work out."

"Yeah, I just couldn't get warmed up."

"Was that it?"

Leonard toed the fat man a little, making him roll over on the floor so he could get to the refrigerator. He found a can of beer in there and brought it out and popped the top and took a foam-dripping swig. "There, assholes. I drink your beer. I kick your ass. And you will give us some information."

When Conners and the fat boy were back in their chairs, Leonard took the sap out of his pocket, said, "Just so you know, I'm ready to warm you up again."

"Tell us about the hit folk," I said. "We're tired of getting shot at. Tell us about who you sent after us, and just to make it easy on you, don't say you don't know what we're talking about. Just talk or I'm going to give you to Leonard again."

"We just do as we're told," Conners said.

"And why is that?" I said.

"Why do you think?"

"Money," I said, "and now that you're in, you don't want someone coming after you, am I right?"

"Something like that."

"But you're a bigger dog in all this than you've let on. You, and probably your fat friend here—certainly your fat friend—you pick the hitters, so you're pretty well connected. What the fuck is your name, fat friend?"

"Sykes," he said.

"I prefer Fat Boy," I said. "Now, how goes it, Conners? How's it work?"

"I've made some connections over the years," Conners said. "I'm a cop. You meet people that know people, and you find you can make deals."

"Sweet deals."

Conners nodded.

"So, to get right to the fuckin', no foreplay, where is the woman you hired to kill us?"

"Woman?"

"Yep. She hit one of our pards, and blew up Hirem's kid and girl-friend, and put me and Leonard in a hospital for a while, and just so you know, we're mad."

Conners smiled. "Vanilla Ride. I didn't even know it was a woman. I got her contact a couple years back. She's made ten hits for what you call the Dixie Mafia. She's made hits for others. Made them through me. Sometimes those hits are more than one person. You two are supposed to be dead."

"It wasn't from want of trying," I said.

"I've never even seen her, or a lot of the hitters. I got contacts, I told you."

"Tell us how to contact Vanilla Ride. Me and Leonard thought we'd drop in, say hello."

"I contact her by mail. No e-mail. No phone number. I drop her a letter from a false address to a P.O. box, and the letter has names on it, some general information, where these people are. Then we get a FedEx from her with the names we gave her and she's got a line drawn through them when the job is done, and then the big dogs pay her at that P.O. box. She, huh? A woman. Now that's something. I thought Vanilla Ride was some big guy with a shotgun. And you guys, you were on her list with lines drawn through your names, drawing flies somewhere. That's what I was thinking, what I was hoping."

"She speculated a bit too much," Leonard said. "We're still here. Tired and pissed off, but here. She was on our tail, but she got cocky."

"Got a question," I said. "Did Vanilla Ride return the money?"

"No, not yet," Conners said. "Someday it'll just turn up on the right doorstep. No one will see who dropped it, it'll just show up. She knows everyone in the business, where they live, what they do. That's what makes her so deadly. Damn, a woman. Sounds like my kind of broad."

"What's the address?" I said.

"I give it to you, you'll kill us," Conners said.

"You don't give it to us I'll kill you," I said. "I'm in no mood to play games, man. Give me the address."

"You'll let us go?" Conners said.

"I don't want any more blood on my hands than I already have."

Leonard looked at me. I said, "I mean that, Leonard."

"Yeah," Leonard said. "I know you do."

"He wants us dead," Sykes said.

"Yep," Leonard said. "I do."

"So how's it gonna be?" Conners said.

"It's gonna be nice enough, you give us that address."

"It's a post office box in Arkansas."

"All right. Give it to us, and let me just say this. If we go on a wild-goose chase, or anyone gets on our tail, we will come right back to you and kill your asses dead, and then shoot you daily for a week just to make ourselves happy. Tell us what we want to know, this is a way you get out of it scot-free, but you screw with us, we hold a grudge."

"Hell, I hope you find her," Conners said. "No idea she was a woman, but you find her, from what I know of her work, you'll wish you hadn't."

"You tell us how to find her, you get to live," I said. "Hell, man, it's your choice."

Leonard looked at me like a puzzled dog, said, "They hired Vanilla Ride for the Dixie Mafia. She tried to kill us. What makes these assholes so special?"

"I want who hit our man and those kids and took the money and tried to blow us up, so I'm willing to trade."

"How do we know your word is good?" Conners said.

"You know as much as we know yours is good," I said. "Make a choice. Now."

50

Stopping by the all-night station/store in No Enterprise, we bought some traveling goods and filled up the gas tank and I looked for the guy in the garage, but he and his fuck book were not present and the door was locked. It was too late to work and too late to read. Maybe he was home doing what he had been reading about. Most likely he had the book in his left hand and himself in his right.

One of the things we bought was some bright blue stationery and envelopes. I wrote down the address Conners had given us on it, put it to Vanilla Ride, and then I wrote Conners' address, which he had been so kind to give us, in the left-hand corner as the sender. Since they couldn't phone her or find her any quicker than we could, I wanted to get things started. I wrote "Hi" on a piece of the blue stationery and folded it up and put it in the bright blue envelope and laid it on the dash of the car, waiting until we could buy a stamp.

We started for Arkansas, cruising along not listening to music, just quiet for a long time. We had left Conners and Sykes tied up in their kitchen with lamp cords and stripped sheets. I figured they'd work themselves loose in a couple hours or so.

Leonard finally broke the silence, said, "You know that was stupid, letting them live?"

"I do. But I think I have to draw the line somewhere."

"You draw the line on them but you're traveling all the way to Arkansas to kill Vanilla Ride."

"It seems a little more personal."

"I see them all as one big nest."

"I'm sure you're right, but I guess I've decided to focus my anger all on one, the one put the bomb under the car and killed Tonto and those kids and gave us a stay in the hospital."

"All right," Leonard said. "But you know those guys aren't through with us."

"Yep."

"We'll deal with them again."

"Yep."

"I thought Conners was at the top of our list. You said to put stars by his name."

"Yep."

"So why didn't we just nip it in the bud?"

"I've tried my best to explain."

"And your explanation sucks."

"I just couldn't shoot them out of their chairs like that, in cold blood."

"What if Vanilla Ride is sitting in a chair?"

"I'll ask her to stand up."

"You'll be killing a woman."

"She may be of that gender, but she's no woman to me. I'm not even sure she's human. Conners and Sykes do it for money, and Vanilla Ride gets paid, but, man, I got a feeling she loves that stuff. She liked baiting Tonto along like that, getting him to the point where he thought he was gonna get him a piece, and then, wham, he's out of there. That's cold, brother. And those kids."

"I still don't see a difference. She took the money. In the end, it's all about money and they all want the money."

"Maybe, Leonard, truth is, in the end, there's no difference at all. Them. Us. We're all killers, and in the end, the worms sort us out."

There was no real address for Vanilla Ride, just the P.O. box Conners had told us about, and the rest of the address was a town called Sylvester, Arkansas. What I had in mind was staking out the post office, waiting till she came to collect her mail. It wasn't exactly a plan up there with Robert E. Lee, but then again, it was me and Leonard. We're not dumb, but strategy is not our long suit.

It was about three hours to Arkansas, and it was still night when we got there, and we stopped at a station and put more gas in the car and checked our map to make sure we were heading the right way, then pushed on, like Mounties after our man, or in this case, our woman.

Daylight was breaking as we drove into the mountains amongst the trees, and there was a light frost on our windshield. The roads grew narrow, the trees thickened. Leonard rolled down the window to get some air, to keep himself alert, so as not to drive off a cliff. He let it blow cold on his face for a while, then touched the electric window button and sent it up. I looked ahead at the sun-stained road and the countryside and listened to the hum of the heater.

51

Sylvester looks almost unreal, a kind of holdout from frontier days, but the truth is it isn't all that old. It was founded some fifty years ago and built to resemble a frontier town, and they've kept it that way. Traffic was pretty intense for a place that claimed twenty thousand people, but the traffic would be the tourists, because there's a nice lake nearby with plenty of fish and the scenery is beautiful. It's the kind of place people come to rest and not Jet-Ski or mountain-climb or party all night. There are a few restaurant clubs, and from what I could see they catered to the older set as well. We parked and headed toward the post office. I read on a sign for a place called the Buckin' Horse Saloon that it opened at four for dinner, had entertainment, and closed at ten. If the horse bucked, it did it quietly and at reasonable hours.

At the post office, which was one open window commanded by an old man in a plaid shirt with a postal name tag (Jake), I bought a stamp for our bright blue envelope and mailed it. We walked around the post office and saw there were rows and rows of mailboxes with thick glass windows in them so you could see when you got mail, and finally we located the one that went with our envelope.

"All right," Leonard said. "She has to come here."

"Except she won't," I said.

"Surrogate?"

"Of course. She'd be too easy to find otherwise. Why do you think I got that bright blue envelope?"

"Ah, but what if she gets lots of mail and whoever picks it up mixes it with other envelopes, and we're watching from a distance. What if it's night?"

"Oh. Well, I didn't think about that."

Leonard sighed. "Guess we got what we got."

We walked across the street to a hotel and Leonard stayed outside to watch the post office while I went inside. At the desk I talked the clerk into giving us a window facing the street, so we could enjoy the view, and then I took Leonard's spot on the sidewalk and he walked back to the car for our little bit of supplies.

For the next week we hung out in that hotel room, looking at the post office out the window, hoping we'd be able to spot the blue envelope come out in someone's hot little hands. From time to time one of us would walk over to the post office and look through the little window of her mailbox, and we could see the blue envelope was there, waiting, and no one had been in to get it.

We took shifts so one or the other could go out and buy food. We also bought underwear and we didn't shave, under the odd notion that maybe if Vanilla Ride saw us she wouldn't recognize us unshaved. It was lame, but again, it was what we had.

First day we were there we started seeing some interesting-looking guys showing up at the post office, watching for what we were watching for, I guess. But had they been smart enough to send her a brightly colored envelope? I thought not.

They couldn't hang around the place any more than us, but they did get a room in, you guessed it, our hotel. I passed one of them, a lean, greasy-haired fellow, on my way out to pick up some sandwiches. He was sitting in the lobby, and when he saw me, he watched me go out, and I didn't let him know I was watching him. Across the street, in front of the post office, another guy sat in a car, getting out now and then to feed quarters into the parking meter. He was tall and fat, with very little hair on his head. Sometimes he moved the car and parked elsewhere, but he was always parked so he could see the post office. I guess the other two were out buying sandwiches and underwear, same as us. But they all swapped out from time to time, and it was my guess they weren't lawmen and they weren't from the IRS and I doubted they were the men in black since their wardrobes were varied. All I was certain of was I had seen four of them over a period of time.

Back in the room with our sandwiches, Leonard said, "You know, this sucks. Those guys were sent here from Conners, and had we put a hole in his head, him and his fat friend, we'd be sitting here without contention, except for Vanilla Ride herself. But now, thanks to you, we got her and them."

"I know."

"You don't mind?"

"Hell, yeah, I mind," I said. "But I did what I could do, Leonard. That's it. I don't know what to tell you. It's my flawed nature."

Leonard shook his head and patted me on the shoulder. "I love my little idealist. In a gay sort of manly way, of course."

"Of course."

"Look at it this way: if we'd killed those two, you wouldn't have to kill these four. Or, worse yet, get killed by them."

"You are a goddamn sage, Leonard."

52

One day we're in the hotel room, looking out the window, having sucked down too much coffee, my personal plumbing backed up to where my insides felt like a brick factory, and I'm thinking a little fruit juice might be good, when Leonard, who is nibbling around the edges of a vanilla cookie, said, "These guys, they here for us or Vanilla Ride?"

"Maybe both," I said. "Could be they've decided she needs to go too. Maybe because she hasn't returned the money."

"You think she'll keep it?"

I shook my head. "I don't think that's her plan. I think she's a professional. But I also think the people she's dealing with are falling apart. The talent they've sent out has cost them big-time, and it would probably be nice to get the money back, but they want us because we're a couple of amateurs who have survived everything they've got, including Vanilla Ride. My guess is they haven't paid her because she didn't finish the job, because we didn't die, and now she's got their money on top of having not wiped us out."

"She's got more money than they think," Leonard said.

"That too."

"So, Hirem lied about the amount of money, which was probably because there was extra he was going to give the Mummy and his friend to make sure his son got a good deal with the FBI, and then they got whacked, and then we got the money, and then Vanilla Ride got the money, and she's thinking, well, they don't pay me, I got a little windfall. They do pay me, I keep the rest."

"That's the way I figure," I said. "And the Dixie Mafia is thinking they're running low on guys, and they aren't considered such bad dudes if they can't stop a couple of yokels from East Texas, and if they just quit, that looks bad too, so they got to keep them coming. And now, since Vanilla didn't finish the job, and we're on her tail, they're starting to see her as expendable. That way they don't pay her and she's dead and they're rid of her. I bet on top of all that, finding out she was a woman chapped their ass."

"If only she had been black," Leonard said.

"Yep, that would have been aces."

"And gay."

"Better yet. And we may have it all wrong," I said. "Guys following us could be just very persistent insurance salesmen."

53

One night I'm at the window, and the brilliance of the streetlights is all there is in the way of action, and what do my wandering eyes see but a lemon-colored Volkswagen pulling up at the curb in what might be called a sprightly manner, or what I might call in my East Texas vernacular, pretty goddamn fast. A young man, gangly as a puppet, with a dark mustache and a cap from under which shoulder-length black hair hung, got out and went into the post office, walking heavy.

I looked at my nifty Warner Bros. Looney Tunes watch with all the great cartoon characters on it with my flashlight and saw the time was three a.m. The post office lobby was always open. You could go in at any time. Just an old-fashioned town with an old-fashioned mailbox connected to an old-fashioned killer who liked to live quietly in Arkansas. I figured not a lot of folk were out and about at three a.m. in a town like this, and if they were, how many just decided it was necessary to check the mail at this time of night?

It could happen, but it made me curious.

He came out quickly and got in the Volkswagen and started up the hill. I yelled Leonard awake, and since he was already dressed, he only had to roll into his shoes, and then the two of us were on our way downstairs, pulling our coats over our holstered handguns and our manly buttocks.

The fat guy had his turn in the lobby chairs, and when he saw us he stood up and a magazine fell out of his lap and flapped to the ground. Leonard gave him a little wave. We went out and got in our car,

Leonard driving, and he cranked it up and started up the hill in the direction the Volkswagen had gone. I looked back and saw the fat man was on the curb with a cell phone to his ear. They weren't any niftier than we were, which in real life is often the case. There just aren't that many James Bonds or Mike Hammers outside of the pages of books or the brightness of film.

Of course, Vanilla Ride, now she was another matter altogether. That woman was spooky like Tonto was spooky, only more so, because she had killed Tonto right when he thought he was about to visit the fun house.

That's just mean.

The road wound up through the mountains, and at one point, going around a curve, I could look back through a split in the trees and see car lights moving along the road behind us. I said, "I figure that's them."

"Yeah," Leonard said, "that is some good deduction there, Sherlock."

We hadn't caught up with the Volkswagen, which had to be hauling some serious ass, and we weren't all that far ahead of our friends the ugly thugs. I said, "When we get around this corner coming up, let me out."

"Are you nuts?"

"If it goes well, I'll catch up with you at the bottom of the hill. If you look back and see it isn't me running down the hill to leap into your arms, and instead it's them in their car, or even on foot, then I suggest you drive like you're in a stock-car race."

I climbed over the seat and pulled the backseat down and got the sawed-off shotgun out of the trunk and a box of shells. When we climbed up the hill and got to where it curved, Leonard stopped and let me out, said, "Nice knowing you, dumb ass."

"You just watch for me."

He motored away and I got back in the woods a bit and hunkered down and waited. More time went by than I expected, or so it seemed. Out here there were no streetlights and the moonlight wasn't much, and it took me a while to start to adjust to being able to see in the dark. My mouth was dry, and hunkering down like that was starting to hurt my calves, and I was about to switch positions when I saw headlights coming and then I heard the roar of a car.

When I could see the car well enough to determine that it was the car I had seen our trackers in, I braced the shotgun against me and waited until the car was almost even with me, and fired a little in advance, the blast lighting up the night and knocking the right front tire to shreds. The car swerved and twisted and threw up dirt as it went over the other side of the road and down a hill and out of sight. I heard a crash, trotted across the road and looked down. It was about a thirty-foot drop, but they had most likely rolled most of the way, and the slant was just enough so there weren't a lot of hard falls on the trip down, at least not as hard as I would have liked. The car was lying on the driver's side, and the right-side passenger doors were heaved open, and out came the four dark figures. No, seven. They had been stuffed in that car tight as impacted turds in a colon. One of them fell out on the ground, then got up to one knee and stayed there a moment. I could see the car was near a little deer path down there that dipped into the woods and ran back in the other direction, up toward the road where they had been driving. It wasn't much of a path, but if they could get the car upright, and if it still ran, they might be able to drive out of there.

I turned and started running up the road as fast my legs would carry me. I could tell when I was about halfway up the hill that I needed to get back to road work because my heart was pounding against my ribs hard enough to break them and my vision was a little blurry. I looked back and saw one of the thugs coming up over the edge of the hill, carrying a long gun of some kind. I took to the woods and went along there, getting whacked in the face with limbs for a while, and then when I was sure the road was sloping down, I stumbled out of the woods and went down the hill where I saw Leonard's car, and Leonard outside of it, standing by the passenger side with the deer rifle.

I huffed out some cold air and waved the shotgun above my head and started down at a speed I didn't know I had in me. Leonard got in the car and cranked it up, and when I made the passenger side, I was nearly out of wind. Climbing in, closing the door, I looked over at Leonard, said, "There are seven of them."

He said, "You dumb ass."

54

"Now where's the Volkswagen?" Leonard said. "You've caused us to lose it."

"But I managed to knock the bad guys off a hill and now they're on foot."

"Okay, I guess that's something. You get a pass. Seven, huh?"

"It was like a goddamn clown car."

We continued driving and where there hadn't been roads going off the main road there were now plenty. Leonard said, "He took one of these, or we would have caught up to him by now. I'm driving this thing like it's got a real engine in it."

Pausing at a dirt road that turned to the right, I got out of the car and bent down and tried to check the ground in what little light there was. Finally, Leonard backed the car so that the lights shone on the ground, and then I could see there were recent tire marks.

I got in the car, and Leonard said, "Well, Hawkeye?"

"There are tire tracks that look fresh," I said. "It could be him. It could be someone else, but it could be him."

"It's what we got," Leonard said, and started down the road. It was dark down there and the trees ate up the sides of the road until there was only room for the car, and then we came to a bridge that looked as if the headless horseman ought to be on the other side of it. We rattled over it and went around a curve that climbed through some trees with winter-dried moss hanging down. When we broke over the hill there was a clearing and an A-frame house, not too big, sitting at the peak of the hill and we could see the Volkswagen parked in the yard. There was a little road that went into the trees on the right and there was one on the left. Leonard took the one on the right and we drove down it a piece and found a place where the road was a little wide and parked on the right-hand side and got out, me with the shotgun and him with the rifle. We were carrying our handguns and we each had a nifty blackjack and a jaunty stride.

When I loaded up the shotgun, Leonard said, "Here, you're a better shot. I should have the shotgun."

We swapped, and I gave him the shells. I took the box of shells for the deer rifle and put the whole box in my coat pocket.

"How long will it take them to get up here on foot?" Leonard said.

"A lot longer yet," I said, "and then they have to be smart like us and look at the tracks."

"I'm going to give them that much smarts," Leonard said. "Let's get this over with. Maybe we can be in and out and in our car and down the hill before they realize it's us coming back and they'll be so startled they won't shoot at us."

We started crawling up the hill, down close to the earth, in line with the Volkswagen. It took about a century for us to make it that way, but we thought it might be preferable to being spotted and shot. When we got to the Volkswagen, I stood up behind it and glanced in. My blue envelope was on the seat next to the stationery I had written "Hi" on, and beside it was a black mustache and a cap with a headful of black hair.

I hunkered back down behind the Volkswagen, said, "Unless the driver has some kind of skin disease and his mustache fell off in the altogether along with all the hair in his hat, the guy who picked up Vanilla Ride's mail was Vanilla Ride."

"A master of disguise."

"Well, I think maybe for us she doesn't have to be all that masterful."

"That's certainly true. Now what?"

"I think the now what is I get my wind back."

"Too many late dinners and not enough exercise, Hap. I've been telling you that."

"Yes, you have. Now shut up."

"So, in a couple hours when you get your wind back, what do we do?"

"We split up. You go right and I go left."

"That's it?" Leonard said. "You complained to me that we didn't have a plan last time, and now your plan is you go one way and I go another."

"Okay, what's your plan?"

Leonard was quiet for a moment. "I go left and you go right."

55

We were about to start our plan when we heard boots on gravel, looked up into the smiling face of Vanilla Ride, standing by the Volkswagen pointing an automatic pistol at us. It certainly seemed to be a big automatic. She had come up like a ghost while we were putting our war room together. She had her golden hair tied back in a ponytail, and she looked like some kind of female goddess of war.

"I have systems on top of systems," she said. "I knew you were here the moment you entered my perimeter."

"Damn," Leonard said. She got a determined look on her face, like she was about to pass an anvil through her bowels, extended the automatic, ready to pop us, and then a shot rang out and the window on the Volkswagen above me splintered and some of the glass rained down. Vanilla took a turn around the Volkswagen on one end, and Leonard and I scrambled around to the other side. We ended up behind a tire, close as lovers, and Vanilla was behind the other tire. When I looked at her, she jerked the automatic at us.

"Truce," I said. "They want us too."

She studied me for a long moment.

"You're wondering if you can trust us," I said, "and I know this isn't much right now, but we keep our word. Truce. For now, anyway."

After a moment, Vanilla Ride nodded, said, "I can kill you anytime I want."

There was an explosion as a low bullet caught the tire we were behind and rang off the rim and the pressure of the exploding tire blew us back about three feet. Vanilla darted for the A-frame, and Leonard grabbed me by the coat collar and started dragging me. I let him, clinging to my deer rifle like a child with a teddy bear.

When we were inside and the door was slammed, glass began to come out of the windows as shots rained down. It was a two-story house with a short stairway up to what was more a loft than a room. The middle floor had a low section and some standard couches around it. Except for some exercise equipment off to the side of the living room, the place looked as impersonal as a cheap motel room.

I got off my belly and on my knees and looked at Vanilla Ride. She was crawling across the floor toward the corner. She popped the flooring up there with remarkable deftness, took out a long, sleek black weapon with a very large banana clip, and she pulled a spare clip out of there too. She crawled back to where the glass was still dropping from the big window. The glass splattered around her like falling stars and she stood up and let the spare clip drop to the floor and cut loose with the gun. Down below, where their shots were coming from, the dirt leaped up in heaps and the trees whipped and then she went down again, behind the high windowsill where Leonard and I were lurking, but on the opposite end. We were bookends. Same alike. Except we were guys and she was a girl and she had a big gun that would shoot faster than ours.

"They got their car out of the ditch," Leonard said.

"It was more of a drop-off than a ditch," I said. "I didn't think they could turn it off its side and drive it out. Not that easily."

"You were wrong," Leonard said.

"Yep," I said.

"You didn't do as good as you thought."

"Nope."

"Kind of typical, isn't it?"

"It is," I said.

"You see, they got it running, and now they are after our ass, and here we are with"—Leonard turned and looked at Vanilla Ride—"her."

Vanilla looked at us and smiled. Damn, she was a beauty. "How have you two lived this long?" she said.

"Our sterling personalities," Leonard said. "We charm just about everyone."

I eased over so I was near the corner of the windowsill and the wall, and then I raised up. I could taste the cold air coming in through the shattered window and smell the pines down the hill, and I could see one of the men coming along where the hill spread up toward the house, and though there wasn't much light, I could see him well enough. He was the greasy-haired guy and he was stooped slightly, his head down, running for the Volkswagen, the only real cover he had.

I rose up and beaded in and shot and hit him in the top of the head and knocked him rolling down the rise.

I sat down behind the wall and looked at Leonard. He said, "Haven't lost your touch."

Vanilla Ride smiled at me.

Leonard said, "You wait until there's some real light, he can shoot the balls off a dog tick."

"My guess is they won't wait until it's light," I said. "They like it better this way. Daylight comes we can see them better from here than they can see us, and we got cover. In the light, they got dick, so they'll either cash in now or come soon. I vote that they come ahead."

Leonard looked at Vanilla Ride, said, "They may not even be after you, though I'd say that shot hit the Volkswagen was close to all of us."

"It doesn't matter," Vanilla Ride said. "They've invaded my home. So have you."

"But we have a truce, right?" I said.

"You came to kill me, didn't you?"

"That's right, we did."

"You're not too good."

"We're tougher and smarter than you think," I said. "Except for getting sneaked up on. That part, well, we're not so good."

"You want the money?"

"It's not about money," I said. "It doesn't even belong to us. You killed a couple of kids and a friend of ours."

"Business," she said.

"It didn't seem like business to us," I said.

She shifted slightly to a kneeling position, behind the wall. The gun she held shifted too. She said, "I don't have any reason to believe you two about anything."

"No, you don't," Leonard said. "But I will say this: I just saw one of those bozos cutting low across the bottom of the hill, moving to the left of the house. They're trying to circle us. They got six and we got three, and we got the house, so in one way we're better off. In another, they know where we are and we don't know where they are, and there are more of them than there are of us. So that's the situation. How's it gonna be?"

Vanilla Ride was quiet for a few moments. She said, "I keep my word."

"We keep ours," Leonard said.

"Then we have to trust one another, don't we?" she said.

"So we're going to maintain the truce?" I said.

"Certainly," she said.

It wasn't like I expected. They were brave. Either that or stupid. They came at us hard and they came at us quick. What they did was they opened up with automatic weapons that made the walls jump apart and a splinter from the wall popped into my cheek and it felt like fire. Without really thinking about it, Leonard and I crawled toward the center of the house, toward where the floor was lowered and the couches circled it. We crawled down in there and kept our heads ducked while the stuffings leaped out of the couch and things came off the walls and glass broke.

I looked up once, and there was Vanilla Ride, standing up, bullets buzzing around her like hornets, and she was letting down on that automatic weapon, and it didn't even seem to jump in her hands, and I could see through the big open window where she was shooting that the ground was churning up, and I could see one body there where she had caught one of the guys, and then everything went silent. She hit the floor and the clip went away, and she pulled the other clip out and slipped it on the weapon smooth as a gigolo sliding on a condom.

The back door burst open with a kick and we raised up, saw a tough-looking guy with a shotgun. Leonard raised up and shot at him and missed. I lifted the rifle as the intruder's shotgun wheeled toward us, and just before I fired, I knew he had me beat, so I jumped and covered Leonard. The shot tore at the couch and I felt pellets hit my ass so hard one butt cheek slammed against the other. I came up scrambling and firing the rifle twice, and both shots hit the shotgunner as he pumped another load and I saw one of his eyes go big and red and then he was down and two were coming through the front window.

Vanilla Ride was no longer at the window. I wheeled around to shoot, but by this time Leonard was up, and he fired, caught one of them in the kneecap and he dropped with a yelp. Then a shot came from upstairs, and the other one took it through the right side of his head as he was stepping over the spot where the window had been. He seemed to lean against the sill, and then he turned his head slightly, like someone had called his name, sat down hard on the sill, dropping his weapon, his head falling forward in his lap. The guy Leonard had hit in the knee was screaming loudly. It was so loud and strange it made my skin knot up. He quit screaming when Vanilla Ride leaned over the stair railing and shot him through the head. He just lay quietly then, bleeding out.

"That leaves two," Vanilla Ride said.

56

"Someone's got to die!" a voice called from outside.

"That would be you," Leonard called out.

"Why don't you chicken farts just come out and face us?" the voice said. "What's stopping you?"

"Bullets," Leonard yelled out.

"Chickenshits," the voice called.

"Absolutely," Leonard said. "Why don't you just come and get us? We'll put the coffee on."

"We got two, you got three," the voice said.

"You started with seven," I said.

"Vanilla Ride," the voice said, "we ain't got nothing against you. We want them."

"You fucked up my house," she called out. "You nearly shot me trying to shoot them. You pick this moment to come after them. No. I think you're ready to retire me because I know too much. Me and you, we aren't friends."

"I don't have any friends," the voice said.

"That makes us even," Vanilla Ride said.

They went silent out there and time slipped by slowly and the beginnings of light seeped in under the trees and rose up between them like a gentle flame. The back door was wide open, and it made me nervous, that and the big front window open as well. I moved once, just to see if I could make it to the back door, and a bullet plowed into the couch about a quarter inch from my face, so I got down and played it close to the floor, my ears perked.

This went on for a long time, and Leonard said, "Fuck it. Let's you and me go get them."

"You can't hit the ass end of an elephant with a shotgun at two paces. That would be some shoot-out."

"I can hit most anything," Vanilla Ride said. "And you seem to be a good shot."

I looked up at her on the landing, in the shadows.

"With a long gun," I said.

"What about a short one?"

"Nowhere as good."

"But he can hit stuff," Leonard said. "His bad is someone else's good. He's got an instinct."

"My instinct is to stay right here," I said. "I don't like where this is going."

"I'm tired of waiting," Vanilla Ride said. "You can go, or you can stay." Then she turned her attention away from me and yelled outside. "Hey, you still out there, loudmouth?"

"I'm out here," came the voice.

"You two, you show yourself, handguns only," she said. "I'll meet you outside, guns by our sides."

"You mean that?"

"Hell yeah, I got better things to do with the morning."

"Oh, you aren't going to end up doing all that much today, Vanilla."

"I guess we can find out, swizzle dick."

There was a long moment of silence. Then the voice yelled back. "Deal."

"Damn," I said to Leonard. "You know I got to do it now."

"Yeah, I know. I'll do it, you know that, but—"

"You can't shoot for shit."

"Bingo," Leonard said.

I took a deep breath and put the rifle on the floor and pulled the automatic from my belt. Leonard said, "If you get killed, I'm running out that back door like a goddamn rabbit."

"No you won't."

"Yes I will."

"No. You're a macho queer."

"Oh yeah, that's right. Maybe. Christ, Hap, let them come for us."

"Either way scares the hell out of me," I said. "I'm always scared. I'm not like you."

"Hey, I'm scared. You get killed, John doesn't take me back, where am I to stay?"

Vanilla Ride came down the stairs carrying her automatic pistol in her hand. I eased away from the couch and along the wall near the window. I said to her, "Think they'll keep their word?"

"Of course not," she said.

Easing over to the edge of the window on her side, she called out: "There will be two of us, and two of you."

"That sounds good," came the voice from the dark.

"One of us will step out, and you'll show one of you, with a handgun only."

"High noon," the voice yelled out.

"High morning," Vanilla Ride said. She stepped through the gap where the window had been. A tall man with dark hair came up over the rise. He had his hand down by his side. I could see a handgun in it. I stepped out, but kept close to the edge of the windowsill.

The other man came up over the rise. I could see his handgun. He held it in such a way that it was in front of him and resting against his thigh. The sun was still coming up, and though the sun in our eyes should have been a hazard, this early in the morning and coming through the trees it wasn't so bright and all it did was outline our targets neatly.

"Let's walk out a ways," said the tall dark-haired man.

"They're going to fuck with us," Vanilla Ride said so only I could hear.

"But we're going to go on out a ways in spite of that, aren't we?" I said.

"We are," she said. "I got to tell you, I always wanted to do this."

"Not me," I said, and I could feel my hands shaking. It was all I could do not to break and run.

"What happens we get killed?" she said. "What about your friend?"

"They'll have hell coming in and getting him," I said. "It won't be any cakewalk, that you can depend on."

"Good," she said.

"Do we have to do this?" I said.

"No."

"Then what the fuck are we doing?"

By now the two had spread out. One was going wide, in the direction of the Volkswagen, and I knew he was my guy, as he was on my side. The other guy going the other way, I decided not to think about him. He belonged to Vanilla Ride.

My guy brought his gun up and a shot went by my head so close I felt the heat from it. I jerked my automatic up and fired. If I hit him, he didn't show it. He started running low along the ground, and I fired again. He did a kind of bunny hop and went down. I heard shots to my right, but I didn't turn my head. I could still see out of the corner of my eye that Vanilla Ride was standing.

She said, "Goddamn," and then my guy leaped forward from where he lay, grabbed at an automatic rifle he had planted earlier, in the dark, hid it there waiting to grab it and cheat. I stepped forward and took my time, aiming one-handed, the way I had been taught, not with two hands, and when he lifted up I shot him somewhere along the jawline. It took part of his face off and he rolled on his side and lost the rifle, but he came up then, as if the pain had given him a jolt of power. He stumbled forward. He had another handgun, drawn from under his coat, and he was coming toward me fast, his face seeming to drip. He fired a shot and I found myself standing sideways all of a sudden, looking in the wrong direction. And by the time I had turned, having realized I had been hit, he was firing again, and this time one of his shots punched my coat but missed me, and I took careful aim and fired, hitting him in the center of the chest, but he kept coming. I fired again, and he must have been firing too, because there seemed to be shots popping all over, and I'm thinking I missed, but he went down, propped on a knee. I shot him another time and his body jerked and he went to his right side and lay there, his ruined face in my direction, his body kind of horseshoed behind him.

Turning, I saw Vanilla Ride was standing with her arm to her side, her gun in her hand. Her man lay on the ground squirming, holding his groin.

"Right in the goober," she said, and started walking toward him.

He saw her coming. One hand went away from his groin and

clawed in the dirt for his dropped handgun. He never got to it before she stood over him and shot him twice in the head.

She came walking back toward me. I could see her right side was stained with blood. She didn't seem to notice. My left arm had grown heavy, and then I felt as if it was being set on fire. The way she walked, the way she was coming toward me made me nervous. I said, "We still good?"

"We are," she said, and walked right past me.

57

"If she hadn't been good," Leonard said, "I was going to shoot her."

He was standing at the edge of the house with the deer rifle. He had gone out the back door. He said, "You'll find the guy you shot, he's also got a rifle shot in his chest."

"I thought I missed."

"Nope. You hit him. I just hit him again."

"That was cheating," Vanilla Ride said to Leonard. "Ganging up on the guy."

"Damn straight," Leonard said. "You think I'm going to let that motherfucker kill my brother?"

She grinned at him.

My knees buckled and I fell down.

Inside the house on the couch, Leonard looked at my wound. Vanilla Ride came over. She had removed her shirt and was wearing a sports bra and a bandage around her waist, different blue jeans. She said, "I got hit, but it went through."

"He's still got the bullet in his arm," Leonard said, as he pulled the splinter out of my face.

She took hold of my arm, looked it over, making me wince. "You'll be all right, tough guy. We got to push the bullet all the way through. It's in the fat of your arm. You didn't lose a lot of blood."

"Any is too much . . . what did you say?"

"You're lucky it missed the serious muscle," she said.

"About that pushing it all the way through business," I said.

She went away for a while and I lay on the couch, kind of going in and out. She came over and I looked up and she had a kitchen knife, about half of it glowed red-hot.

"Now wait just a goddamn minute," I said.

"Hold him down," she said.

Leonard got on top of me and kept my back pinned to the couch, held my injured arm down and at my side. "It's for your own good, dumb ass," he said.

"I hate you," I said.

Vanilla Ride took the knife and stuck it quickly into the wound and pushed and I felt the knife touch the bullet inside of me, and then I passed out. When I woke up, she was cutting at the back of my arm, freeing the bullet. I passed out again.

When I came to I was bandaged up and sick to my stomach. There was a lot of sunlight now, but it was very cold. Leonard was sitting on the couch with the rifle across his knees. He said, "She's gone," and when he spoke a cloud of white mist came out of his mouth. "We should have killed her, I guess. She had it coming, Tonto, the kids and all. But she did help save our ass."

"What?"

"Gone. She left us four hundred thousand dollars. Took the Volkswagen, told me to tell you if she was older, or you were younger, you might be her meat."

"She said that?"

"She did."

"But we came to kill her."

"Doesn't seem to hold it against us. I feel sort of mission unfinished, you know, but she patched you up, brother, so what was I gonna do?"

"What?"

"You keep saying that."

It was because I was so stunned, I didn't know what to say. After sitting there stunned for a moment, I found a few words. "The money. I don't get it."

Leonard patted the duffel bag, which was lying next to him on the couch. "Look, man. Focus. She gave me three hundred thousand to return to the Dixie Mafia, with her regards, and gave us a hundred thousand to keep, or pretty close to it—minus what the kids spent, we spent, and she spent. But, man, it's still over ninety thousand. She kept a hundred thousand for herself."

I sat up on the couch. "She trusted us to return the money?"

"I know. What you gonna do? She asked for my word."

"And you gave it?"

"Of course."

"And she accepted it?"

"Duh. I got the money, don't I? What the fuck is wrong with your hearing?"

"I don't know," I said. "The world feels like a big banana."

"What?" Leonard said.

"I don't know," I said. "It don't mean nothing."

"You're delirious," Leonard said.

"Maybe," I said, and passed out again.

58

It was a few days later and I had my arm in a sling, courtesy of a veterinarian Marvin knew who wouldn't report he had treated a gunshot wound. He said whoever had done the first aid had done a good job.

Anyway, there I was in a sling and we were in No Enterprise sitting in the little station/cafe with connecting grease monkey shop. It was me and Leonard and Marvin Hanson, Conners and his fat friend, and two other guys. One of them was Cletus Jimson, and he was a fortyish guy with tattoos on his knuckles that I couldn't make out but were meant to be some kind of symbols. I guess they were Chinese, which, considering he was supposed to be a stone racist and the current head of the Dixie Mafia in this part of the country, seemed odd to me. Marvin had managed to get us in touch with him through Conners. The guy with Jimson had a lot of bulges in his coat. Some of them were muscles, some of them were guns. His head was shaved and he had a crease on the side of his head that looked to have been put there by a blunt instrument.

"So, you kill a bunch of our guys, and you want to come and make a truce?" Jimson said.

"That's about right," I said. "We also bring gifts."

"Gifts," Jimson said. "What kind of gifts?"

I had a box with me and it was tied with ribbon. I picked it up and put it on the table and he untied the ribbon and picked up the lid and looked inside. I knew what he was looking at. Three hundred thousand dollars.

"That's not a gift. That's what's owed me."

"Not by us," I said. "We sort of came into this deal sideways."

"Yeah?" Jimson said.

"Yeah," I said.

"He come over and pistol-whipped us," Conners said.

"Actually, most of it was done with a blackjack if I remember correctly," Leonard said. "Oh yeah, and there was that part where I just plain ole pure-dee whipped your black ass with assholes and elbows."

"Yep," I said. "That's the way I remember it too."

"So you brought me my money home," Jimson said.

"Courtesy of Vanilla Ride," Leonard said.

"She really a woman?" Jimson said.

"Oh yeah," I said.

"How about that," he said. "A split tail that's a gunner. That's some precious stuff, that is."

"Precious," I said.

"Conners here," Jimson said. "He tells me he knows Marvin here, says Marvin says you guys went to kill her and didn't, but killed my guys instead."

"That Marvin, what a blabbermouth," I said.

Marvin Hanson chuckled.

"It seemed like the right thing at the time," I said.

"I don't like that," Jimson said.

"Get some better guys," Leonard said.

Jimson sat back in his chair and looked at Leonard. If he thought Leonard was going to flinch he was out of his mind.

"So," Jimson said, "you two, you're tough guys, huh?"

"That's about it," Leonard said. "But we'd like to end this. We got put into this when we didn't want to be."

"How's that?"

I explained.

"That's some story," Jimson said when I was finished.

"It's true," I said. "I say you've wasted a lot of guys on us, and I say it'd be best we didn't shoot at each other anymore. There's your money back."

"It wasn't about the money," he said.

"I know that," I said, "but it's our peace offering, your money back."

"Yeah," Leonard said, "and now we're going to sweeten it." He reached inside his coat pocket and brought out ten thousand dollars in ten one-thousand-dollar bills.

"That's nothing," Jimson said.

"It's ten thousand dollars," Leonard said, "and it's money we don't owe you. Call it a present, a peace offering." Of course, Leonard failed to mention that there was a little over eighty thousand dollars we had left for ourselves.

"Like I said," Jimson said, "it's not about the money. I spent more trying to have you guys hit."

"And what they're telling you," Marvin said, "is why spend any more?"

"I could pop you right here," Jimson said. "All of you."

"No," Leonard said, "I don't think so. You could try, but I don't know it'd work out."

"You people," Jimson said, "you always got to be smart-asses."

"When you say 'you people,'" Leonard said, "do you mean queers or niggers? I'm a little perplexed on the matter."

"You're queer?" Jimson said.

"I'm so queer queers call me queer."

"Wow," I said. "That's pretty queer."

"Isn't it?" Leonard said.

"You aren't going to do anything here," Marvin said to Jimson. "That would be plain stupid."

"I got some law here," Jimson said. "I could make it look the way I want."

"Maybe," I said, "and maybe not, but it won't do any good if you're dead, now, will it?"

Jimson grinned. "All right. All right. You guys, I give you this, you got you a set, both of you, queer or not."

"It's just me that's queer," Leonard said. "I'd rather not be included with heterosexuals. Bad for my reputation."

Jimson turned and looked out the window, then picked up his coffee and drank. "We call it even, that means you stay out of my business, right?"

"Unless that business gets into our business," I said. "And I don't know how Vanilla Ride feels about things. Me and Leonard and her have a truce. But you guys, I don't know. She might not like you sent men to kill her."

"I sent them for you."

"Well," I said, "far as I know, they're still in Arkansas."

"I'll worry about Vanilla Ride," he said.

"Just a polite warning," I said.

"Fair enough," he said.

"But we owe them one," Sykes said. "Me and Conners."

"That's your problem," Jimson said. "Me and them, we're done."
He hesitated a moment, then turned to Conners and Sykes. "And you
know what, you two, you're done too. Leave them alone. They come
around on some other matter, that's something else. But on this, you're
done. You took a lickin'. Learn to like it."

"Good advice," Leonard said.

"Don't push it," Jimson said, stood up and pushed his chair back.
His man got up at the same time. Conners and Sykes got up too.

Leonard said, "Been good doing business with you, and just one last
thing. Keep your word. We expect it. You don't, we won't like it."

Jimson smiled. "Say you won't?"

"Absolutely," Leonard said.

"Yeah . . . well," Jimson said, and he and his man and No Enterprise's finest walked out and got in their cars and drove away.

We ordered pie.

59

Couple months later, upstairs in our bedroom, my arm all healed and wrapped around Brett, she said, "You're not exactly hot with the flesh pistol tonight."

"No," I said, "I'm not."

"A lot on the mind?"

"You know it."

"You told me everything, didn't you? Got it off your chest?"

"Yep. But I still feel like I have a hole in me."

"You're healed up fine."

"I don't mean that, and you know it."

"It'll pass, baby."

"I hope so. I just don't think I was cut out to do what I do and not feel bad about it."

"Leonard's not bothered."

"No, he's not. He said, 'If they deserve it, I got no problem. They don't deserve it, then I got a problem. They deserved it.'"

"Words to live by."

"I guess."

"Vanilla Ride . . . Leonard said she sort of liked you."

"He has a big mouth. And I think she said what she said as a kind nod to my courage. Truth was, I was scared to death."

"But you went out there and did a stupid thing knowing it was stupid."

"That's called stupid, not courageous."

"I have to agree."

"I guess I was caught up in the moment. Thing I got to think—to consider—is Vanilla Ride. Beautiful young woman like that, what was done to her? Why is she like that? Why did she learn the skills she learned?"

"Some man is at the bottom of it, I can promise you that," Brett said.

"Most likely. Probably childhood. Bottom line is she killed Tonto. He wasn't any friend, but he was our partner, so we were supposed to do something. The kids, they didn't deserve it. They were just stupid. Shit, she tried to kill us. All that, and in the end we let it slide."

"But she helped you against the others."

"True."

"And she cut out the lead in your arm."

"Also true. It makes the whole thing kind of confusing, at least in the sense of trying to figure where loyalties lie."

"So, she was beautiful?"

"Not like you."

"You liar."

"Really."

"Keep on."

"You are the beauty of all beauties."

"That's what I want to hear. Bet her real name isn't Vanilla Ride."

"Bet you're right."

"But you're thinking about her, aren't you?"

"She's got me stumped. She let us go. She could have killed us."

"You like that she had a sense of honor, don't you, baby?"

"I guess I do. But I still wonder why she is the way she is. The killing part . . . I'm not like her, am I?"

"You do what has to be done and for the greater good. She does it for money."

"That's what I keep telling myself."

"You do odd jobs, Hap, and you're an honorable man, but you don't do psychology. Quit trying to figure her out, or yourself. There's no clear answer."

"Yeah, you're right."

"Say you could figure out all the ills of the world, it wouldn't stop them from happening. Humans suck."

"When you're right, you're right. How was it in Arizona with Marvin and his family?"

"It blew. I like Marvin, hate his family. Gadget is a little bitch who not only needs rehab, she needs a daily beating and someone to cuss her for an hour every Thursday."

"You're open for that, aren't you?"

"If it was a paying gig. What about Leonard and John?"

"You talk to him all the time. Why are you asking me?"

"I didn't want to ask him about that. I thought it might make him sad."

"But I can ask him?"

"You two talk about stuff like that, and you know it. What's the skinny?"

"Not working out. Not yet anyway. They talk now and again. Leonard has his own place, not a motel room but an apartment. Just got it. Me, I'm not that hopeful they'll work it out, but then again, tonight I'm not exactly full of cheer."

"You have half of eighty thousand dollars," she said. "A gift."

"A little more, actually. Leonard split it right down to the penny."

"Well, that's good."

"I keep thinking about where it came from. Women flat-backing and dumb asses mainlining, or whatever."

"So it's bad money you can put to the good for eating and renting this house and you also don't have to work out in the weather for a while."

"Yeah, I thought about that. A lot."

Brett snuggled up close to me and rubbed my stomach. "You want to try again?"

"Not just now. I think he's sleeping."

"It's okay. I love you even if you are a failure sexually."

"Thanks. I needed that."

"You know I'm joking."

"Sure."

"Now don't brood. There's always tomorrow morning. And afterward, I'm going to make waffles."

We snuggled awhile, and then Brett fell asleep. I thought about Vanilla Ride and the way she had looked, the way she had marched around with that bandage across her stomach, and wondered if she had been hit worse than she let on. I had wanted to kill her badly, and now I wondered where she was and why she was what she was, and if Brett was right about me and Vanilla Ride being all that different. Down deep it seemed to me that at some point, me and her, we were exactly the same.

I lay there trying to sleep, my head turned, looking first at the dim outline of the photograph Brett had framed of me and Leonard and Cindy the Bear. It was on the nightstand. I rolled over and looked out the window. The moon had turned nearly full and it was very bright out and the light came through and fell onto the carpet and onto the end of the bed. I felt funny about that light, like if I stretched my foot out, it would move away. It was as if something inside of me had shifted and gone deep inside of myself, into the shadows, and no matter where I sat, stood, or lay, no light would, or ever could, shine on me.

Joe R. Lansdale has written more than a dozen novels in the suspense, horror, and Western genres. He has also edited several anthologies. He has received the British Fantasy Award, the American Mystery Award, seven Bram Stoker Awards, and the 2001 Edgar Award for best novel from the Mystery Writers of America. In 2007 he won the Grand Master Award at the World Horror Convention. He lives in Nacogdoches, Texas, with his family.

A NOTE ON THE TYPE

This book was set in Janson, a typeface long thought to have been made by the Dutchman Anton Janson, who was a practicing type-founder in Leipzig during the years 1668–1687. However, it has been conclusively demonstrated that these types are actually the work of Nicholas Kis (1650–1702), a Hungarian, who most probably learned his trade from the master Dutch typefounder Dirk Voskens. The type is an excellent example of the influential and sturdy Dutch types that prevailed in England up to the time William Caslon (1692–1766) developed his own incomparable designs from them.

Composed by TexTech, Brattleboro, Vermont
Printed and bound by Berryville Graphics, Berryville, Virginia
Designed by Virginia Tan